## Attica prison the year 2051

"On the lock in, gentlemen. On the lock in, lights out, time to hit the sack." As the correction officer made his rounds to check his count assuring that all inmates were accounted for, I was reading a letter that I had received from my daughter. She had gotten married to a very succesful doctor and she had sent me pictures of the wedding. Such a beautiful girl, she had my attitude and her mother's looks. As I finished the letter, I folded it up, put it back in the envelope, and put it with the rest of the letters I had from both my son and my daughter.

    Here I sat in a cell at 67 years of age, day after day, month after month, year after year, watching my young skin wrinkle. I had spent the last 40 years incarcerated and locked away for damn near the rest of my existing life, playing cards and walking the yard, listening to old and new war stories from convicts, sun up to sun down. One day, my children will get a phone call from the warden saying, 'I'm sorry but your father passed away'—what a way to find out that your old man just died. If you would have told me 40 years ago that I would be spending the rest of my natural life behind bars, I would have laughed like it was some Andrew Dice Clay joke you just told. I would have responded by saying, 'Well, if they got a prison in hell for the dead, I guess you're absolutely right—because the grave is the only place I'm heading to and fast'.

My cellmate was a young Italian kid about 28 years old, who had a bright future ahead of him. He just got caught up hanging with the wrong crowd. He was actually a well-known book writer, who was up and coming, and would talk my fuckin' ears off in the middle of the night about how he was on his way to becoming a huge film writer, and wanted to begin his own production company. I never spoke much to him or anybody in the prison, for that matter, but I have to admit this kid had spunk—I actually liked the kid. Every night, he would read me letters that his wife and his family wrote him but other than that, conversation between me and him was extremely limited. For 40 years, I hardly said 5 words to people other than my children. I was mentally sheltered and was living in my own sheer misery. As I put my letter away, I turned around only to see this kid standing right behind me.

"How come you never mention your family or your kids?" he asked, in a concerned but firm voice. "I mean, come to think of it, you don't say anything. Ever since I've been your cellmate, you have said all of maybe 10 fuckin' words, bro. I've been your cellmate for five years, and I've only heard you spit out 10 fuckin' words. Ya know I walk around this prison and alls I hear are stories—all kinds of stories—love stories, war stories, I-almost-got-away-with-it stories, every kind of story exists in this hell we're in. For Christ fuckin' sake, the warden even told me a story one day when I was in his pig pen. And to tell you the truth, it was a very interfuckin' resting story. I think I've conversated with every old man in this hellhole except you. You never say anything. At times I wonder if you're just a little fuckin' koo koo, bro."

In the back of my head I'm saying to myself, this is some kid, he's gonna be OK in this cold world, just as long as he keeps his nose clean. "Kid, that's the problem in this joint. Everybody's gotta fuckin' story to tell," I replied, adding, "Half of them ain't worth listening to anyway. I mean what the fuck do you want me to tell ya? How my kids have had to come back and forth to this fuckin' joint just to see their dad who is extremely lucky that they even want me in their life anyway? War stories are like a GED in today's society, they ain't worth shit and they ain't gonna benefit you anyway, so why tell 'em, and even better, why listen to 'em. But hey kid, you wanna hear a story, huh. Come over here and sit on this bottom bunk because this is the only time I'm gonna let you ever sit on my fuckin' bed. Now… I'm gonna tell you a real fuckin' story.

A Suicide Story
©2021, A Beautiful Mind

All rights reserved. This book or any portion thereof may not be reproduced or used in any manner whatsoever without the express written permission of the publisher except for the use of brief quotations in a book review.

ISBN: 978-1-09835-886-0

ISBN eBook: 978-1-09835-887-7

# A SUICIDE STORY

WRITTEN BY
A BEAUTIFUL MIND

40 years earlier New York City, 2013

# CHAPTER 1

It was Monday morning. I woke up to the sound of Anastasia putting on her clothes. Anastasia was one of my night fling things. For three years, we'd known each other, and for three years, we'd been sex partners. The first time we met, we came to a mutual agreement that our relationship was gonna be just sex. When I rolled over to see what time it was, my eyes lit up, I sat straight up in the bed, and shouted, "OHHH SHHIT!" It was 10 am, and I was supposed to be at work at 8. I couldn't even find my clothes because they were scattered all over the room. Anastasia and I had been out partyin' at night and when we got back to her place, we were so damn ready to fuck that we just threw our clothes off. As a matter of fact, I remember taking off her high heels, tossing them across the room and hearing them crash onto her dresser, knocking off all of her perfume bottles.

Anastasia had already dressed and she was in the mirror fixing her hair. She had showered and gone the whole nine, and I was still looking around for my clothes. "Goddammit Anastasia, why didn't you wake me up? You know I had to be at work by 8." Anastasia's phone was ringing so she just ignored my ass, and answered her phone like the snotty bitch that she was. I knew that I was in some real shit. This was my fifth time being late and I already had been written up twice for being late. I hated my fuckin' job with a passion—that's why I never took it seriously. I didn't even take a shower—when I found all my clothes, I just threw them on. Anastasia finally got off the phone, and said, "Damn, Casual, you late for work again. You know they're gonna fire your ass, don't you." 'Casual' was my nick name, everyone called me that because I dressed so casually, no matter what the occasion was.

My real name is Damion DeVoh, I am about 6'1" with hazel eyes, medium build, short wavy hair with a caramel complexion. I am your average 25-year-old black kid with big dreams and little pockets. To me, in order to be somebody big in life, you had to think big, so I was a superstar in my own little world. My only problem was that I didn't wanna work hard; I just wanted to play hard. So when Anastasia told me that they were gonna fire me, I just shrugged my shoulders like I didn't give a fuck—and I really didn't give a fuck. Anastasia kept on talking my ear off about how I'm so irresponsible and how I need to get my shit together. Anastasia was 28 years old; she had a Master's degree and a good job working as the weather reporter for Channel 5 News. She was a tall, Nestle Crunch bar-colored, half-Panamanian half-Korean girl with a matrix haircut. She was the classiest 28-year-old female I had ever met. I knew older women that didn't have their shit together like Anastasia had hers together. Anastasia lived on the west side of Manhattan on W 29th st, and I worked all the way in Brooklyn at Models, so I knew that I really had to rush. I didn't even say bye to Anastasia; I just rushed out, hopped on the train and headed to work. It was December 22nd and everybody was doing all their last-minute Christmas shopping, so I knew the store was gonna be a madhouse.

When I got there, I walked in and I bumped right into my man, Rick. Rick was really the only person I spoke to at work. Other than him, I kept to myself. Rick and I would fuck with every woman that came into the store, and what was good about it was that we worked in the Sneaker Section. So, when a broad came through to try on a fresh pair, we would freak it, especially me. I would put their shoe on for them, and at the same time, I would gently massage their foot in a slick, sneaky manner. Now I was already a fly mothafucka, so that basically sealed the envelope. Rick would run right up to me and give me a pound, knocking all the customers out the way like they weren't even standing there.

Rick was a loud talking Jamaican with a shiny, bald head, who was funny as hell because his accent was so deep that you couldn't understand what he was saying. And let me tell ya, half the time, he really wasn't saying shit. He would always mispronounce words and say them the way he wanted to instead of the way they were really supposed to be pronounced. I remember one time he was trying to tell me a story, and I couldn't understand a fuckin' thing that came outta his mouth. Normally, I would just nod my head like I understood what he was saying but this time, I really wanted to hear the story, so, after he was done telling the story, I paused for a minute and just looked at him. Rick talked so loud and fast that you couldn't cut him off, so you actually had to wait until he was finished with what he was saying before you said to yourself: what the fuck did this mothafucka just say! So, as I was looking at him, he said to me, "What ya eyeballin' me like dat for?" I just shook my head, and said, "Yo, Rick, I really seriously didn't understand what the fuck you just said bro, seriously." Rick cocked his head to the side and had the nerve to tell me, "Oh what, ya not understand English?" I couldn't believe he actually had the audacity to say that shit—he was the most non-English speakin' brotha I ever met. What I really wanted to say to him that day was, 'Well, maybe if you spoke English, I would be able to understand you,' but I just shut my mouth.

After Rick gave me a pound, he said, "Yo Casual, ya late again, and ya not just late, ya two hours late for work, for godsake, what da fuck iz da sense of even showin ya bloodclot face afta two whole hour? Ya know, Romondo iz tired of this fuckery that's goin' on wit ya."

'Fuckery' was one of Rick's made-up words that meant 'nonsense'. So, translated in English, he said Romondo is tired of my nonsense. Rick seemed to think it was funny because he was laughing at the fact that I just might get fired today. He put his hand on my shoulder, and said, "Yo Casual, me hope ya got cash in ya bank account cuz afta today ya done workin here."

"Yeah, Yeah, Yeah… Whatever, Rick, if I get fired, I get fired. It ain't no big deal to me. It ain't like this is my fuckin' career." I said. As I was brushing what Rick was saying about me getting fired off my shoulders, I headed towards the back, into the break room to hang my coat up. As I entered, who do I see—of course, my pain-in-the-ass boss Romondo, not to mention Ursula, my assistant manager, and Erick, the scheduling manager. For some reason, I just had this gut feeling that they were all talking about how they were gonna terminate my ass. My boss Romondo was a real dick. For some reason, he thought he was this big-time executive, and on top of that he had this dull sarcastic way about himself—I mean this guy actually thought he was fuckin' funny. He was this fat Puerto Rican guy with long hair, and wore way too much cologne. I knew somethin was going down when my assistant manager and my scheduling manager got up and walked out.

As I started to hang up my coat, I heard Romondo clear his throat before saying, "Hey, Damion, don't bother hangin' up your coat because you're not stayin'. Why don't you come over here and sit down, so yet again, for the hundredth time, I can talk to you about being on time before I terminate you." As I walked over to sit in the chair across from him, I gave him a real nonchalant look—just to let him know that I really didn't care. Me and Romondo were just alike in a way—we both had egos the size of New York City, and we both used sarcasm like an assault weapon. So whenever we bumped heads, it was a quick draw. Like two cowboys outside the saloon going at it. The whole thing about the situation that Romondo didn't know was that it really didn't matter to me if he fired me or not. So as I looked at him, I leaned back in the chair and put my feet up on the table in a real cocky manner. The room got quiet for about 30 seconds—it got so quiet in there that you could probably here an ant crawl across the floor.

Romondo finally opened his mouth, and said, "Hey, Damion, how many times do we need to go over the rules about being on time before it finally sinks in that this type of thing is not acceptable, especially when you're working for me?" I suppose he was asking me a question, so I damn sure wasn't gonna do him the honor of answering him. I pulled out my gun first, and fired at him with a smart remark. I slouched down in the chair a little more and got comfortable before I spoke. My body language was extremely unprofessional—it was like I was in-charge and Romondo had to prove himself to me. I rested my hands behind my head and said, "Look, Romondo, I really don't have time for this shit. Why don't you just hurry up and terminate my ass? Ya know, Romondo, you would be doing both of us a favor."

Romondo just kinda smirked when I said that, and played it cool. I could tell what kind of game he was playing—he wanted to lay back and try to piss me off, so that eventually, I would blow up and make a fool outta myself. Romondo cleared his throat, sat up in his chair, and calmly asked, "Now what makes you say that, Damion?"

"Aww… Come on, Romondo, don't sit up there and act like you like me. And secondly, don't act like you don't know that I don't like you. So basically what I'm sayin', Romondo, is when I say that you're doin' both of us a favor by terminatin' me, I mean it would be such a relief to the both of us that we don't have to ever see each other again. I mean I know it would be a relief to me at least."

Romondo wasn't shocked at all that I spoke to him in that manner because he knew how I was. When I first had my interview, he even admitted how he admired the way I carried myself in such a confident way. But Romondo was no dummie, and he was just as cocky and just as arrogant as I was. He took a shot from the barrel of my gun and bounced right back. Like I said, me and Romondo were like two cowboys outside the saloon, just firing at each other. Romondo said calmly in a real soft voice, "Look, Damion, me not liking you has nothing to do at all with the fact that you simply can't own up to your responsibilities. It's quite obvious that you have a lot of growing up to do, Damion, and that's all I have to say about this whole situation."

I didn't even wanna give Romondo the satisfaction of telling me that I was fired, so I simply told him that I quit. I got up and walked out the break room, and left Romondo sitting there. I couldn't work there anymore; it just wasn't me; and it wasn't because I was lazy. I graduated high school at age 17 at the top of my class, and went on to attend 4 years of college at Stony Brook and received a B.A. degree in communications. The thing about it was that I just was confused about what I wanted to do with my life. Rick saw me as I was walking out, and he came over to me with this grin on his face like he just knew that I got fired. I walked right past him and said, "Yo, I'll call you." As rude as it seemed, I just didn't wanna hear what Rick had to say.

Alls I wanted to do was go home and sleep, so I went and hopped on the train straight to Greenwich Village. That's where I lived with my little brother, Derrick, who was only 6, my twin sister, Heaven Lee, and of course, my mom and my crazy pops. We were livin in Greenwich Village for the moment—it was right by Washington Square Park on Waverly Street. When I say we lived there 'for the moment,' I mean any given day we could have been moving someplace else. We were always moving. I grew up in Queens on Sutphin Boulevard, then when I turned ten, we moved to the Bronx, over on Gun hill Road. We stayed there until I was fifteen, and then we came to Greenwich Village. My mom was a social worker and a damn good one too. Her job was always transferring her—that's why we were always moving. My dad was a cop who worked for the 73rd Precinct, and he would always come home with these crazy-ass stories about who he arrested.

When I got home, I was so hungry that I went straight to the fridge. I noticed a big plate of food on the bottom rack, so I picked it up and looked at what it was. When I opened the aluminum foil, the smell of fried chicken, mashed potatoes, broccoli with cheese and macaroni salad made my mouth just water. I thought to myself, 'This plate must be mine because I didn't come home last night—my mom must have made me a plate'. I didn't waste no time. I put that plate right in the microwave. As I looked next to the microwave, I noticed a big piece of chocolate cake with double frosting. I said to myself, 'Aww yeah, moms is the best—she even saved me a piece of cake'. Finally the bell went off to let me know the food was done, so I took it out, I grabbed my cake and a fork and went into the living room to park my ass right in front of the TV. I took a bite of that fried chicken and I was in heaven. My mom was such a good cook, plus she could bake her ass off. I was scarfing the food down, so I could hurry up and get to that cake. It didn't take me long at all to tear that food up because I hadn't eaten ever since the day before. Plus I had been out drinking and getting high, so I had the munchies like crazy.

As I bit into the cake, I heard my pops come in through the front door. He was in his uniform, so I figured that he probably forgot something. "Hey, son, what's goin' on?" "Hey wassup, pops, did you forget somethin' again?" My pops was always coming back home because he forgot something. But he usually forgot things in his room—this time, he didn't go to his room, he went straight to the kitchen and opened the fridge. He was standing there for a good thirty seconds, looking up and down, side to side. Finally, he shouted for my mom. "Hey Regina!" My mom must not have heard him, so he called her again. "Hey Regina!" She finally heard him, came into the kitchen, and asked, "Eddie, what do you want?" Ya see, my pops was a real funny dude… I mean real funny. He had his hands on his hips, and asked, "Did you make my lunch last night?" "Yes, I made your lunch, Eddie. I packed you the leftovers that we had last night. There was three pieces of chicken, some mashed potatoes, macaroni salad and broccoli." Still looking in the fridge desperate to find his lunch, my dad said, "Well, if you packed it, Regina, where the hell is it—'cuz it damn sure ain't in the fridge." "Eddie honey, you just ain't lookin.'" My mom pushed my pops outta the way and started looking for the plate herself.

I said to myself as I swallowed the last little bit of cake, 'Oh damn, I'm in some shit now.' I thought for sure that my mom made that plate for me. "Well, Eddie, I don't know where the plate is." When my mom said that, my pops got mad, and said, "What the hell you mean you don't know where it is—you made it." "I know I made the plate Eddie and I put the plate in the fridge." Right when she said this, my nosey-ass sister came into the kitchen, and said, "I saw mommy make the plate, daddy, and she put it in the fridge." So now my pops was getting real mad. He put his entire head in the fridge, and said, "Look y'all, I don't see no damn plate. So I guess the plate just got up and walked out the damn house huh?"

All of a sudden, my mother stuck her nose up in the air, and asked, "Hey, do y'all smell food?" As soon as my mom said that, she looked in the living room and saw me. The only thing that I could say was, "Hi, mom." She walked right over to me, looked down at the plate, and said, "Here you go. Your food's right here, Eddie." My pops slammed the fridge door as my sister was laughing hysterically. Even my mom had a little grin on her face, but when my pops came into the living room, she wiped that grin right off and acted like she was mad at me. My pops came and stood right in front of the TV, just looking at me with that no-you-didn't-just-eat-my-food look. We just looked at each other for about a good minute before he said, "Well, now ain't this some shit." He came over towards me, and picked up the chicken bones, and said, "So, was it good? And what the hell you doin home anyway? Ain't you supposed to be at work?" This just wasn't the time to tell my pops that I had quit my job, so I lied, and said I was off for the day.

My mom put her hands around my pops, and said, "Look, baby, just go over there and get that chocolate cake." My mom must not have seen the little plate that was next to my pops' lunch that had frostin on it. As my pops walked towards the kitchen, he yelled out, "Where's the cake at, Regina!" My mom responded, "It's right next to the microwave, baby." My pops went over to get the cake, and said, "It ain't over here, Regina." My mom finally recognized the little plate that she put the cake on, and just shook her head. Now I knew that my pops was gonna get mad because that cake could have fed about four people. I was telling my mom to hush and keep her mouth closed, but my little six-year-old brother—who I didn't even know was in the room—yelled out, "Ooooh daddy, he ate the cake too."

My father came storming back into the living room, and said, "Now I know you didn't eat all that damn cake, boy. I know you ain't gonna sit up there and tell me you ate all that cake without savin' none for nobody else. Shit, we all like cake too. That don't even make no damn sense, boy. You ate that whole damn cake plus my fuckin' lunch." Turning to my mom, he said, "Regina, is this my son? Please tell me that this boy isn't my son because I don't think any child of mines would do such a damn thing."

My pops was so mad that he just walked out and slammed the door. My mom, my sister and my little brother were just sitting there looking at me. Then my mom came over, sat next to me, and asked, "Now, Damion, why did you eat that food?" "Ma, I thought you saved that food for me since I didn't come home last night." My mom just looked at me when I said that, rolled her eyes, and said, "Oh, Damion, please, when was the last time I saved you a plate? You run the damn streets so much, I'd think that you would have enough sense to feed yourself." She continued, "And when do you go back to work because I need to get your brother some sneakers. What I'm gonna do is just give you the money to get them the next time you go in—and please make sure you get a 13 in little boys, please."

I knew I was gonna have to tell my mom or my pops about my job sooner or later. I knew if I told my pops, he would sit me down and tell me one of his long, boring stories about how every boy in his house had to have a job. And if they didn't, they had to get out. Plus I knew he wouldn't be too happy because this would be the fourth job that I got fired from in a total span of six months.

The last job that I had had, my pops had actually hooked me up with. He got me a job working as a security guard at the Bronx Zoo. But that didn't last long at all. One day, I got so high before I went to work—I mean I was a fuckin' wreck. I knew I should've just called out that day, but I said, 'Fuck it. I can handle it.' I smoked two whole bags of weed, and had a tab of the finest acid ever sold down in the Village. You know that shit that will have you trippin' for 24 whole hours. What happened to me that day was the most embarrassing moment in my crazy life. I had got a call on my radio that an old woman had passed out from the heat. After all, it was hot as hell that day. It was so fuckin' hot that I thought even I was gonna pass out. It was also so hot that all the women were walking around with almost nothing on. Everywhere I looked, there was a sexy-ass woman strutting by with her titties or her ass hanging all out. As I approached the location where the old lady was lying, I saw two men and another older lady giving the lady who was passed out what appeared to be water. I really couldn't tell because I was about 150 feet away from where it happened.

As I proceeded to drive towards the old lady, I saw this black woman walking with her kids, and she was fine as hell. For a moment, I left the Bronx Zoo, my mind took me to a place of pure bliss, everything and everyone just disappeared except me and this woman. Her skin was the color of chocolate milk, she had long cornrows, and her pants looked almost as if they were painted on her thick legs. She had this pink lipstick that matched her fingernail polish and her toenail polish. She was radiant and irresistible. But as I kept staring at her, that acid that I had taken earlier just took over my brain and my ability to think clearly and separate a deep daydream from reality. I blinked, and all of a sudden, she was naked—her chocolate skin was glistening under the sun, her long cornrows were blowing in the wind, and she whispered in a sexy voice, "Come take me, Casual, take me now." Then she walked right up to me, leaned forward, and puckered her juicy Barbie doll lips out so she could give me a kiss. As I leaned forward to kiss her, I heard a voice yell out, "What the hell are you doin' kid? You're gonna hit her!"

Reality came back to me at the last minute. That same sexy woman, who was naked and leaning forward to kiss me, had disappeared. She really didn't just disappear—she just kept walking with her kids minding her business as she was doing all along. The funny thing about it was that this woman didn't even know that I was looking at her in the first place—she didn't even know that I existed. By the time I snapped outta this daydream I was in and came back to reality, it was way too late—the damage had been done. I had hit the old woman. And I didn't just hit her—I ran her over. I couldn't believe that I had hit her. I got out the cart to check the woman and everyone was yelling at me asking me, 'What the hell is wrong with you—are you a nut?' This one old guy looked at me and asked, "What's the matter with you? Are you on drugs?" Little did he know I was on drugs. I don't have to continue with the story—you can figure out the rest. They drug tested me and fired my ass. My father was mad as hell, but he was more embarrassed than anything. All his friends down at the Precinct were laughing about the whole thing. He had got me the job through one of his friends who worked part-time at the zoo as a security guard when he wasn't on duty.

After my mom told me to get the shoes for my brother, she got up to start her morning chores. She was on vacation from her job for the holidays. I grabbed her by her arm and pulled her back down on the couch. She looked at me and asked, "Boy, what's wrong with you, grabbin' up on me like that?" I said, "Hey listen, ma, I really need to tell you somethin' but you have to promise me that you won't tell pop."

She asked, "Boy, what do you have to tell me now?" And again I said, "Ma, listen if I tell you… you can't tell pop at all. I'm serious, ma." My mom gave me this look that she always gives me when she knows that I have done something wrong. She took a deep breath, and said, "Alright, Damion… Tell momma what you did now."

    I paused for a minute, and then I came out and said it so fast that she didn't understand what I said. It came out like "maIgotfiredfromthejob". I said it like it was all one word, and I said it real quick too. She looked at me like I was crazy, and asked "Boy, what the hell did you just say?" I finally got it together, and said, "Alright, alright, alright… I got fired from the job ma. But please don't tell pop. Please don't tell him, ma. I really don't wanna hear his mouth." My mother was just sitting there shaking her head. "Damion, this don't even make no sense. You can't keep a job for nothin." I assured her, "Ma, don't worry, I got some other stuff lined up, I swear. Just don't tell dad, OK." My mom looked at me and promised that she wouldn't tell my pops. She got up, still shaking her head, saying "Boy, you getting too old for this irresponsible nonsense. You better get it together."

# CHAPTER 2

New Year's had passed. It was January 1st 2005, and it was bone-shivering cold out. I had gone to see the ball drop with my sister and a couple of her friends, and got so drunk that I threw up on the train. The next morning, I had such a hangover that I didn't realize that I had slept for half the day. All of a sudden, my mother came pounding on my door telling me to open the door because I had a phone call. I opened my eyes and slowly got outta my bed. My head was still spinning and I felt sick to my stomach. It was the kind of feeling that you get when you eat something and then get on one of those rides at an amusement park that just go in a complete circle, like the Gravitron. I got up from my bed, took my first step and tripped over my clothes that were all over the floor. I was so weak that I couldn't break my fall by putting my arms out. By the time my brain had got the message that I was falling, I had already fallen and hit my head on the corner of my dresser. I heard my mom say, "Boy, what are you doin in there? Hurry up and come get this damn phone because I'm tired of this girl calling here. She dun called here ten damn times already, now come get this phone." I was so weak that I couldn't even get up. I just lifted my head from off the floor, and in a slow sloppy voice, I asked, "Hey ma, who is it?"

"It's Kit Kat, Damion. She said you was supposed to come and get Michael this mornin,'" my mom replied. Kit Kat was my son's mother, and boy, let me tell ya, she made my fuckin' life miserable. She looked, acted, and spoke just like Jada Pinkett-Smith but twenty five times worse. I was supposed to pick my son up that morning, but of course, I forgot, and I knew I was gonna hear Kit Kat's mouth. I finally made it to the door and grabbed the phone. I didn't realize how bad I looked until my mother said, "Boy, you got throw up all over your shirt." I just closed the door and went right back over and plopped on my bed, and said, "Hello." As soon as I said 'hello', Kit Kat started her shit. "So what bitch was you with last night, huh Casual? What bitch was so damn important that you forgot to come and pick up your son?" I'm sick of this shit, Casual, that's why I'm takin your ass to court for child support because I can't depend on you to do shit. So tell that bitch that's layin next to you that you got shit to do."

Kit Kat was always assuming that I was out with some other girl—that's why we just couldn't be together. I remember when we first got together, she accused me of dating my mother! One night, my mom and I went out to the movies together because we were dying to see this movie that had been out in the theater. Now Kit Kat lived all the way in Jersey. How she found out what movie theater I was at shocked and scared the shit outta me, because it just let me know how capable she was of finding my ass.

When my mother and I came out the theater after the movie was over, I couldn't believe what was before my eyes. It was Kit Kat, just standing there with her hands on her hips. She walked right up to me and my mother, and said, "Now who the fuck is this bitch, she needs to be ashamed of herself, robbin' the cradle with her old ass." Turning to my mother, she asked, "What the fuck are you doin' with my man, bitch?" I couldn't believe what was happening, I immediately grabbed Kit Kat by her arm and brought her over to the side. "Are you fuckin' crazy, Kit Kat? Are you seriously fuckin' insane? What the fuck is wrong with you? That's my mom, Kit Kat."

Kit Kat was so caught up on the fact that I was cheating on her that she didn't believe that my mom was my mom. She thought I was running game on her. She started getting loud shouting out, "Don't lie to me, Casual, I know that ain't your motha. Nigga, you ain't slick. I can't believe that you're gonna actually sit up there and lie in my face." To make a long story short, she still didn't believe me. She followed me all the way to my house just to make sure that my mom was actually my mom. My mother thought it was funny. I was really surprised that she didn't get mad but my mom is way too much of a lady to act out of character.

Kit Kat was those kind of girls that just kept on nit-picking at you, talking about 15 words every 3 seconds. She was so annoying, you would just wanna choke her and kill her. So, after about 10 seconds of listening to her accuse me of having another girl next to me, I just put the phone down next to me and closed my eyes because my hangover was really starting to get to me. When I finally heard silence, I picked up the phone, and asked, "Are you done yet?" I don't know why my dumb ass said that. I thought to myself I should know better by now. I had to really watch what I said to Kit Kat because she would just turn whatever smart remark that came outta my mouth into something else to argue about. I would actually have to walk on thin ice when talking to her, so I would say things like, 'Yeah, I know, Kit Kat, Yeah, you're right, Kit Kat. Yeah, Kit Kat, I know I'm an asshole.' So, instead, when I said 'Are you done yet,' she started to yell at the top of lungs like a mad woman, yelling and screaming, "Are done being an irresponsible father? Are you done being a sarcastic bastard? And are you done sleeping around? Don't fuckin' ask me am I done yet, hell no, I ain't done yet, mothafucka." She continued, "Ooooh. Don't piss me off, Casual.

Please don't piss me off because I'm already in the mood to just come to Manhattan and punch you in your fuckin' face. I bet you went to go see your daughter, didn't you? You'll do whatever in the world for her and that white bitch. You tell her, when I see her, I'm gonna slap her rich stuck-up ass."

Kit Kat was referring to Lacey, my daughter's mother. Lacey was an actress. She was pretty, always dressed nice, and had my daughter, and what Kit Kat really didn't appreciate was the fact that she was white. But this is what really took Kit Kat's top off—you don't hear about this happening too often. Both my son Michael by Kit Kat and my daughter Onyea by Lacey were born on the same day. That whole day, I had been with Lacey. We were on 5th Avenue doing some shopping for her mom because it was her birthday. Now I knew that Kit Kat was in the last stages of pregnancy but she hadn't called me all day to say she was having any pains, so I thought she was OK. Lacey and I were walking around when all of a sudden, her water broke. We hopped into a cab and headed to the hospital. When we got to the hospital, I left my cell phone in the cab—I was so caught up in the moment of my daughter coming out, I didn't realize I left it in the cab.

The next day, my mom, sister and my pops came up to the hospital to see my daughter. My mom had this look on her face like 'boooy, you in trouble'. I asked, "Ma, why do you look like that?" My mom wasn't the type to keep secrets from Lacey or Kit Kat, so she just came out and said, "Kit Kat had your son yesterday. He was 7 pounds 6 ounces. Need I say more?" She didn't have to say more. I knew I was in some shit. I knew Kit Kat must have been calling me off the hook, and I knew she was gonna be mad as hell. Now that right there is the biggest reason that Kit Kat hates Lacey.

Now it was gettin to the point where Kit Kat was starting to get on my nerves. I wanted to hang up the phone but I knew if I did that, she would let me hear about it. So I told her that I would have my mom pick up Michael, and I just hung up the phone. Right after I hung up the phone, it rang again. I thought it was Kit Kat, so when I answered it, I said, "What do you want, Kit Kat? Listen I'm sick and I wanna sleep." "Ohhh Casual, you know what I want—I want you to come and fuck the hell outta me. Ohh Casual, fuck me now, fuck me now, God, I wanna feel that black dick in my pussy right now." Only it wasn't Kit Kat—it was my best friend, Rodger.

Rodger was always joking around. He was a really, really, crazy, fuckin' white boy. He was about 6'8" and weighed about 268 pounds. He was big, crazy, and didn't give a fuck about nothing. I would always tell him that he wasn't normal—I mean normal people don't walk around with paint on their face, earrings all over the place, tattoos all over their body, and wear a Mohawk. And this wasn't no ordinary Mohawk that he wore—the Mohawk had spikes. He was bald on both sides but he had big, thick spikes going from the front of his head to the back. One side of his face was painted black, and the other side was white; he had rings of skeletons and dragons on every finger; and he wore a big thick chain around his neck with a lock on it about the size of a toddler's head. Let me tell ya, when this fuckin' guy came walking down the street, everybody moved outta his way. He looked insane, and not only did he look insane, he was fuckin' insane. He was the lead singer of this band called Suicidal. There were five of them, and they were all fuckin' crazy, if ya ask me. They were a rock group that sang about everything under the sun that had to do with hell on earth. They would even diss other rock groups that had record deals—they would say that they were too commercial and they would call them 'chumps'. Rodger and his crew considered themselves to be the underground of Megadeath. As far as I was concerned, their music was just a bunch of noise. I couldn't understand what the fuck Rodger would be saying on the microphone because he would just scream like a madman and jump around like he had no sense.

I met Rodger when I was in college through this girl I use to fool around with. I needed money on campus, so the girl and I started sellin LSD and heroin to make money. She was into all that Megadeath shit, so she knew Rodger. She was from the Village—all of us Village kids pretty much stuck together in college. Rodger was also from the Village. He was a heavy drug user and would also sell a lot of shit too. So this girl introduced me to him because he sold LSD cheaper than we were getting it for. Ever since then Rodger and I been the best of friends—we had pretty much the same things in common besides music but that was cool with me. It was funny though because everytime we went somewhere together, it looked like I was his damn lawyer. I was a clean-cut brotha, who dressed very casually, and here I was walkin with this 6'8" 268-pound lunatic with spiked haired and a painted face, who used profanity every time he opened his mouth.

I really didn't feel like talking to Rodger that day because I was feeling so fucked-up that I just wanted to sleep. Plus he had his music blasting in the background, so he was screaming into the phone. "Duude! What the fuck are you still doin' in the fuckin' bed, dude? Get the fuck up—the day is half fuckin' gone already." I couldn't take it—he was screaming into the phone because his music was so loud. "Yo, Rodger, can you please turn that shit down? I have a headache and you're makin it worse."

He said, "Duude, what the fuck did you just say? You gotta speak up, dude, I got my music on, and can't hear you."

"Well, turn that shit off, Rodger, and you might be able to hear me."

"Duude, hold on, I still can't hear you. Hey guys, turn the fuckin' radio down, am tryin' to talk on the fuckin' phone here."

Of course, they couldn't hear him because the radio was so loud. So he had to scream to tell them to turn the radio down. Alls I heard through the phone was his loud voice saying, "I said turn the fuckin' radio down. Duude, what the fuck are you fuckin' deaf. Turn the fuckin' shit the fuck down."

I couldn't take it any longer. I knew all of them were in there high as hell on LSD, and couldn't function straight, so I just hung up hoping that he wouldn't call me back. But he did. I knew it was Rodger's ass, so I didn't pick up the phone. When the phone finally stopped ringing, I said to myself, 'Yes, finally some peace and quiet.' But before I could get comfortable, I heard my door open—it was my pops. He was always just coming into my room without knocking, so I said, "Yo pop, can you knock before you come in, please?" My pops just gave me this funny-ass look, and said, "Boy, do I tell you to knock before you come into my house or do you just come in?"

He came over by my bedside and bent down on one knee just looking at me. I was a little confused about why he was even in my room, so I said, "Yo pops, why are you lookin' at me like that?" He scratched his head, and said, "Son, listen to me, son, and trust me, it's real hard for me to sit here and call you 'son', because I swear they must have switched you with my real son at the hospital." If you didn't know my pops, you would say, 'Damn, that's some harsh shit to say to your son.' But my pops was just a tough-lovin' funny-ass guy. He was like Richard Pryor and Bernie Mac all in one. He said, "Son, is everything OK with you, because you can tell me... Did me and your mother do something wrong? I mean, at what point did we mess up with you son?" I didn't know what the hell my pops was talkin about, so I just said, "Yeah, everything's cool, pop." Then he asked, "Well, why the hell can't you keep a goddamn job, Damion. This don't even make no sense boy. Your mother told me that you got fired last night."

I couldn't believe it. I just put my hands over my eyes in total disbelief. I couldn't believe that after all I said to my mother about not telling my pops about me getting fired, she told him anyway. I took my hands from my eyes and said, "Don't listen to ma. She got the story all twisted, pops." He just looked at me, and said, "Oh does she really? Well, untwist it for me, Damion, because I would love to hear the real *E! True Hollywood Story* of why your ass don't have a job this time."

Before I started to tell my pops about what had happened, I thought to myself maybe if I told him I quit because the job wasn't for me, he wouldn't get as mad. As I started to tell him, I noticed this look of pure interest on his face—like he just couldn't wait to hear what I had to say. I cleared my throat and came right out with it, "Listen, pop, that job was bringin' me down. I felt like a damn caged bird. I mean, come on, pop, as smart as I am, and with all the capabilities and potentials I possess, I felt like I was wastin' my life. So instead of lookin' at this as a backstep, I'm lookin' at me quittin' that job as a step forward. I can't be no shoe salesman, pop—that just ain't me."

My pops didn't even say anything—he just shook his head, got up, and walked towards the door. Right before he walked back into the hallway, he turned to me, and said, "Damion, that was the dumbest thing I ever heard in my life. Now you either go out and find you a job that your ass is gonna keep, or you're gonna be lookin for a place to live."

# CHAPTER 3

My ears were ringing. My eyes were getting tired from adjusting to the flicker of the strobe light. I couldn't breathe. It was hot and crowded. I started to feel weak—my legs were tired from standing all night. You would think that I'd be used to this by now. Rodger was performing with his band, and of course, I had decided to help out. My job was to hand out free T-shirts and promo CDs. I liked doing it because I met a lot of people but tonight was just a little too much. As Rodger's band was doing what they did best on stage, which was jumping around and screaming like a bunch of lunatics to their smash song, *The Devil lives upstairs from me*, the crowd went absolutely fuckin' nuts. I mean everyone who lived in the Village was practically a fan of Suicidal—not to mention every other bunch of headbangers, skaters, and skinheads that lived in the city. Rodger's band was considered the best underground Megadeath group in the city. People loved them so much, it confused me that Rodger didn't wanna be signed to a deal. Their band logo was a man pointing a .38 caliber pistol at the temple of his head, pulling the trigger, and blowing his brains out. You actually saw the bullet exiting from the other side of the man's temple along with the blood oozing out of the bullet wound. The song, *The Devil lives upstairs from me,* was actually one of Rodger's favorites. It was about his life and just how fucked-up it was, from his father beating him and his mother up every night, and how he feels like his life is worth nothing sometimes. Rodger's parents were also stone-cold drug addicts. His father was a member of the Satin's Assistants motorcycle gang and was just a renegade, period. Rodger's pops never even really wanted him to be born, so he just simply took it out on Rodger's mom. Then Rodger's mom would get upset and take it out on Rodger—it was some real crazy shit. So everytime Rodger performed this song, he would put his all into it—not like he didn't put his all into every song that he screamed or sang, if that's what you wanna call it. To me, it was just plain ol' screaming, but this one song in particular, he would just put extra energy into it. And when Rodger put his all into a song that he was performing, the crowd would go fuckin' bananas.

That's just what was happening right at that very moment. As Rodger started to jump around and scream at the top of his lungs, the crowd started to form what was called a 'mosh pit'. Now this is where I just said to myself, 'This don't make no damn sense'. These people would form a circle and just pound each other like they hated each other. I mean they would punch, kick, slap, slam, push, and do all kinds of other violent shit. And this was considered dancing to them—it just boggled my brain that they would even consider calling it 'dancing'. It's like saying, 'Hey, ya wanna dance?' and then just punching the other person in the face as hard as you possibly can. It just didn't make any fuckin' sense to me, but then again when I looked at the people that were doing it, half of them smoked up their last little bit of sense any damn way. Why wouldn't a guy with tattoos all over his face wanna dance like that—it's not like he can go to a regular club and ask a pretty girl to dance regularly with him. A pretty girl with brains, anyway. And I say that because a 3rd of the pit was filled with girls who were into this slam dance shit. So here you have a guy and a girl beating the shit outta each other, and calling it dancing. How attractive! Sometimes I wondered if this was how the girls picked who they wanted to go home with at the end of the night. Ya know, by judging who beat them up the most.

One time, I asked Rodger if that's how these people have sex. I asked, "Do you slam the bitch down on the bed and choke the shit outta her while you're fuckin' her?" Rodger would just laugh and then with a straight face, he would ask 'why'—almost as if he was guilty of such behavior. Sometimes, he would get offended because I referred to his fans as 'those people', but I didn't care because it was fuckin' ridiculous behavior. It was primitive and barbaric and it almost made me sick. Rodger would say, "Duude you haven't lived until you've slam danced." I would just look at him, and say, "Well, then I must be still fuckin' dead, and if that's livin, who the hell would wanna be born."

Then all of a sudden, I turned to look at Rodger to see what type of crazy shit he was doing while performing, and he just stage dived right into the crowd. I swear, I never thought a 258-pound man could jump so high. But what I really couldn't believe was the fact that his fans actually caught his ass. I mean he just jumped right out into the crowd, and they caught him. I thought to myself they must really love his ass because I would have let his ass fall right on his mothafuckin' face.

After the show, I was standin out in the parkin lot next to the van that we drove in, waiting for Rodger and his band to finish getting all their groupie love. I never wanted to be a part of all that attention because it didn't make me any difference if a slam dancing headbangin' chick with tattoos all over her body wanted to go home with me or not. So while I was waiting by the van, this group of guys approached me, and one of them asked me, "Hey, are you a part of the Suicidal band?" I responded by saying, "Now do you think someone dressed like myself would be a part of this?" Then I added, "Nah, I'm just fuckin' with you. Yeah, I'm with the band. Why what can I do for you?"

The kid looked kind of scared—I could tell because he was shaking—and he started off by saying, "Listen, bro, I think you guys are so fuckin' awesome, man. I mean you guys are the hardest rock band around in the underground." He kept rambling on and on about how he loved how we rocked, and I was getting tired of hearing him because after all, I knew what he wanted. Rodger had been looking for a new guy to play the guitar because his guitar man had gone to jail for almost killing a guy during a bar brawl. So I knew this guy was gonna give me a demo CD so that Rodger could listen to it. And as quick as I figured out what he wanted, he reached into his bag and took out a CD,, and said, "Look, man, do you think Rodger can check out my CD and get back to me? I mean I know I have the potential to rock on stage with him. I know my skills are just as good or if not better than what he's heard, bro, so can ya take this CD?"

I politely grabbed the CD, and opened up the back of the van where Rodger kept all the demo CDs that people gave him. There were so many of them that when I opened the backdoor, some of them just spilled out. I knew once he saw how many CDs were in there, his confidence would come right back down to size. I took the CD and just chucked it right in the van—when it landed, it hit a bunch of other CDs and they all fell right on top of the CD that he had given me. I put my hand on his shoulder and said, "There, hows that?" As I bent down to pick up the CDs that had spilled out onto the ground, I noticed that this guy was still standing in front of me, like he wanted me to do him some sort of special favor. So I stood up, and said, "Is there something else that I can do for you?"

It took him a while to answer because firstly, he was probably shocked at how many demos were in the van, secondly, he was probably disappointed at the fact that I had just chucked his CD in the van like I didn't give a fuck, and thirdly, he was probably even more disappointed at the fact that when I chucked it, all the other demo CDs had fallen on top of his. After taking a deep swallow of his saliva in total shock, he finally said, "Hey bro, how do I know that Rodger is actually gonna get to hear my CD? I mean how does he find the time to listen to all those demos?" I paused for a minute before responding because I really didn't wanna hurt this kid's feelings, but I didn't know what else to tell him except the truth, so I just said, "Ummmmm... well, ya know, it took him some time to come up with this but he's finally figured out a system where he just doesn't listen to any of them. And it seems to be workin' out pretty good for him. So if you'll excuse me, I have to pick up the rest of these CDs." The guy just walked off, and I closed the van door while waiting for the next asshole to give me a demo.

After Rodger and his band finished with all that groupie love shit, we all hopped into the van, and headed back to Rodger's place. I guess performing their own music wasn't enough because as soon as we pulled out, Rodger turned on the radio, and turned it up full blast. I couldn't take it—I wasn't gonna take it—I refused to listen to anymore of that shit. "Yo Rodger, can you please, please, turn that shit off, I mean really." He didn't turn it off but he did turn it down. When he turned it down, I swear I never thought the sound of the New York City streets and the air blowing in from the open windows could be so soothing. It's amazin how noise can relax you after your ears have been surrounded by noise. It sounds weird but the noise from Rodger's band was so fuckin' loud and irritating that the noise from the New York City streets was like a massage to my eardrum. As I sat back in the seat trying to relax myself, I noticed one of Rodger's band members, whose name was Bad News, and who was sitting next to me, fixing to shoot a load of heroin in his arm. With a look of disgust and a slight smirk of my lips, I said "Damn, you just can't wait till you get back to the house, huh? A hard night's work calls for a shot of dope, huh." He looked at me and smiled with the little bit of teeth that he had, and asked, "So how did you like the concert?" Laughing almost hysterically because I couldn't believe that he would even ask me, I responded by saying, "Well, let's see... uhhhhh it was noisy." Bad News was shocked by what

I said. "That's all you can say, that it was noisy? Dude, were you there or what?" he said to me while spraying spit from his mouth because of the missing teeth that he had in the front. At that point, Rodger then jumped into the conversation, and said, "Hey Bad News, it's useless, dude. Casual doesn't like our shit. He'd rather listen to that rap shit." Rodger hated rap music—he thought it was unoriginal, repetitious, and way too violent against its own kind. So then Bad News said, "You think that rap shit is better then what we sing? Aww, come on, Casual, you gotta be shittin' me."

"Look Bad News, first of all, you guys don't sing anything, you fuckin' scream it. And I'm not gonna sit here and argue with you about how beautiful and inspiring the music that I listen to is, because that means that I would actually have to talk intelligently to you, and that's like talkin' astrophysics to a fuckin' retard. So on that note I'm goin' to sleep."

"BEAUTIFUL!!!! INSPIRING!!!!! Excuse me, bro, but there is absolutely nothin' at all inspiring about your music. Alls you guys talk about is, bitch this, bitch that, selling drugs, I'll fuckin' pull my Tech 9 out and shoot you, or if not that, you guys are talking about how big your fuckin' cock is. How inspiring is that?"

I could see that Bad News wasn't gonna give up because he kept on talking down rap music. So finally, I sat up, looked over at him jamming that needle in his arm like it was his saving grace, and said, "I don't think that you're in any position to downplay the ghetto mentality, especially when you're jamming that poison in your arm. So, that same shit that you say we're talking about all the time can't be so bad because you're putting it in your arm right now as we speak." Rodger couldn't help but laugh, and Bad News was so stupid and fried from just being on drugs all the time that he was laughing as well.

When we got back to Rodger's house, I was really debating whether I should have just had him take me home because I knew once I stepped foot in Rodger's house, the smell of funk was gonna hit me. Rodger always kept a filthy place—I mean his apartment was just disgusting. But it was too late. We were already too close to Rodger's apartment for me to just come out and say, 'Take me home'. When we got inside Rodger's apartment, it looked like the police had raided the apartment or a hurricane had just blown through it. He had clothes and shit all over the place—you couldn't even see the floor. And on top of that, he was a fuckin' pack rat—Rodger loved to collect things—stupid things that people would put on the street as garbage. But then here would come Captain Save The Trash to save the day. Rodger would take it off the street, clean it up, and put it right in his apartment. As far as I was concerned, it looked better on the damn street than in Rodger's apartment because alls he would do is clean it off and put it in with the rest of the junk that he had. I was so tired that I just wanted to pass out, but an obstacle had to be overcome. Finding a place to sleep that night was an actual obstacle in Rodger's house. The rest of the band was comfortable—they found a spot wherever and just laid down. So I said to myself, 'Fuck it.' I walked over to the couch and prepared myself to lay down.

As I was about to plop on the couch, I was suddenly stopped by a nasty plate that looked like someone hadn't finished eating. The plate was full of food—it was as if someone had taken a couple of bites and just left it. The disgusting thing about it was the fact that this wasn't a plate that had been left out from last night or earlier in the day. This plate had to be at least a month old; it was growing mold and it smelled horrible.

"Hey Rodger, what do you want me to do with this nasty plate that you have on your couch"? I asked. "Oh just leave it, duude, I'll get it later." I wasn't surprised at all by his response. He thought that I was trying to straighten up but I wanted to lie down. I mean Rodger was a really disgusting mothafucka. Anybody who drinks leftover hot dog water is just ridiculously nasty. Yeah, this guy actually drank hot dog water. I remember one time I was cooking hot dogs in his apartment, and I went to dump out the water in the sink so I could wash the pot and he ran over towards me like I was pouring out a whole bottle of Grey Goose liquor. He ran over to me so fast that he was huffing and puffing, and in between each breath he took, he said, "Duude, are you crazy? What the fuck are you doin—don't dump that. I love hot dog water. Ya see, duude, what I do is I put it in the fridge and wait until it gets cold, and then I drink it."

I remember that day like it was yesterday, so now I'm thinking of how I'm gonna get this plate off the couch without touching it with my hands. I finally just said, 'Fuck it. I'll sleep on the fuckin' floor.' So I'm lookin back and forth between the floor and the couch, trying to figure out which of the two is less dirty. And I say 'less dirty' because neither one was even close to bein clean, so deciding which of the two was cleaner wasn't one of my options. Now you can understand what I mean when I say finding a place to sit or lay down was an obstacle. My choices were either a couch with a moldy dinner plate on it, dirty underwear on the arms of the couch, holes in the pillows, and not to mention whatever was livin in those holes. Then there was the floor, well… I couldn't see the floor because it was covered in clothes and junk, so I guess if I chose the floor, I would be speaking of dirty laundry. I tell ya, if I could've slept standing up, I would've.

As I was trying to make a decision on where I was gonna lay down, Rodger's girlfriend came out of their room lookin like hell, of course. Her name was Patricia. And she was a weird mothafucka; let me tell ya, she actually scared me at times. She was one of those atheist chicks that thought there was no such thing as god. She had long, jet-black hair, and these scary, bright green eyes that made her look wild. About two years ago, she had one of the nicest bodies I had ever seen on a white girl, but hard drugs had changed all that. She was on every drug that was on the market—she popped pills, sniffed coke, took LSD, heroin, and all that. But what she really loved to do was shoot crack.

I never understood it. I remember the first time I saw her shoot it like it was yesterday. I always thought crack was supposed to be smoked, but she took the shit, put it on top of a spoon, and heated it up with her lighter until it went from solid to liquid. And when it turned, she stuck her needle in it. She would then hold her breath, so the vein in her neck would stick out, and she would have Rodger insert the needle right in her juggler vein. According to her, it was better than smoking it because it goes straight into the bloodstream. She called it 'rush'—I mean it was still crack but down in the Village, they called it 'rush'.

Rodger and Patricia had a real strange relationship. To me, it was 'drug love'. The only time they really got along was when they were high. Rodger liked to smoke dust and take LSD, and when he mixed the two, he became a fuckin' madman. Now he was already a madman any way, but when he was high on dust and LSD, he would become a nice guy actually. They would get into these heated arguments, and Rodger would end up beating the shit outta Patricia. But she was always getting back up and getting in his face. The thing was—she was just as sick in the head as him. Sometimes, I would have to get in between them and break it up before Rodger killed her, because no matter how hard he would hit her, she would get right back up. And all this shit would happen when they were sober, or when they were coming down off of a good high. But when they got their hands on some goods, they were in love all over again—that's why I called their relationship 'drug love'. When they were high, they would be kissing all over each other and whispering 'I love you' and shit—it was just plain downright 'drug love'.

It was getting close to morning, and my eyes were getting real heavy. I cleared a little path through the mess that was on Rodger's floor and I laid down. I propped my head up on my leather coat and used it for a pillow. I turned over to the left to close my eyes and fall asleep but they were quickly reopened because Patricia was making so much noise in the kitchen talking to Rodger. She had been waiting for him all night to bring home her fix—her nightly dosage of rush. "I hope you brought my shit Rodger," she yelled out, "I've been waitin' on you all fuckin' night." She was walking back and forth, pacing around the kitchen waiting for Rodger to put her to sleep. It was a crying shame how this girl needed that shit to go to sleep. She even needed it when she woke up—she was jammin it in her system before she would even brush her teeth. Then during the course of the day, she needed it to function, not to mention all the other goodies she was mixing in with it. "Come on, Rodger, hurry the fuck up. I need my shit—let's go." she yelled. "Alright, alright, Patricia. Shit, will you stop bitchin'? I'm heatin' this shit up for you," Rodger replied.

As Rodger continued to heat her fix up, Patricia sat down in the kitchen and stuck her arm out. I thought to myself, her neck vein must be shot because she used it too much, so now she's using her arm. Rodger tied the strap tightly around her arm and inserted the needle in her arm. The shit was like magic. She let out a big sigh as her eyes rolled in the back of her head. Then Rodger picked her up and brought her into the room.

# CHAPTER 4

It had been a couple of weeks since I had seen my daughter, so I called up Lacey to let her know that I was on my way. Lacey's parents pretty much took care of our daughter because Lacey was always away on some shoot for a movie, and I was just a deadbeat dad—to cut a long story short. Of course, when I got to her house, Lacey and her parents were about to sit down and have dinner, so I sat down next to Lacey and joined them.

"Hey Damion, you're just in time for dinner. How would you like to bless the table before we eat?" Those were the exact words that came out of Mr. Broshere's mouth as he stared me down with such hate in his eyes. Mr. Broshere was Lacey's father, and the only reason he tolerated me was because I was the father of his granddaughter. As I pushed my chair in, I turned to my left and noticed that Lacey's face had turned red, "DAD!!" she shouted, "He doesn't have to bless the table if he doesn't want to." While pouring a glass of his favorite wine that he always drank, he looked right at me while he spoke to Lacey saying, "He can say grace, Lacey. I'm quite sure that he is more than capable of doing so." "MOM!!" Lacey screamed across the table at her mother.

But I put my hand on Lacey's shoulder, and said, "Shhhh, don't worry, I'll say it." "No Casual, you don't have to bless the table. My dad is just being stupid." That was another thing Lacey's dad hated—he hated it when his daughter called me 'Casual'. Ya see, Lacey was a rich, spoiled rotten, white girl from the Upper West Side of the city. She was born with a silver spoon in her mouth, and she got whatever she wanted. She was an only child and her father hated the fact that his only daughter was parenting a child by a black man.

Now it was lights, camera, and action—the table got quiet. Everybody bowed their heads as I prepared to bless the table. I cleared my throat and took a sip of water. Now I'd never said grace before, so I didn't even know how to start, so I just set it off with, "Dear Lord… Ummmmm, thank you Lord… Thank you for… this… wonderful, wonderful food." I couldn't think of any more shit to thank God for, so I faked a cough, acting like something was stuck in my throat, stalling for time so I could think of something to thank God for. As I cleared my throat for the 80th time, I continued to bless the table with the words, "Oh Lord… Oh great, mighty, strong Lord… You are indeed a great mighty, strong Lord." Then it came to me! As I lifted my head a little, I looked at all the food that was on the table. I said to myself, 'Fuck that! I'm just gonna thank God for every fuckin' dish that's on this damn table, starting with the meat.' So now that I knew what I was thanking the Lord for, it gave me a little enthusiasm about blessing the table. I continued, starting off with, "Oh mighty Lord, we thank you for these fine, juicy pork chops, and these delicious mashed potatoes, and these peas, and this white rice, and this cheesecake. We thank you, oh good Lord, Amen."

When it was finally over, as soon as I said 'Amen', Lacey's father looked up at me, and said, "Why thank you, Damion, that has to be the most uplifting blessing I've ever heard at a dinner table in my whole life."

"Oh don't mention it, Mr. Broshere. I do this type of thing all the time at my house."

"Yes, I can tell, Damion, I can feel your spiritualism from across the table. Your family must be very religious."

I knew that Mr. Broshere was being sarcastic. But I liked fuckin' with him, so I was getting ready to say something slick, until Lacey pinched my thigh from underneath the table, signaling me to shut up. Not only did Mr. Broshere hate me because I was black, he also hated me for turning his daughter from a good Catholic schoolgirl to a drug addict. After all, it was because of me that she went into rehab. I had her trippin' on acid and lacing her weed with coke on a daily basis. And rehab didn't even work—she still gets high on a daily basis. Her mom really didn't seem to mind anymore. After a while, she just said, 'Oh the hell with it, the damage has been done'. Her mom was actually cool with me now.

After dinner, I went into Lacey's room to wake up my little girl. I picked her up and laid her right across Lacey's bed. Lacey and I were shooting the shit for about a half hour while I played with my daughter until Lacey said somethin stupid. "So have you thought about us getting back together?" she asked, in a soft, whispering, guilty voice. I didn't even look at her—I just said, "No, I haven't, Lacey. Whatever happened to that underwear model—he ain't fuckin' you like you wanna be fucked?"

Ya see, Lacey had left me for some underwear model that she had met while she was on one of her movie shoots. He was some French fuckin' pretty boy, who had a muscular body and just the right amount of fame to slide right into Lacey's panties. And he came just at the right time—when I wasn't paying any attention to her. I mean you couldn't tell me shit—I was dating a rich actress from the Upper West Side of Manhattan, who was on my dick so bad a good Jewish lawyer couldn't get her off. I was the mothafucka, but it all got to my head. I started taking advantage of her, and she ran off with another dude. After all, I use to say to myself, we couldn't be together any way because Lacey was just not my kinda girl. She was way too passive. She would do anything I asked her to do—I mean anything.

So as we were on her bed, talking about how I'm never gonna get back with her, my cell phone rang. Lacey snatched my phone from off my hip before I could get to it because she wanted to talk about our relationship.

"Yo, gimme my fuckin' phone, Lacey, I don't have time for this shit."

"Ill, Casual, what's the attitude about?"

"I don't have no attitude, Lacey, you're sittin' here, playin' games with me, snatchin' my phone so we can talk about a fuckin' relationship that's never gonna happen."

"Well, damn, Casual, we do have a daughter together. I think it would be best if we were together so we can raise her properly."

"Yeah, whatever, Lacey, ya should've thought about that shit when you were suckin' that underwear model's dick."

Lacey's mouth opened real wide when I said that, and she stood up, and pointed her finger right in my face shouting, "Ya know, Casual, you weren't exactly Mr. Fuckin' Wonderful when we were together. You treated me like I didn't even exist." While Lacey kept rambling on, my cell phone went off again and I took advantage of the opportunity and snatched it back from her.

"Hello."

"Yo what's up duude! Where the fuck are you? I've been lookin for you all day." It was Rodger, of course, and once again, he had the fuckin' music blasting in the background.

"Yo, Rodger, can you turn the radio off please? I can't hear you."

Almost yelling at the top of his lungs, he responded by saying, "Duude I can't hear you. Speak up."

This always happened when Rodger called me so, I screamed into the phone, "TURN THE MOTHAFUCKIN' RADIO DOWN, AND MAYBE YOU'LL HEAR ME, RODGER."

"Yo, Duude! Stop yellin' man. You're hurtin' my ears." I couldn't believe he said that to me, so I just hung up. As loud as his radio always was, he still tells me to stop yelling, and that I'm the one hurting his fuckin' ear. I knew he would call back because he always did, and 5 seconds later, my phone went off again.

I quickly picked up my phone, and said, "What do you want, Rodger"?

Rodger was huffing and puffing like something was up, so I knew he was gonna ask me for something. "Yo, duude, ya know how my girl usually takes the trip with me out to Englewood to drop the goods at my cousin's house for some cash?"

"Rodger, don't tell me you need money."

Rodger made runs out to Englewood every now and then to drop off some of that good dope that he had. It was called 'heaven' because as soon as you inserted that shit in your vein, that's where you went. Ya see, his cousin couldn't get that shit out in Englewood so Rodger would take it out to him and overcharge him because his cousin didn't know any better anyway. It usually went down like this. Rodger would put the dope inside of a balloon and have his girl swallow it. He would also give her some Ex-Lax to make her shit, so by the time they got to his cousin's house, she would just shit it out. It was a smooth operation, and the money was alright but this time there was a slight problem.

I could hear Rodger's girl in the background yelling at the top of her lungs at him, "YOU PIECE OF SHIT. I FUCKIN' HATE YOU. ALL YOU CARE ABOUT IS YOUR FUCKIN' MUSIC. I'M NOT DOIN' SHIT FOR YOU. GET ONE OF YOUR LOW-LIFE FUCKIN'

FRIENDS TO DO IT." Right then and there I knew what the problem was. I knew that they had gotten into some fight, and Patricia didn't wanna mule that shit to his cousin's house. What was on my mind now was—what the fuck did Rodger want from me.

So I said, "Yo, Rodger, I can hear your girl in the background talkin' shit to you, so I'm guessin' that she ain't about to mule those goods for you. But what I'm boggled about is why the fuck are you callin' me? Because I'm tellin' you right now—if you're even thinkin' about what I think you're thinkin' about, then you're a bigger dummy than I thought."

Rodger just started laughing and said "Duude, I would never ask you to swallow that shit, but what I'm gonna ask you is do you know anybody that will?"

"Rodger, why the fuck are you askin' me some dumb ass shit like that? I ain't no fuckin' dealer."

"Duude, chill out, Casual, I just figured that you might know some slut that would do it for a small fee."

As soon as Rodger said that, I kinda got a little tingle in my brain—like the kind you get when you're thinking about doing something when you know you can get something out of it.

So I said "What the fuck do you mean 'a small fee'? What the fuck is a small fee?"

"Duude, what I'm sayin' is, if you can find someone to mule this shit for me, I'll give you some of the cash."

The way I needed money in my life at the moment, a lightbulb went off in my head. Rodger was talking business now. I immediately put my daughter down on Lacey's chest, and asked, "So how much?"

I knew Rodger was a cheap mothafucka, so when he said, "Don't worry. I'll hook you up," I told him, "Fuck that shit. I want at least 300 or I ain't doin it."

Ya see, I knew that Rodger was muling at least 2,000 dollars worth of shit because everytime he went up there, he made out with at least that much or more. So when he told me that if I found someone, he'll cut me at least 300, a smile appeared on my face that made Lacey ask what we were talking about. And little did she know, she would find out what it was that we were talking about sooner than she thought. As soon as Rodger said "OK, 300," I looked straight at her with that smile on my face. "Yo, Rodger, let me call you back in like thirty seconds," I told him.

Lacey was the perfect one for the job. Ya see, I knew Lacey would do it because first of all, Lacey would jump off the fuckin' Brooklyn bridge if I told her to. Plus she felt guilty anyway for cheating on me with that model, so I knew she would do it. I pushed up on her and started kissing her on her neck because that was her hot spot. She started giggling, and said, "OK, Casual, what is it that you want?" I looked her in her eyes as if I was in love with her all over again, and said, "Yo, you wanna do daddy a favor?" while I ran my hands up her skirt. She looked back at me so innocently, and asked, "What?" As my hand went further up her skirt, I started rubbing her pussy as if I wanted to fuck her, while I whispered in her ear what it was that I wanted her to do. And like magic, as she moaned, she whispered back into my ear, "Only if you fuck me first." As disrespectful as it sounds, I called Rodger with my left hand, as I put my dick inside of Lacey with my right hand, and told him, "Yo, don't worry about it. I got it all under control. Just call me when you're ready because right now I'm takin' care of some shit."

I hung up with Rodger and continued making Lacey happy. Dumb me, I didn't even have a condom on but I said, 'Fuck it. Let me just make her happy so we can get this shit done.' Now you would think that a guy would have more respect for his daughter's mother but not me—300 dollars was on my mothfuckin mind. The very next day, we were ready to go. I got Lacey drunk so she wouldn't freak out about swallowing the balloon, but hell, the way Lacey sucked a dick, this wouldn't be a problem for her. Now I had a big cock—a real big cock—and Lacey would practically swallow that shit when she was giving me head. So I knew that she wouldn't have a problem swallowing this balloon. The only problem was that Rodger didn't have any balloons this time, so we had to use a little plasticwrap sandwich bag.

Before I knew it, we were on the road, me, Lacey and Rodger. Lacey let us drive her car—she never used it anyway because here in New York, you really didn't need one. While we were riding, Rodger pulled out some of that good ol' Village town coke to keep us company on the way. I sniffed up about three lines, and I was lit. Rodger always had good shit, no matter what it was. He also had some weed. We were getting fucked-up so much that I started to swerve on the road. Lacey started to get a little nervous, and said, "Alright, Casual, you've done enough, you're all over the road." But I didn't pay any attention to her. I kept on hitting that weed.

Rodger and I got so high, we got into this real deep conversation about God. We always got into deep conversations about shit when we were high. Ya see, Rodger didn't think that there was such a thing as God—basically, he was an atheist, like his girl Patricia. His life was so fucked-up that he just got comfortable with the fact that there can't be a God. As we were going back and forth, I noticed that Lacey's head was tilted to the side and her eyes were closed. I reached over to wake her up but Rodger said, "Chill, duude, just let her sleep." That was cool with me because that meant that I could take another sniff of that caine without hearing her fuckin' mouth. So Rodger passed me a line, and I sniffed it up.

I was so fuckin' high at this point that I felt like I was just floating. I turned to Rodger, and said, "Yo, look at this girl, Rodger, for Christ's sake, she's a fuckin' TV star, and she's sittin' over here with a sandwich bag full of dope in her stomach. I'm goin' to hell for this shit for real,

Rodger." Laughing his ass off, he grabbed me by my neck, and said, "Not only is she a fuckin' TV star, duude, she's your daughter's mother." We were both laughing like two clowns, as if this was a funny situation. We were almost there, so Rodger and I decided to stop acting like clowns. His cousin lived with his parents—Rodger's aunt and uncle.

As we got off the Exit, I turned to wake up Lacey and said, "Yo, Lacey, wake up, baby girl. We here." When she didn't answer, I just thought that she was in a deep sleep. So I started shaking her and shaking her, "Yo, Lacey, wake up baby, we here." When she still didn't respond, I started yelling out her name, and shaking her like a rag doll. When she still didn't wake up, I knew something was wrong. I started to panic and raised my voice, almost screaming, "YO, LACEY, WAKE UP, LACEY... LACEY... YO, LACEY, WAKE THE FUCK UP." Even after me screaming and shaking her, she still didn't wake up. I started to slap her in the face—I had to have slapped her at least 7 fuckin' times, and she still didn't respond. I was a fuckin' wreck.

Rodger was trying to calm me down by saying, "Yo, duude, she's probably in a deep sleep." I was so scared, I yelled at Rodger, "A DEEP SLEEP! A DEEP FUCKIN' SLEEP! RODGER, THIS IS MY DAUGHTER'S MOTHER. I KNOW HOW SHE FUCKIN' SLEEPS, AND THIS AIN'T NO SLEEP, ASSHOLE." I started smacking her so hard that her face turned beet red. Then I noticed that her lips were blue, and her face was paler than usual. "Yo, Rodge, I think she's fuckin' dead, man. She's fuckin' dead, man. We gotta do somethin', Rodge. We gotta do somethin' now, Rodge. Oh shit, oh my fuckin' God, oh my mothafuckin God, LACEY, GET THE FUCK UP, GET UP!"

I was a mess, and on top of that, I was high as hell. Rodger's aunt was a doctor, so he immediately called his cousin and told him what was going on. When his cousin answered the phone, Rodger calmly said, "Jason, we gotta serious fuckin' situation, dude. Meet me at the front door right now." Rodger's cousin must have asked him what was going on because Rodger yelled, "DUUDE, DON"T ASK QUESTIONS. JUST DO IT!" Right after Rodger just screamed at his cousin, he just hung up his cell phone, and directed me to where his cousin lived. I drove right up on their lawn like a madman.

When I put the car in park, Rodger's cousin was standing outside, in his pajamas. With a look of pure shock, he put his hands on his head, and said, "Are you serious you, asshole. Rodger, what the fuck is wrong with your friend? Jesus Christ, you're on my father's lawn. He's gonna fuckin' kill me." Jason was more shook up than we were—he was always nervous about some shit. He went to a private school because his parents didn't want him to turn into a Rodger. So he was caught in between being a nerd for his parents in the day time, and being a hardcore drug addict at night. I mean he played it off kinda cool but this day, he was gonna have do some explaining to his parents.

As soon as I pulled up on his father's lawn, I got right out, and ran over to open Lacey's door. Jason walked right over to Rodger, and because he didn't wanna alert his parents, he spoke in a real low voice, grinding his teeth, and said, "Rodger, you wanna tell me what the fuck is goin' on before my pain-in-the-ass mom, slash your-pain-in-the-ass Aunt comes down here?" Rodger and I were just totally ignoring Jason so we could get Lacey out of the car, and into the house. And let me tell ya, it wasn't far—I was not fuckin' around at all—I drove that mothafuckin car right up to the front door. I mean the car was practically in his damn house. Jason had his hands over his eyes in total disbelief. He was pacing back and forth, saying, "Dude, this is not fuckin' happening. Please tell me that I'm dreaming. Please tell me that there's not a car parked three quarters of the way into my goddamn living room." Rodger didn't waste any time telling his cousin that Lacey had overdosed on the dope that he was selling to him. As I laid Lacey down on the couch, alls I heard outta Jason's mouth was, "WHAT! Dude, what the fuck did you just say! I know I didn't hear what I thought I heard.

Look at her, for Christ's sake, Rodger, she's dead. She's fuckin' dead, bro. I can't believe you just brought a dead bitch into my house."

Immediately, I started to lose my patience, and said, "Yo, where the fuck else were we suppose to go?" Still pacing back and forth, Jason looked at me, and sarcastically said, "Dude, do you think that just maybe the fuckin' hospital might be able to help? I mean really, here you've gotta bitch who just swallowed enough dope to pay a monthly mortgage in the Hamptons, and you bring her here. Boy, if that ain't thinkin' like a hero, I don't know what is." Then outta nowhere, Jason's mom came over and just pushed all of us outta the way, and asked, "What's wrong with her—is she OK?" We just kept our mouth shut—we didn't say a word. When we all didn't say anything, she looked up at us all, and said, "Well, what's wrong with her? Let's not all talk at once, boys." Right then and there, Rodger came up with the dumbest reason ever. He said, "Oh Aunt Karyn, she got stung by a bee, and I think she's allergic." Now outta all the fuckin' reasons in the world that he could have came up with, he says she got stung by a bee! Rodger's aunt didn't waste any time. She immediately called the ambulance, and off to the hospital we went.

## CHAPTER 5

It had been two weeks since Lacey had been released from the hospital. It was like a boulder had been lifted off my shoulder. Ya see, what had happened was, the plastic that we had put the dope in somehow opened inside of Lacey, and the dope went into her bloodstream, causing her to pass out and damn near die. And let me tell ya, she should've fuckin' died—anybody who swallows that much dope has no chance in hell of coming back from that. God must have really been with her through that shit.

But what was so fucked-up was the fact that she got a warm welcome from the press as soon as she walked out that hospital door. There were cameras, news reporters, all kinds of magazine writers and photographers just waiting for her to come out so they could get some info on what went down. Ya see, Lacey was starring in this HBO series called the *Rotten Apple*, in which she played the daughter of this big-time, dangerous mob boss. The series was mainly about how this mob boss balanced his home life and life with the mob. I never watched it because I was never a real big TV watcher, plus I was always too busy hanging out. Everybody was really dogging Lacey. I started to feel sorry for the poor girl. From *Star* magazine all the way to Fox Five News, everyone was talking about this. Even the radio stations were talking shit—it was sickening. They shouted out her drug habit, shouted out how she doesn't take care of our daughter like a mother should, they even shouted out her steamy affair with that underwear model. Little did I know, he was a married man with kids—that's why they were calling it an affair. So not only were they calling her a drug addict and a drug mule, they were calling her a whore and a home-wrecker. But what really pissed me off was the fact that they blamed all this shit on me. These magazine writers and these radio people didn't know me from a hole in the fuckin' wall but they were still talking shit about my ass. Jesus Christ, they were even calling me Bobby fuckin' Brown—in this one magazine, they wrote that it was all me that got her hooked on hard drugs, which was true but all that shit about me hitting her and taking her money to get high, was crazy.

Besides all that, I had to face Lacey's parents. Of course, her dad wanted me locked up in jail. He tried to get me arrested but it didn't work. And her mom…the little bit of love that she did have for me was gone—she just flat-out told me to stay out of Lacey's life, and that I would never see my daughter until some court issues on custody were settled. My parents were red hot, especially my dad—ya know with him bein a cop and shit, he was mad as hell. I even got kicked outta my house. My mom didn't want me to go but my pops was like he's getting the hell outta my goddamn house. If ya ask me, I think he went a little overboard about it all—he started calling me a drug dealer. I told him, "Damn pop, if that was the case, I'm the brokest drug dealer in New York City because I damn sure ain't got no money." My sister thought it was funny as hell—she said that everyone at her job was talking about it—I was like the talk of New York. And Kit Kat was the worst. She actually said, "Good for that stuck-up little bitch. She shoulda died, dumb-ass, white bitch swallowing all that shit. Now how's Hollywood treatin' her ass?" I couldn't stomach being around her that day, so I just picked up my son and left. Ever since what had hap

pened, I became a bigger drug user than usual. It really fucked me up—my mind wasn't right after all that shit. I actually thought that I killed my daughter's mother—I was even having nightmares about it.

So, to stop me from thinking about this, alls I did was sit around with Rodger and get high all fuckin' day. It was Friday night, and I was with Anastasia all day—we had just come from Rockefeller Center because she wanted to go ice skating. When we got back to her place, alls she wanted to do was talk. My mind was set on getting her back to her place, fuckin' her, and leaving. But for some reason, she just was talking my fuckin' ear off, and that was one thing I hated about Anastasia—she talked too fuckin' much. So about five minutes into our conversation about nothing, I just cut her off, and asked, "Can we fuck now or what?" She just looked at me with these big eyes, and said, "Damn, Casual, is that all you want from me—is sex? Can't we spend one night with each other, without havin' sex?" I immediately let her know what the deal was when she said that—because it sounded like she was getting a little serious on me. "Listen, Anastasia, it is what it is. Let's not fool ourselves. I'm here to spend a little time with you, talk, have dinner or whatever, and then have nasty sex—and that's it."

"Excuse me, Casual, but it would be nice if we just spent the night with each other without having sex." Anastasia was not about to get the upper hand on what I had intended on this relationship, so I quickly said, "Wait a minute here, see this is what I'm sayin', Ann. Who said I was spendin' the night tonight anyway? Listen, if it's not too much trouble, I would love to fuck you right now, so can we please just... ya know... Let's do the damn thing, girl." Right after those words came so strongly from my arrogant mouth, Anastasia moved the hair that covered the left side of her face with her long, red fingernails, and softly said, "Casual, get outta my house. Get outta my house right now." She didn't have to tell my cocky ass twice. I stood right the fuck up, popped the collar on my leather coat and stepped out. As I was on my way over to the door, I heard her mumble under her breath that she couldn't stand my ass. I knew I had fucked-up because actually, I really wouldn't have minded staying the night at Anastasia's because God knows that the only place I could crash at was the place that I really didn't wanna stay at… Rodger's house.

When my pops kicked me out, Rodger told me not even to sweat it because I could always stay with him, and that's right where I ended up at. When I got to Rodger's house, of course, he wasn't home, so I had to enjoy the company of his crazy-ass girl, Patricia. The weird thing was when I walked in, there was this guy who was on his way out, which was kinda unusual because I didn't know him. When he walked out, I asked Patricia who he was. She looked at me all stoned outta her mind, and said, "Oh, that's the goodies guy. That's where I get my shit from whenever I can't find Rodger." I didn't pay any attention to it because to me, it was like well… she's a druggy, and she's gotta get the shit from somewhere. As I took a seat on the couch before removing a handful of clothes, Patricia was holding up another magazine that was talking all kinds of shit about Lacey. Then outta nowhere, she just started reading out loud what it said—as if I needed or even wanted to hear what it said! So I just rudely interrupted her by saying, "Soooo… Patricia, are we still worshipping the devil these days?" And boy, if that didn't shut her up real quick! She put the magazine down, and put her hands on her hips just staring at me with those big, bloodshot, scary, green eyes.

"How many times do I have to tell you, Casual? I'm an athiest, not a devil worshipper."

"Oh, I'm sorry, Patricia. I really didn't realize that there was a difference."

Almost enraged by my comment, she responded by saying, "And, of course, an ignorant bastard such as yourself wouldn't think that there is a difference. Ya see, Casual, atheism is not a belief in any sort of superhuman power, nor is it categorized by worship in any meaningful way." I just looked at Patricia when she said that.

Shaking my head, I then leaned forward, and said, "Hey, Patricia, why don't you go somewhere and get high OK?"

"Fuck you, Casual. Ya know, you can sleep the fuck outside."

I could see that Patricia was offended by what I said, so I apologized to her. "Listen, Patricia, it's just that I've been through so much, with too many people talkin' about what happened, and it's getting' kinda old, so I really don't like talkin' about what happened."

I had to be an ass to think that Patricia would understand my position because she just laughed, and said, "Oh, get over it, Casual. The shit is the talk of New York right now. So get used to it. Me and Rodger talk about it all the time—we think it's fuckin' hysterical."

"Wow, ya know, that's great, Patricia. So tell me, what does Rodger do? Jam that needle in your arm and tell you a little bedtime story every night about how I almost killed my daughter's mother because you wouldn't mule that shit up to his cousin's house for him?"

Patricia just crossed her legs and with no remorse for how I would feel about it, said, "He suuure does, and ya know what else, ya left out the part where we fuck ourselves to sleep right after that." Patricia was a real asshole sometimes, I didn't wanna argue with her, so I just asked her where Rodger was and what time he was coming back. She responded in a snooty manner, without even looking at me, "How the fuck should I know? He's probably runnin' the fuckin' streets like always. I'm surprised you don't know where he is." As I started to get comfortable on the couch, I couldn't help but to pick up the magazine that Patricia had. Curiosity about what kinda shit they were saying about poor Lacey was eating me. It was basically saying the same shit that everyone had been saying, so I just started to skim through it.

While reading the magazine, I felt Patricia staring at me. So I pulled the magazine down from in front of my face, and damn sure, she was looking right at me. "Patricia, is there a reason why your fuckin' just sittin' there starin' at me?" I asked. Then I noticed that in her right hand, she was holding a needle full of that liquid crack, cocked back and ready to be inserted in her bloodstream. That's how much of a feen she was—she cooked that shit up so quick, before I even knew she took the shit out the bottle that it was in.

So with the needle in her right hand, cigarette in her left, she looked at me dead in my eyes, and said, "Well, don't just sit there. Help me the fuck out, dickhead."

I stared back at her with both of my eye brows raised, and said, "Fuck you, Patricia. I ain't touchin' that fuckin' needle. Knowin' me and my bad luck, I'll probably slip or some shit and stick myself with that nasty-ass needle."

"Oh, shut the fuck up, Casual, and help me out here."

"Look, Patricia, I am not touchin' that needle, so you can kiss my ass. You better wait till Rodger comes home or somethin' because I ain't doin it, fuck you. And on top of that, I can't even stomach watchin' Rodger do that shit to you. That shit is nasty, Patricia, and I don't want no part in that shit."

Patricia just started to laugh at me. She was laughing so hard that she dropped the needle on the ground, and it rolled under the lazy boy. I couldn't believe how she reacted when she dropped it—she was acting like she had just dropped a diamond ring. She dropped down to her knees and looked for that needle like a mad woman. When she couldn't find it, she shouted, "YA SEE WHAT THE FUCK YOU MADE ME DO! NOW I CAN'T FIND IT!" She then started to panic and went crazy. She stood up, pulled her hair, and growled—she was really starting to scare me. "Holy shit, hoooly shit! What the fuck am I gonna do now, Casual?" While Patricia was pacing back and forth, wondering what she was gonna do now that she couldn't get high, I glanced over by the lazy boy, and saw that the needle had rolled to the back left of the chair. But I wanted to be a dick, so I just sat there watching her go crazy. "Are you gonna help me or are you just gonna sit there like an asshole? That was my last little bit of money, ya know," she pleaded.

I really wanted to fuck with Patricia, so when she said that, I simply folded my hands behind my head, and said, "Why don't you pray to whoever it is that you worship—maybe it will help."

"Fuck you, Casual, maybe you should sleep on the train tonight, asshole."

"Hey, I'm just tryin' to help."

"You're not tryin' to help me, Casual. If you was tryin' to help, I would have been high already. When I told you to stick me, you should've just did it."

"Oh, so now this is my fault. It's my fault that you lost your fuckin' needle and can't get high huh?"

"Casual, just shut the fuck up and drop dead."

Patricia was really getting irate. I actually thought she was gonna have a damn panic attack, so I just told her where the needle was. When she found it, she picked it up and kissed it, as if it were her child that had been missing for months—it was really sick. Patricia didn't waste any time. She reached into her pocket, and took out ten dollars. "Look, Casual, take this ten and please do this for me." I looked at that ten-dollar bill for a hot second, then I looked at Patricia, and said, "Hurry the fuck up. Let's go." It was sick, and it was a shame but my ass was homeless, and I needed to eat. Plus if I didn't do it, she was bound to get someone else to do it. Ya see, Patricia was a wild girl. If I didn't do it, she was the type who would've gone out into the street, and had just any mothafucka do that shit for her. And I figured, it was a small price to pay. I mean she was letting me live there until I got my shit together. I had to keep that in my mind as I stuck that shit in her neck vein. I grabbed a handful of her hair, pushed her head to the side, and inserted the needle. I was wondering why she didn't have me stick it in her arm because I knew her neck was all abused up. I even could see all the tracks in her neck, it was so disgusting, but I just said, 'fuck it'. She held her breath for about a minute so that the veins in her neck would come out, and then, when I found the biggest one, I gently stuck the needle in her neck. She was instantly relieved—I mean at this stage of the game, this shit was like her medication, she was a stone-cold junkie, and I was no better for accepting a measly ten-dollar bill to do it for her. The shit went straight to her head, so she immediately laid back in the chair, like a tranquilizer had hit her.

About fifteen minutes later, Rodger came storming through the door with the rest of his headbanging buddies. All sloppy and drunk outta his mind, he said, "Duude, I thought you were gonna be at Ann's house tonight." I said, "Yeah, but she got on my nerves yo. She wouldn't give me no pussy. She wanted to talk all night, so to make a long story short, she kicked my ass out." Rodger just busted out and laughed when I said that—like I said something hysterically funny. He just kept on laughing and laughing, to the point where he almost choked. When I took a closer look at him, I knew he was on something—something good at that.

I knew Rodger for so long that I had gotten accustomed to the way he acted on certain drugs. And when he laughed like he was laughing that night, I knew he had some good mescaline. Mescaline was this tiny little purple pill that made you hallucinate and laugh like hell. I loved it—it was one of my drugs of choice. I grabbed Rodger by his shirt, and told him to ante up, and he knew just what I was talking about. He reached into his pocket and pulled out a bag full of mescaline and some other shit that I thought was something else good. "Awwww shit, Rodge, you got some coke too! Yo, I'm gettin' tore up tonight—mescaline mixed with coke—it's on now boy!"

Rodger and his headbanging buddies just paused from what they were doing and looked at each other with little smirks on their faces, like something was going on. Then they started sniggling like little grade school girls, and it was starting to piss me off. That's when Rodger cocked his head to the side, and calmly said to me, "Hey, Casual, you wanna fly through the sky above the city like the pigeons, and look down on all the low-life that scowls the streets of Manhattan." I still didn't know what the hell Rodger was talking about, so I looked around the room at everyone as they looked back at me with the same smirk on their faces. "Yo, Rodger, just cut the shit alright. What the hell are you talkin' about, and why is everyone lookin' at me with a stupid grin on their faces."

Rodger didn't answer me. He took the powdery substance and poured it on the table. Pheelix, who was one of the band members that played the guitar, passed Rodger a bag of angel dust. Rodger took the angel dust and mixed it with the powder, plus some weed that he had and rolled up two blunts. As he finished twisting up the last Dutch Master, he began to explain what he was about to get me into. Still with that smirk on his face, he said, "Duude, we are about to take flight, strap on your seat belt and let's head up to the roof." At this point, I didn't give a fuck what we were about to do. I just followed them up to the roof and joined the crew. "Alright, Rodger, what the fuck are we about to do?" I asked. Flicking the lighter to set fire to the tip of the blunt, Rodger began to smoke. He inhaled deeply after three hard pulls, and then closed his eyes. Exhaling the smoke through his nostrils, he passed me the blunt, and said, "Get ready for the ride of your life." Now I knew that this blunt had weed, coke, and angel dust in it, so I couldn't wait to take a puff. Right before I put it to my lips, Rodger said, "Duude, I know you think that's coke but it's not. What you're about to inhale is methamphetamine, so take it easy, duude." I had never smoked methamphetamine before, not to mention I had never even smoked dust. And now, I was about to smoke dust and methamphetamine mixed together. But the way I was feeling, I didn't give a fuck. Instead of taking it easy like Rodger said, I took about five big deep hits and just inhaled that shit like it was pure oxygen. We stayed on top of the roof just passing that shit back and forth to each other, getting so high that I started to question myself on whether I should take another pull. Alls I remember was we all woke up the next morning laid out on the roof of the building.

My life was a total mess—I mean a mess—two whole years had passed, and I had become a stone-cold drug addict. I was hooked on coke, meth, LSD, pain killers, weed and heroin. The only thing about heroin was that I wasn't about to stick that shit in my veins because of the fact that I could catch AIDS from a dirty needle. Plus I didn't like needles. So I just sniffed it. I was no better than any other heroin addict. I just put my fix up my nose rather than injecting it. We were living like savages—me, Rodger, and his crew. From time to time, Rodger would perform and get paid, but besides that, we would do anything to get money. None of us had jobs—we would rob, steal, and do anything we could to get money. It was amazing how we were able to pay Rodger's rent every month, and still be able to get high, but we did it.

Rodger had stolen a sawed-off shotgun from his father's apartment one night, and ever since then, we were doing stick-ups all throughout New York City's Village area. Our main thing was burglarizing houses. Patricia was a damn wizard at picking locks and sneaking into people's houses—this girl was a professional cat burglar. We were in and out like thieves in the night. As a matter of fact, we got so damn good at the shit, we were robbing mothafuckas in the middle of the night while they were asleep. It was funny as hell when we couldn't find anything valuable to sell because Rodger would go into the master bedroom and point the shotgun right at whoever was lying in the bed, and say, "Wake the fuck up—you got some company." These people would literally shit on themselves when they saw Rodger standing over them with that shotgun in their face. We didn't wanna hurt anyone so we just told them to give up all their goods and we would be on our way, and it actually worked.

Slowly, we got cocky. We were so good at doing the shit that we would spend up all the money on drugs and food until we were at our last dime, and not worry about it. We didn't care, we would just rob another house when we got low on money. It was like clockwork—there was nothing to it. But we had to really kick the bottle the night I burglarized my own parents' house. We needed money in the worst way, and Rodger's rent was due, but most of all, we needed that fix. We had no way to get high at all, and we were running outta options. So to cut a long story short, I had decided to sneak into my parents' house late at night. I knew that they hadn't fixed my window because I had broken the lock trying to sneak in one night and I never told my pops about it.

The plan was to steal my parents' living room television along with the DVD system, and sell it. But stupid me—I had forgotten that my mother sleeps like a fuckin' bird. She heard us trying to disconnect the TV, and alerted my father. Rodger and I were both dressed in black from head to toe, so when my father came tiptoeing out, he couldn't tell it was just me and Rodger. Now with my pops being a cop and all, he had his gun drawn, cocked, and ready to shoot. I almost fuckin' froze when I heard his voice. He shouted, "DON"T MOVE. STAY RIGHT THERE MOTHAFUCKA." As Rodger and I stood up and tried to run, I heard two gunshots. It was like slow-motion, but it was amazing how fast Rodger jumped out the front window. What I couldn't figure out was why I couldn't move—alls I know was I dropped to the floor and I started to feel a hot burning sensation in my leg. Then before I knew it, my father was standing over me with his gun in my face. He didn't press charges on us but he did disown me—he didn't even visit me in the hospital. The only person that came to see me was my mother, and let me tell ya, it was hard for her. She was crying the whole time she was there—she couldn't believe what her son had turned into.

# A SUICIDE STORY

Two months had passed since then, and it was a Thursday. We had been running the streets all day. It was so hot outside. I had been sweating so bad that I decided that I was gonna take a cold shower. As I was in the shower, I heard the bathroom door open. I couldn't see who it was because I was rinsing the shampoo out of my hair but I figured whoever it was would have the decency to say, 'oops, my bad', and just walk out. And I say that because Rodger had no shower curtain in his bathroom, which wasn't surprising for such a filthy dude. So, if you were in the shower, not only did you have to worry about spilling water all over the place, you had to worry about someone seeing you while you were washing your ass. As I was wondering if whoever came into the bathroom had left, I heard a voice—a female voice, may I add, say, "Oh my God, I gotta pee so fuckin' bad." Now this voice wasn't Patricia's—it was a new voice, a voice that I hadn't heard before. I quickly wiped the water from my eyes, and looked over toward the toilet, to see a pretty-faced girl with long, black hair just sitting on the toilet taking a piss.

When we made eye contact, I didn't waste any time at all. I said the first thing that came to my mind, which of course, was a smart-ass remark. I firmly and very rudely said, "Hey, let's not waste any more time. Your pants are down; I'm naked. You're a pretty girl and I know you see the size of this big, black cock—so let's just fuck right here and get it over with." She replied by saying, "Well, isn't that just a polite way to introduce yourself."

"Shiiiiiiit, it ain't no more polite than you just walkin' your ass in here and takin' a piss when you see someone in the shower—not to mention a shower that has no curtain on it. So let me introduce myself. I'm Casual," I said. I walked out of the shower, dick swinging with soap suds all over me, and stuck my hand out. Meanwhile the water mixed with lathered soap suds from my hand was drippin onto her thigh, and dribbling down her knee into her pants. I guess the both of us were playing mind games with each other because what she did next was even ruder than what I had just done. She slightly lifted up off the toilet grabbed the toilet tissue, wrapped it around her hand and proceeded to wipe herself. And right after she finished, she stuck out the same hand that she used to wipe herself with, and shook my hand. She had this real firm grip about her handshake—like this was some professional introduction between the both of us, and in a real snobbish voice, she said, "Well, I guess it's my turn to introduce myself. I'm Summer, Patricia's cousin. I'm here visiting from California."

"Well, Summer, welcome to New York," I said. As I proceeded to get back into the shower, I thought to myself, well, if she's visiting, where the fuck is she gonna sleep. So being the upfront guy that I am, I asked her as I stepped into the shower, "Hey, where are you gonna be staying at, may I ask?" Right before she left the bathroom, she turned to me, and said, "Ya, now you sure do ask a lot of questions for a man who thinks it's rude for his privacy to be invaded so nonchalantly by a stranger." I didn't even have the energy to entertain her wise mouth. Plus it wasn't all that important to me, any damn way.

Later on that night, Rodger and his band were performing at a local club around the area, so of course, I was once again surrounded by skateboard punks, skinheads, and every other freak of the night that crowded the streets when Rodger and his band performed. So it was me, Summer, Patricia, and the whole Suicidal crew. Summer and I just sat by the bar like the civilized human beings that we were, while everyone else banged their heads like wild and crazy cavemen, to the beat of Rodger's music. And Patricia was right out with the rest of them—and who could blame her—she didn't have any sense in her head anyway. I mean acting civilized was just not these people's idea of having a good time.

About a half an hour had passed by, and I hadn't said a word to Summer, nor did she say a fuckin' word to me. Finally, she just came outta nowhere, and said, "So what's your fashion story. Why are you dressed like you're about to attend a formal affair." I turned towards her and positioned myself directly in front of her, as if I was gonna lean over and start tonguing her down, and said, "Yeah, that's because I'm a formal mothafucka. Now I know you're probably thinkin' in the back of your head right now that this guy is way too overdressed to be in a place like this. But ya see, you're probably not used to somebody like me, and it's probably gonna take some time for you to get adjusted to someone like me. I'm highly unorthodox. Very, very, highly unorthodox."

I couldn't even get all of what I wanted to say outta my mouth because she cut me right off by putting her pointer finger right on top of my lips, insinuating for me to shhhh. Then she called over the bartender, and told him to send over two Long Island ice teas. She just totally brushed off what I said, and directed her attention towards the bartender. When the bartender came back with both drinks, I was kinda impressed by the fact that she had ordered me a drink. But when I went to grab the drink, she slapped my hand, and said, "That's not for you." I was a little boggled when she said that, so I simply said, "Well, who's it for, if it's not for me? I know damn well you ain't gonna drink both of those glasses." As soon as I said that, she guzzled down the first glass, put it back on the table, and then picked up the second one and guzzled that one down. It really fucked me up because I was sure that she had bought that drink for me.

After gulping down the second glass, she said, "Listen Cash, or Cashew, or whatever the fuck you call yourself, because I know that in the back of your head, you're thinkin' 'I know this bitch didn't just order two drinks and not offer me one'. But if I wanted to buy you a drink, first of all, I would have asked what are you drinkin', or better yet, do you even want a drink. Second of all, I've dealt with assholes like you before, so don't think that you're some unique fuckin' guy that women aren't used to. You're just a typical self-centered, egotistical, unorthadox dickhead. I mean, you're not even interesting enough to make me sick. When I look at you, I just see an artificial, wannabe GQ that's not the least bit smooth. I mean you're so rough around the Mac Daddy edges that it hurts to even hear your corny ass talk."

I just started laughing when she finally finished—I mean I was literally in fuckin' stitches after hearing all that shit. We already had some serious eye contact going on, so I just looked deeper into her eyes and began to clap. I started clapping and shouting out, "Bravo, bravo." Then I said, "You know that was the most exhilarating, and exuberating diss I've ever heard come out of a female's mouth towards me—and believe me, a lot of females have dissed me. But I gotta say… ummm Spring or Winter or whatever-the-fuck season you call yourself, that was fuckin' great. I mean the passion that you put into that shit you just said about me was fuckin' marvelous. Hey bartender, excuse me, bartender, send me over two more of those Long Island iced teas, please." It didn't take long for the bartender to send over the drinks. As soon as he sent them over, I grabbed one of them, gave her the other one, and said, "I'd like to propose a toast."

I couldn't get out what I wanted to toast about because she just walked away from me. At this time, Rodger and his band had finished performing, and came right over to the bar to order drinks. But of course, every dick-riding fan of theirs had to follow them and crowd them, screaming and yelling over them as if they were big-time rock stars. But here in the big city, I guess they were. They weren't internationally known, but they sure as hell were locally accepted. I always hated it when we were all surrounded—I fuckin' hated it. Among all the dick-riding fans and the slut-groupie-girls that wanted them, there was this guy that was trying to get Rodger's attention. I mean this guy was getting pushed and shoved around by the other fans but he still got right back on what he was focused on, which was getting Rodger's attention. There was something about this guy that just made me click and say, 'I gotta get Rodger to pay this mothafucka some attention'.

# A SUICIDE STORY

As I thought about it for a minute, I saw that he was with another guy that was holding a camera, not to mention he was holding a notepad. So immediately I said to myself, this fuckin' guy is either with some record label, a small-time low-budget TV show, or a magazine writer. I really didn't give a fuck which one he was but I was gonna get Rodger to talk to him. So I told everyone to back the fuck up and let him through. As soon as he came up to me, he said, "Thanks man. I really dig what you just did but I wanna talk to that guy right there."

I laughed, took a sip of my drink, and said, "Listen, that same guy that you wanna rap to is my best friend, now knowing him for as long as I've known him, I'm gonna tell you right now that he ain't gonna wanna talk to you. But for a small fee, I could get him to at least consider sayin 'hi' to you." I guess this guy must have thought I was bullshitting because he just walked past me and put his hands right on Rodger's shoulder as if he knew him, which was mistake number one, because Rodger hates it when people touch him. Rodger didn't even turn to see whose hand it was that was on his shoulder, he just grabbed this guy's hand and squeezed it, and in a real hateful voice, he turned and said, "Dude, I will totally rip your fuckin' arm right outta the fuckin' socket. Don't you ever put your hands on me."

Even as Rodger was saying this, his whole crew just swarmed around this poor, little guy, like starving lions, and they looked down on him as if he were a piece of bloody flesh. Their eyes filled with pure hate, fists clenched and ready to fuck something up. It was just comical the way this poor, little guy turned towards me with fear written all over his face, as if I was supposed to just stop him from getting his ass whipped. "Oh, so now you want my help, huh, dickhead?" I shouted out. But then I thought to myself, I said ya know I probably could get Rodger to talk to this mothafucka but I was gonna get him to pay first. And I knew he would, because anybody that thirsty that's gonna push their way through a crowd of brainless Megadeath thugs and skinheads will do anything for a picture or an interview. "Hey, Rodger, let him go for a minute, I wanna talk to him."

Rodger was so fuckin' mad that he just threw him over to me like he was some fuckin' rag doll. "So who the fuck are you? You must be part of somethin', because I can tell. So what is it? Are you with a label or some shit?" I asked him. This guy was so scared to talk, he just looked at me. But his co-worker, who was with him, said, "Nah, dude, we're with *Electric City* magazine. We wanna do an interview with Rodger and his band." Now *Electric City* was Rodger's favorite magazine—he had all their issues in his apartment, and when he would have any spare time, he would read it. "Well, I'll be fuckin' damned. *Electric City* magazine wants to do an interview with my best friend—it's the biggest rock-n-roll magazine around. Well, I'll tell ya what boys, and this time maybe you'll listen to me. I can get you that interview, but you're gonna have to pay for it."

I have to say that I was quite amazed with the response I got from these guys after I told them that they had to pay. The guy holding the camera pulled out a one hundred dollar bill and said, "Here, dude, it's yours." And like a fuckin' magic trick, we were all back in Rodger's filthy-ass apartment so these guys could get an interview. It took some talking but I finally convinced Rodger to talk to these mothafuckas because he really wasn't gonna do it. He walked up to the guy, and said, "So you wanna know about me and my band, you little faggot—you actually wanna sit and talk to a madman like me?" The guy didn't have anything to say, he just nodded his head, and said, "I'm ready if you're ready."

Rodger just gave him an ice-cold look, and said, "Alright. Now don't be actin' like a little fuckin' pussy when you see what we're really about." As we were in Rodger's apartment, everyone did what they usually did—break out the drugs and get high until the sun comes up. There was absolutely no shame in our game. We were sniffing up lines, smoking dust, and cooking up heroin. As Rodger was answering questions from the guy that was interviewing him, he was cleaning out his shotgun. So the guy asked, "What do you have a gun for?" Rodger didn't answer him right away; he took a long, heavy pull of angel dust, inhaled it, and blew the smoke right in this guy's face. "I carry this gun because I'm fuckin' suicidal, and I haven't really figured out how I wanna take myself out. I don't know if I wanna get real high and just go on the top floor of this building and just jump the fuck off… Sometimes I think about just stickin' this here 12 gauge in my mouth, and blowin' a hole in the back of my fuckin' head." You shoulda seen the look on the guy's face—he looked like he was doin an interview with the devil himself. If I were a blind man, I could've smelled the fear that he was wearing on his face. I really wasn't too enthused about this whole interview thing. What was on my mind was that bitch, Summer—after thinking about what she said to me and just how we met in the first place, I just wanted to choke the fuck outta her. Her and Patricia ended up going someplace else instead of coming back to the house—where that place was, I had no clue.

I was in a daze, I must say, for about ten minutes… just thinking about her bitchy ass. I was so much in a daze that I took my attention off of the interview. But when I snapped out and looked over towards what was going on, I couldn't believe what I was seeing. I mean it wasn't exactly shocking and surprising, but it was a bit extra for my taste. Rodger had the barrel of his 12 gauge shotgun pointed right in between this fuckin' guy's eyes, and was asking him if he was scared to die. So, of course, the guy doing the interview was scared like hell, and told Rodger that he was scared of death. Rodger started going into his deep speech about how nobody should be afraid to die, especially when we live in a fucked-up world.

He then stood up and cocked his gun in such a manner that you would almost believe that he was gonna pull the damn trigger, and said, "I'm gonna sing a little song to ya that my daddy used to sing when he came home drunk right before he started to beat on my mother. It went a little something like this, 'ohhhh I'm soooooo tired of living, but I'm toooooooo afraid to diiiiiie, cuz I don't know what's up there in that great big ol skyyyyyy.'" And then after he had finished singing the song, he whispered to the interviewer calmly, "I hate my father so much that I just wanna be able to say, 'hey, you know what, pops, because of you, I hate living my damn self, but the difference is… I ain't afraid to check out'. Now get your little, pussy ass up and get the fuck outta my castle—your time with me is up." Those interviewers were so damn scared that they didn't even say thank you for the interview—they just hauled ass without looking back.

## CHAPTER 6

"Ooooooh yeah, oooooooh yeah, spread them fuckin' legs, spread 'em out so I dig that fuckin' pussy out."

"Ohhhh shit yeah, whose pussy is this, huh, whose fuckin' pussy is this?"

"It's yours, it's all yours, baby."

The bed was rocking and shaking, Anastasia and I were going at it again. We always had rough sex—that was the way she liked to get fucked, and that was the way that I liked to fuck, so it all worked out. Now drugs really weren't Anastasia's thing but somehow I conned her into snorting up some coke before we had sex. I told her that it would intensify her orgasm. Ever since the first time she sniffed it up that one night, she'd had a thing for me and a fifty bag of some good coke. It was her mix. She told me that coke and I go together like cranberry juice and vodka to an alcoholic. As we both lay in bed, trying to catch our breath all sweaty and wet, Anastasia looked over at me while she rubbed her smooth hands across my face, and said, "Ya know, casual, you really have to start wearing a condom." I just kinda brushed off what she said, and responded by sitting up in the bed and saying, "Now after the kind of sex that we just had, why would you even want me to wear a fuckin' condom, Anastasia—that makes no sense. Using a condom is like drinking non-alcoholic beer—what's the fuckin' purpose?"

"Casual, the purpose is so that I don't get pregnant, and you should be trying to prevent me from getting pregnant, anyway. I mean you already have two kids that you don't take care of." I just laughed when she said that because the shit was funny the way it just came outta her mouth. And right when I got ready to defend myself, my cell phone went off, and who was it, of course, it had to be Kit Kat. I never answered the phone by sayin 'hello' to her. So I just said 'what'. "Don't 'what' me, you no-good-for-nothing, deadbeat, drug-addicted, funky-ass no money-havin' mothafucka. You ain't been over here to see your son in weeks. Oh, I forgot, you're on drugs and you probably forgot you gotta fuckin' son," said Kit Kat.

I didn't wanna argue with Kit Kat in front of Anastasia, so I got up and proceeded to go into the bathroom. The sound of Kit Kat's voice was like nails on a fuckin' chalkboard—her voice was so annoying. So I closed the bathroom door, pulled the toilet seat down, and sat on the toilet, before I began to say anything to Kit Kat, I took a real deep breath, and said to myself, 'Here we go'. I rudely interrupted her, and said, "Kit Kat, I am trying extremely hard to sit here and listen to you without hanging up the phone. I mean, come on, Kit Kat, why can't we just act like civilized parents for once?"

Now I don't know why I even wasted the oxygen in my lungs by trying to have a civilized conversation with her because alls she did was cut me right off with all her screaming and yelling. So I just hung the phone up and opened the door to the bathroom, so I could go back to my conversation about what kind of father I was with Anastasia. As I opened the door, there stood Anastasia, as if she were listening to my whole conversation. And if I were a betting man, I would bet my whole earnings that she was because she was a nosey-ass woman, especially when it came to me. There she stood, naked, hands on her beautiful thighs, gazing into my eyes. "Ya see, Casual, this is why I say you're gonna start wearing a condom. Because I'm not gonna be one of your baby mothers, who is calling you frantically, worrying whether or not you're gonna come and pick your child up." But she wasn't as serious as she would have liked to be because alls I did is gaze back into her eyes with that convincing charm that I was blessed with, and began to stroke her hair and kiss her roughly. Before you know it, we were fuckin' again, and hell no, I didn't have a condom on. I threw her ass over the toilet and fucked her so hard that even I was starting to feel sorry for her. As I was fuckin' her with everything I had in me, I thought to myself, 'Shit, if she's worried about me stuffin' a kid in her womb, I'll just take my dick out right before I cum, and splash it all in her face.' So that's exactly what I did. I turned her around and let my shit just splash all in her face. And I tell ya, she must have loved it because she opened her mouth as I was doing it, signaling that I should put some in her mouth, so I did. The thing was that I didn't want to spend the night with her, and I knew she was gonna want me to. So I told her that I was going to the store to get us something to eat, and I never came back.

 Later on that night, Rodger and I had been just walking around the city, talking about all kinds of shit, until we stopped on someone's front stoop for what I thought was just so Rodger could relax for a bit. But as I looked over at Rodger, he was lighting up some angel dust that he had on him for quite some time. I knew it was dust because I could smell it. Now I never passed up on some good ol' angel dust, so we sat on these people's stoop smoking angel dust, like we lived there. The moon was bright and full, and the sky was pitch-black, the wind was blowing like the devil was actually making a whistling sound with his lips. And I tell ya, with what was about to happen to my life in a matter of minutes, I should have seen the fuckin' signs.

As Rodger and I sat back on these people's stoop, laughing like evil clowns, I noticed that Rodger was really high, because when he is extremely high on dust he gets really violent. He started telling me how sometimes he just wants to shoot his girl in the fuckin' face. And for some odd reason, I thought that shit was fuckin' funny as hell, so I started to crack up. As I lifted my head back up from holding my stomach, Rodger had a .45 pistol held out for me to grab, and said, "So, are you ready?" Now I'm already high as hell, and I couldn't even see straight, and this crazy mothafucka was handing me a pistol.

I grabbed the gun and said, "What the fuck do you want me to do with this?"

"Aww, come on, Casual, don't be a fuckin' retard all your life. What the fuck do you think we're getting ready to do?"

I couldn't believe this fuckin' guy. I usually didn't rob anyone when I was high because I wanted to be on point. So I asked Rodger what the fuck was wrong with him.

He responded with this real evil grin on his face, saying, "Duude, we're gonna run into this fuckin' house, rob this fucker, and come out filthy fuckin' rich."

"Now see, Rodger, this is what the fuck I'm talking about. This is fuckin' stupid. I'm high like a mothafucka right now. I couldn't even hold my dick straight, let alone a fuckin' pistol, you asshole. I wish that you would tell me before you think about doin' some dumb shit, especially when it involves me. And do you even know these people, Rodger?"

I was serious as hell but Rodger was still fuckin' cracking up—he thought this whole shit was funny. "Casual, will you stop actin' like a fuckin' girl? I have it all under control. This is Fritz's house man." After Rodger had told me whose house we were about to rob, he began laughing hysterically again, just for the simple fact that he knew what I was gonna say. Ya see, Fritz was a well-known big-time liquid acid dealer in the neighborhood, and was crazy—this guy was just plain flat-out fuckin' crazy. Ya see, he was a big fan of Rodger and his group, so Rodger would give him free passes to get into some of the underground clubs, and Fritz would hook us up with some good shit. Word in the Village was he had killed at least four times already, and the last guy who owed him money, Fritz had tossed him off the fuckin' roof. I mean we're talking about a 6' 9", 255-pound, crazy Russian dude, with tattoos all over and a scar on his face that went from one side of his ear to the other. Oh, and I forgot he's missing half his teeth and has only one eye due to a bar fight where he was stabbed. There was no way in hell this fuckin' guy was gonna let me and Rodger rob him.

The story was that Rodger had told this guy that we were coming over to buy a shit-load of liquid acid from him. So this guy knew we were coming. My only concern was that we were gonna have to kill this dude. When I mentioned that to Rodger, he said, "Well, so fuckin' be it. If that fucker doesn't give up that stash and that money, I'm gonna put his brains all over his fuckin' wall." Damn, Rodger! Of all the people who lived in Manhattan that had money, he had to pick this crazy fuck.

The thing about this situation that I was in was that Rodger was just as crazy as Fritz was. So before I could even talk my way outta this shit, Rodger pulled out his gun, cocked it, stood up and rang this fuckin' guy's doorbell. Now it was on. I took so many deep breaths that I was running outta breath. I was scared like hell because I knew that this wasn't gonna go according to plan. I knew we were gonna have to kill this fuckin' guy, and it was a shame because he was cool with me and Rodger. I got myself together, and waited for this dude to come to the door.

As we peeked through the window, we noticed a light came on, and a little girl came to the door—she had to be at least 8 years old. She reminded me of the little girl from *The Cosby Show*, Olivia—she had this little, innocent glow about her that just made you wanna smile. She was a little black girl with two pigtails on the side of her head. She greeted us at the door, and said, "Hey, are you guys here to see Fritz?" Before I could answer her, Rodger had picked the little girl up and said, "Well, aren't you a pretty little bitch, huh?" I couldn't believe this fuckin' guy had said that. But there was no sense in me catching feelings at this point—we were already deep in, and there was no time for pussyness. The look in this little girl's face went from a warm smile to straight terror when she looked into Rodger's eyes. I'm sure she felt a sense of sheer evil. I was so high that I felt like I was in a cartoon. Then in slow-motion, I saw Rodger's hand cover her little mouth and he put his gun right to her head. It was like clockwork the way Fritz came down the stairs. The tension was in the air now, and it was so thick that you could smell it, taste it, and touch it. "Hey, Fritz, how are ya?" Rodger coldly said in a real funny sarcastic but serious way. He added, "Hey, we're just here to pick that pack up, and whatever else you've got in this house. Now by the looks of things, Fritz, you look real angry right now, and you probably are saying to yourself, 'Is this fuckin' guy nuts?' And the answer to your question, Fritz, is yes, I'm fuckin' crazy."

Then a real tender voice came from the background, "Persia, Persia, who's at the door?" Fritz quickly turned, and said, "Don't come over here. Do not come over here." But the dumb bitch came anyway, and when she saw what I was guessing was her daughter in Rodger's godforsaken evil arms with a 9mm gun which he had put to her head, she started to scream. Now being the fact that we had no masks on, we really had to be on our toes, and be serious. For about a good 30 seconds, Rodger and Fritz just stared at each other. I just stood steady gun in my hand shaking, and I was sweating profussley.

"Let's not all talk at once now everyone. Hey, Fritz, why don't you just get everything outta your safe and give it here before shit gets crazy in this muthafucka?" I figured by me sayin this, he would know that we weren't scared of his crazy-ass, and he would just give us the shit so we could leave. But what was I thinking—this was a fuckin' nut we were dealing with, and what he said next really startled me, and made me think that we were definitely gonna have to murder his ass. He turned to me, and in his real thick Russian accent, said, "You fuckin' nigger. You fuckin' no good dirty, black fuckin' nigger. Was this your idea huh? I tell you what, nigger boy, you've got 5 seconds to tell Rodger to put that girl down and let her come to her mother, if not, I'm gonna tear your fuckin' ribs outta your chest."

Rodger started to laugh hysterically when he said that, and I got kinda fuckin' mad. This guy was calling me a 'nigger' in front of this little girl and the woman who was upstairs. The shit really confused me because if he was calling me a nigger, then who was this little girl, and who was the black woman that was screaming. At that point something came over me. I transformed and had no care in the world for this white bastard. First off, this little girl had nothing to do with nothing, and she had a gun to her head, and now she was hearing this asshole call me a 'black nigger' in front her and the woman who was screaming—who I was guessing was her mother. "Oh, so I'm a fuckin' nigger huh. I'm a dirty, black, fuckin' nigger huh. Well, fuck you, white boy. Now you ain't getting this little girl back, and what the fuck are you doin' with a black woman since you're such a racist fuck? Now go get that fuckin' money, Fritz, before I put your fuckin' brain on the fuckin' wall just for bein' a racist."

Rodger was laughing so hard that he dropped his gun from the little girl's head. "What the fuck, is this a race war now? Yo, Casual, you ain't gonna let this bastard call you a nigger, are you?"

"Fuck you, Rodger, I'm pissed the off now," I said. But before I could get another word outta my mouth, Fritz had leaped from the top of the stairs and tackled me. He was trying to take the gun from me but I wasn't even trying to hear that shit. We ended up on the floor with him on top of me. He was screaming at the top of his lungs, saying, "I'm gonna kill you. I'm gonna fuckin' kill you." I mean this guy was growling at me and trying to fuckin' bite me in the face. Now even with Rodger hitting this muthafucka on the back of his head with the gun, he still wouldn't release my arm. He was really trying to get that gun from me. We were really going at it at this point. Rodger and I were both really trying to fuck this dude up, but he wouldn't budge. He just kept getting stronger and stronger, and madder and madder.

The rage that was coming from this dude was incredible. He actually picked me up and tossed me across the room, and then dove back on top of me because even though he tossed me, I still had that gun. Now I would have shot his ass but he jumped back on me even with Rodger on his back. I could tell Rodger really didn't wanna shoot him because alls he was doin was hitting him on the back of his head with the gun. There was blood all over the place. Fritz was punching me so hard in my stomach with his free hand that I thought I was bleeding internally. I couldn't really hit him because I was too busy holding on to that gun, because for one, I was just gonna pop his ass and get it over with, and two, I didn't want him getting the gun from me and popping my ass with my damn gun.

"Rodger, will you just shoot this muthafucka already?" I yelled out in pain as Fritz was pounding me in my stomach. "Shoot him, Rodger, shoot this muthfucka," I yelled. I had no other choice but to headbutt this dude, and when I did, I caught him right in his nose. Blood splashed everywhere—it was all in my mouth and in my eyes. I heard it squirt out when my head hit his nose. The scream of a madman came from the bottom of his gut straight outta his mouth. It sounded like the zoo just let a fuckin' bear out. As soon as I headbutted him, he let go of the gun and I shot him right in his stomach. The pop from the gun made my ears ring. Alls I could see was the spark from the barrel. But even that didn't bring this dude down, he ran back towards me full-speed like a charging bull but I pushed him back into Rodger. Now

Rodger must have been ready to shoot him again because he had the gun pointed at him. But as I pushed Fritz into Rodger, Fritz turned and knocked Rodger to the floor. I couldn't believe how strong this fucker was. I mean I had shot him in the stomach and headbutted him, not to mention Rodger was knocking the shit outta him with the handle of his gun. There was blood everywhere.

Then I heard another gunshot go off. It wasn't from my gun, so I thought that Rodger had popped this guy. But when I looked over, I saw the little black girl holding her chest and gasping for air. I couldn't have tended to her while Rodger and this dude were fighting, so I walked over and unloaded my gun right into Fritz's head, and didn't stop until my gun was completely empty. It was like second nature the way I ran over to this little girl's aid. I didn't give a fuck about Fritz, and I didn't give a fuck about Rodger at this point in time. I held her in my arms and told her to calm down. I was rocking her back and forth, and rubbing her innocent face as if she was my own daughter. She was gurgling blood, and wasn't able to breath. She was fighting so hard to stay alive but the bullet had pierced through her chest as Rodger and Fritz were wrestling on the floor. Her mother—or at least I thought this woman who was her mother—ran over and tried to snatch her from me, but Rodger grabbed her and threw her to the floor, and began tearing her clothes off and kissing her. He was actually gonna rape her but my focus was on this little girl. Alls I kept seeing was my daughter's face—it would flash back and forth from the little girl's face to my daughter's face. I got so scared that I dropped the little girl on her back, and stared into her eyes as she slowly stopped breathing, gasping for air trying to fight for her little precious life—she couldn't talk because the blood was clogged in her throat. I sat there and watched her die. And she died with her fuckin' eyes open.

In the background, alls I heard was screaming and the sound of Rodger violently raping this woman. I knew these were sounds that were gonna haunt my fuckin' life forever. I knew from this point forward, trying to go to sleep at night was gonna be an impossible thing. "Yeah bitch, yeah bitch, take that white cock, take it, take it, take it, take it, UUUHHHHHHHH, UUUHHHHHHHHHH, UUUUUH-HHHHHHHHHH." While I was trying to register what the fuck had just happened, Rodger was fuckin' the shit outta this woman with his hands gripped tightly around her throat, choking her as he raped her. And when he was done, he got up, buttoned up his pants, and ran upstairs. I was guessing that he was going to get Rodger's stash, and that was indeed what he was doing because as he was running up the stairs, he yelled out, "It's time to get paid." I was still stuck in one spot, shocked as hell. Rodger must have known where this dude, Fritz, stashed his shit because he came back downstairs with three garbage bags. "Duude, are you gonna stand there and look stupid or are you comin'? I got three bags full of fuckin' money and dope, let's go, Casual!"

I knew I had to get the fuck outta Dodge but for some reason, I wanted to stay with that little girl. Rodger grabbed me by the back of my neck, and dragged me outside the house, and we ran into the night, covered in blood with three bags full of money, dope, and two bodies on my conscious.

## CHAPTER 7

"Yo, Casual, do all black muthfuckaz got big dicks?"

"What?"

"You heard me. Do all black guys have big dicks?"

"Why the fuck are you askin' me, Rodger? You think I walk around lookin' at other muthafuckaz dicks?"

"Duude, I'm just askin."

"Well, why the fuck are you askin' me? I don't fuckin' know, Rodger"

"Duude, is your dick big? I mean do you have one of those like big-ass cocks that girls go crazy over because they say all black guys have big dicks."

"Yo, Rodger, I'm not gonna sit here and discuss my dick size with you. What the fuck is wrong with, you smoke to much dust, Rodger?"

"Dude, check it out. I think I'm gonna get a penis implant, dude"

I don't know if it was the dust or what, but Rodger was really starting to get on my fuckin' nerves. We were on the roof smoking dust, looking out at the city, and this guy just came out and started talking about black guys with big dicks and dick implants.

"Rodger, why the fuck would you get a penis implant?"

Rodger took another puff and inhaled through his nose with a serious look on his face, and said, "Dude, check it out, and you better not fuckin' laugh either."

"Rodger, please already. I don't give a fuck. I really don't even wanna hear your fuckin' shit right now so come out and say it."

"Alright, alright."

This shit must have really been bothering Rodger because he took a real deep-ass breath about two fuckin' times before he came out.

"Casual, if you fuckin' laugh, I swear to God, dude. One day, Patricia and I were watching a porn flick, and this girl was bangin' this black guy right… and I mean he was really poundin' the shit outta this bitch. I felt bad for her, but this guy's cock was fuckin' huge, dude. Now I'm not a fuckin' homo, dude, and you know that, but holy shit, dude, this fuckin' guy's cock was like a fuckin' fire hose, dude."

"As I was sittin' there listening to this ridiculous shit, I didn't even crack a smile. I thought to myself, 'here we go—he's gonna start askin' me how big my fuckin' dick is'. So I just started fuckin' with him because I knew that he would believe me because Rodger was dumb as a bag of rocks anyway."

"Casual, are you listening to me?"

"Rodger, listen, OK, and listen real good. White men have little dicks—I don't know why but they just do—as well as every other fuckin' race out there but black men. You all have little fuckin' peckers O. I mean shit that muthafucka you saw on that porn, his dick was probably small to me, but to you, his shit was abnormal because you don't have a big dick. It's scientifically proven—black men have big-ass dicks, yeah, that's right."

"No, Casual, this guy's dick was fuckin' insane. I mean it was big and black and holy shit, why can't I be blessed like that? So I asked Patricia right... I said, 'hey, would you ever fuck a black guy, I mean... ya know, would you ever like, ya know... suck his cock and...?' So she looks at me, and says, 'Well, first of all, I wouldn't fuck a black guy because I'm fuckin' you, Rodger. But if I wasn't dating you, yeah I would.'"

Right after Rodger said that, I started to crack the fuck up, because he looked puzzled, it was almost like his heart was crushed. So I asked him, what did he say after she said that she would let a black guy pound that pussy out.

"Duude, she totally didn't say that OK. She didn't say that she would let him pound her ass out!"

"Well, what the fuck, Rodger, what do you think she meant? Of course, she's gonna tell you only what she told you, asshole. What do you think she's gonna come out and say? 'Hell, yeah, I would ride that big, black cock.' Come on, use your brain, Rodger."

I really had his ass going now. He was a nervous wreck—the look on his face went from puzzled to straight 'OH MY GOD. IS MY GIRL FUCKIN' A NIGGER?'

"So, dude, let me get this straight. Are you telling me that my girl wants to fuck a black guy?"

"Rodger, that's exactly what I'm sayin'. All white women think about it—they just don't like to admit that shit."

"Duude, so basically you're sayin' my girl looks at you and says to herself, 'wow, he must have a huge fuckin' cock'?"

I wiped the smile right off my face, so I could really fuck with Rodger, and said, "It's a strong possibility, Rodger. I mean I'm not gonna sit here and tell you that she doesn't when she probably does. And I'm not gonna tell you that she does when she probably doesn't.

But if I were a betting man, I would bet my money on the fact that she is wondering if my cock is huge. Now don't get me wrong—that doesn't mean she wants to fuck me, she's just probably wondering if I have a big cock because I'm black."

Rodger was so fuckin' confused that it was really starting to entertain me. So, of course, he didn't wanna talk about it anymore. We went back inside and went into his room to just look at all the money that we had taken from Fritz, plus all the dope that we had. The whole thing about it was that I wasn't just gonna take this money and blow it. I mean, shit, we coulda died over all that fuckin' money. So the first thing I said to myself was, 'I'm gonna invest this money in Rodger's band, and I'm gonna be the fuckin' manager.' It was like a light bulb went off in my head. I mean practically the whole city listened to that rock shit and loved him, so with my brains, his music and all this money, I just had a real stone-cold feeling about taking this shit straight to the top.

"Yo, Rodger, we gonna take this money, and we're gonna invest it in you and the rest of your band. And I don't give a fuck what you gotta say about it—that's what we are gonna do with this money."

Rodger pretty much trusted my decisions anyway because he knew he wasn't the sharpest pencil in the box. On top of this, he also knew I was a fuckin' slick-talking genius.

"The first thing we are gonna do is make some T-shirts, get our name copywritten, get a business license, and start our own record label." I said.

Now like I said, Rodger wasn't too bright, so the first thing that came outta his mouth was, "Fuck yeah." I mean even if I woulda said, 'Let's spend it all on expensive whores, and get high,' he woulda said the same thing. But the point is, he trusted my judgement.

"Wait, wait, wait, dude, I just thought about something, Casual, I just thought about something."

"Rodger, the last time you thought about some shit, we went into a house and came out some fuckin' murderers. It's not healthy when you think, Rodger. Is this even worth me listening to, Rodger?"

"Aww, come on, Casual, just listen, since our name is Suicidal, our record label can be called 'Already Dead' records. Yeah, I like that—I like how that sounds."

At first, I said to myself, 'Damn, this muthafucka is dumb', but then I sorta liked it. After I repeated it to myself a couple times, I was imagining Rodger on stage in front of a sold-out crowd, and us just livin' the rock life, and people screaming our names. Now it could have been the dust but it did sound good. Before I could even say another word or think another thought, Patricia and Summer barged their way into the room.

"So what the fuck are you guys doin' in here?"

There was a pause after Patricia said that—a pause that expressed pure shock on her face. Her eyes just lit up and it was almost like she had just seen a ghost.

Now, of course, I got mad, I mean first of all, this was blood money, literally blood money. And Rodger didn't tell Patricia how we had gotten the money, so I was a little bit thrown off. And it wasn't like the money was put away—it was all over the place, like we had just thrown it in the air like we were celebrating.

"Oh my God, Rodger, Oh my God, did you like hit the fuckin' lotto or something? Where did you get all this money?"

"Shit, we totally just robbed Fritz, and left his ass for dead. I've been plottin' it for the longest. Remember, I always used to tell you, honey? Aww man, you shoulda been there, babe, it was fuckin' awesome. We took that muthafucka and…"

"OK Rodger, OK," I immediately cut Rodger's ass off in the middle of the fuckin' story that he was gonna tell Patricia. "Are you really fuckin' serious right now? I mean how stupid are you, Rodger?"

I couldn't believe that this asshole actually told Patricia what we had done. I cut him right off in the middle of what he was saying. I was so pissed. But then again, I really can't expect nothing less from Rodger because he was just that dumb.

"OK. Can you guys leave now? I gotta talk to Rodger."

"Oh fuck you, Casual, OK, fuck you! I wanna know where this money came from!"

Patricia said, getting really affended by me trying to keep it a secret. But it was too late now—Rodger had already spilled the beans.

"Chill, Casual. It's cool, man. She doesn't give a shit."

"Oh yeah, yeah, Rodger, fuck it, let's just tell it all, huh. So yeah, Patricia, we robbed him of all his cash and all his shit. Oh and let me not forget—how could I even forget the fuckin' highlight of the night—how could I dare forget to tell you how we blew a fuckin' hole the size of a soft ball in this little girl's chest and watched her die. She won't be able to see her ninth birthday, but fuck it, we got what we came for."

Now I was expecting Patricia to have a shocked look on her face, and maybe cover her mouth in disbelief because of what we had done. But I was dead wrong. I was actually disgusted by her when she responded by saying, "Oh well, at least we're rich," as she jumped up into Rodger's arms, kissing him like he had just done something a genius couldn't have pulled off.

I then turned to Summer and looked at her with a puzzled face— the type of puzzled face that made her just shrug her shoulders.

"Hey Summer, by any chance did you hear what the fuck I just said? I mean did what I just say bother you the least bit?"

In the middle of Patricia kissing Rodger, she heard what I had said, and turned to me as if I was the abnormal person. "Casual, what the fuck are you bitching about? It's not like you can bring the little slut back—she's dead, Casual, get over it. You shoulda thought about that before you did what you did."

"Wow, wow, ya know, Patricia, I'm actually surprised. I mean I know you have no respect for yourself as well as human life, period. But I at least thought somewhere in those doped up veins of yours, there would be some blood pumpin' that had a little love in there. This is a little girl—for Christ's sake—a little girl."

"Oh shut up, Casual, shut the fuck up! It was probably your fuckin' idea anyway. You probably put this shit in Rodger's head."

"Oh yeah! You know us black folks—oops, I mean niggers—you know how we like to rob, steal and kill people."

Patricia and I were just going back and forth with each other like always, until her cousin Summer told both of us to shut up. It then became silent in the room for quite some time. We were all just standing there looking at the money as if we had no idea what we wanted to do with it. You could actually hear each and every single one of us breathe in and out through the nose—that's how quiet it was. But I had already made up my mind about what we were gonna do with the money—we were gonna invest that shit in Rodger and his band, and blow the fuck up into some big-ass rock stars. And I didn't give a fuck what they said about it, so I very boisterously voiced what we were gonna do with all that money.

"Rodger, I want you to listen to me very carefully. I want you, Summer and Patricia to really listen to what it is I'm getting ready to say. Because I am not about to piss this money away. We are gonna invest in Rodger and his band. We are gonna put all this money into a studio, and we are gonna make hits. He's already got a huge fan base, so we know the shit is gonna sell. Then we are gonna come up with our own record label, and we are gonna do this shit the proper way. We're not gonna blow this fuckin' money on drugs and a whole bunch of stupid shit—we've got an opportunity here to turn this money into something, and dammit, we're gonna do it. Now if any of you have a fuckin' problem with it, let me know now, so I can just kill you right here on the spot. We just went through hell to get this money, and I'm not gonna blow it. Now who's got some shit they wanna say, please say it now!"

I guess what I had said really struck Summer, because she looked at me, and said, "Ya know, Casual, I hate to compliment you but I think that's a great idea. I mean Rodger does have a great fan base, and I think if we focus ourselves on makin' this happen with Rodger and his band, I really think that this could be lucrative."

Patricia and Rodger really didn't give a shit, and I could tell what Summer and I had just said involved a little bit of intelligence to comprehend—I mean not really, but to them it involved intelligence. The look on both of their faces was of absolute blankness. Both of them were just concerned with getting high anyway, so alls they said was, "OK. Cool. We're in." Then right outta the blue, she jumped on top of all the money and threw it in the air, screaming and shouting. I couldn't take the shit anymore—I mean I really couldn't—for some reason, she was really pissing me off, so I left the room. Amazingly, Summer followed me and put her hand on my shoulder.

"Hey Casual… ummmm I just wanna ask you… Are you really serious about this, I mean takin all that money and investing it in Rodger and his band?"

At first, I was gonna say something smart, but I thought it about it for a minute after I looked at this girl. Something about this girl had truth all over her. She seemed so real. This girl reeked of smarts and outgoingness. Something told me just get in good with this girl, so I paused for a minute, looked at her with a bright potent smile, and said, "Hey, let's go out for a drink."

She didn't at all seem shocked when I asked her to go out for a drink. She grabbed her coat, opened the door, and said, "After you."

We went to this bar called The Hairy Monkey, and I figured that this was my chance to get into her head. So, after a couple of drinks, I just came out and asked her why in the fuck she was out here in New York.

"Well, Casual, since you seem like you really wanna know, I'm gonna tell you. And by the way, don't think for one minute that you are gonna get me drunk, take me somewhere and fuck the shit outta me because it's not gonna happen."

"Aww, come on, what kinda guy do you think I am?"

"Now do you really want me to answer that, Casual? Do you really want me to answer that?"

"As a matter of fact, I do want you to answer that. I would love to know what kinda guy you think I am. Because coming from a girl like you, I can almost guarantee you're gonna say some pretty offensive shit to me. I mean when we first met, we didn't meet like normal people meet. We met in the fuckin' bathroom, for Christ's sake. I was in a shower with no curtain, and you were on the toilet, taking a piss. I mean who meets like that—you don't even see shit like that on TV."

I managed to crack a smile out of Summer, and it was not only a smile, it was a long, hardy laugh. I really wasn't trying to get into her pants at all but I at least wanted to break some ice with her.

"I do have to admit, Casual, you are a very unique person. Now back to what I think of you—because now I really want you to know what I think of you—to tell you the truth, I still think you're a bit of an asshole. I think you're full of yourself. You probably think you can get any woman you want at any time. And by the way, may I add, I don't find you attractive in any way, so if you're waiting for me to say you're a handsome guy, please stop. To top it all off, you're on drugs. For Christ's sake, you spend your time hangin' with Rodger—I mean how much more of a loser can you really be! But… I do, for some crazy reason, think that I can have a decent intelligent conversation with you. So in that manner, you kinda sparked my interest back at the house when you said the smartest thing that you ever probably said in your life."

Summer was just like me in a way—egotistical, snappy, witty, and just didn't give a shit about what the outside world thought of her. People like me and her stick out—we shine. So, in order for me to get in with her, and get her where I really wanted her, I had to play humble a little, at least for a little while. But I did feel the need to tell her about herself, so I did. My glass of whiskey on the rocks was empty, so I was playing with the ice, twirling the straw around in the cup, making serious eye contact.

"Well… That hurt, so if you don't mind Miss Summer, I'm goin' to tell you that you're absolutely right. I am unique, I am an asshole, and yes, I hang with Rodger and do drugs all fuckin' day. But the part about me bein' not attractive is so wrong. You know I'm sexy—it's just against the rules for people like you to actually tell me that I'm sexy. And I don't want you to respond to that; I just wanna know if you're really down with my idea of takin' all that money and investing in Rodger."

"Absolutely, I mean I think that's a great idea, and not to mention I have so many connects in the mainstream industry, it's sick. So hell yeah, let's rock with it!"

Now something about not just what she said about having connections, but how she said it, really set off a spark of curiosity in my head. So I had to ask her what she meant by that.

"Hey Summer, now I don't mean to be nosey and shit but exactly what kinda connections do you have?"

Immediately, she laughed, shook her head, and said, "I'm sorry, Casual, they're not drug connections, OK?"

"Wow, Wow, holy shit! Are you really that fuckin' shallow, girl? My mind is not even on drugs, and just when I thought we were gonna have an intelligent conversation, here you come with somethin' stupid to say."

Summer laughed so loudly that it almost made me think that I had said something funny. She laughed so loudly that I almost started to laugh myself— for being such a drug addict that this girl thought that everything that was on my mind was drugs.

"Aww… Look at your face… look at your face. You look like a guilty drug addict."

"You know what, fuck you, bitch, because I don't think that you are the least bit funny at all. I asked you a simple question, and now you are really actin' like you know me, and I'm not digging it." I was really starting to get pissed off—I couldn't even look at her anymore—I almost wanted to spit right in her fuckin' face.

"Casual, Casual, is that you?" I heard a voice call my name twice, and it was a familiar voice, so I turned to see who it was—and it was Anastasia. "Hey wussup, 'Stasia, what are you doin in here?"

"Oh, I came with a bunch of people from work. It's my co-worker's birthday, so we decided to come out." Anastasia got real close to me, as if she wanted to kiss me, and whispered in my ear that she misses me. And boy, was I glad to see her because I sure didn't wanna stay there with Summer anymore—she had totally turned me off with her smart-ass comments. I figured that I would just introduce Anastasia to Summer as my girlfriend, and just tell her that I am going home with Anastasia. So that's exactly what I did, I introduced them.

"Hey, Summer, this is my longtime girlfriend, Anastasia, and Anastasia, this is a good friend of mine, Summer." Now they both shook hands and said hello, but what happened next hit me like a fuckin' Mack truck, I mean, totally threw my ass off. Summer threw her drink in my face, and slapped the pure shit outta me—she slapped me so hard—so fuckin' hard.

"How dare you, you son of a bitch! We've been dating for three years, you bring me out here to tell me that you wanna get serious with me, and you introduce this bitch as your longtime girlfriend? You told me that you couldn't stand her. You told me that you was done with her." Now I was thinking to myself, 'Shit, I know Anna is not gonna fall for this. Why would I introduce her as my girl if I'm here with another girl who I am trying to pursue?' But when Summer stormed out and it was just me standing there with Anna, the look on her face told it all. She actually fell for that shit, because she walked away from me too. Even though Anna and I had an agreement that our relationship was just gonna be sex, the way she walked off meant she was starting to get feelings. But I wasn't gonna chase her—no way. And as for Summer's ass, I was gonna deal with her one way or another!

# CHAPTER 8

It was a Saturday night. Rodger and his band were performing at this underground spot called The Vampire Din. It was packed with freaks—I mean these muthafuckaz were some goddamn freaks. Now I don't believe in vampires, and I never really did, and I don't know if it was the angel dust that I was smoking or what, but these people that were in this particular spot were really spooking me out. First of all, it was pitch black in there—the only fuckin' light was the light that came from the stage. Rodger was doing the opening performance for this band called *Brooklyn After Dark*. They were a bunch of crazy-ass looking dudes with paint all on their faces, and wore tight leather clothes—well, the ones that had clothes on anyway. The rest of them barely had anything on. Patricia had some connects with the promoters of the club, of course, because these were indeed her type of people— there was no second guessing that shit. Anybody in New York City who didn't believe in God or thought the devil was the greatest thing, she knew them. I mean it worked out because they also skin popped, which meant they shot heroin, so she hooked me up with them and I was making a killing all night long off these crazy asses.

Now I've been around some dope feens before but these people were like demons, devils, and just straight out Antichrist freaks. I was in the VIP room, well, at least that's what normal people would call it anyway, but these people referred to it as the 'cave'. And that's just what it was—these muthafuckas were in there cutting themselves and havin the person next to them suck the blood, and the crazy thing was they were acting as if they were experiencing a fuckin' orgasm. It was sick—I mean it was fuckin' sick. So here I am—me Patricia and Summer are sitting in this cave. I'm trying to knock off this heroin, and at the same time, I've got my eye on every single last one of these dudes. All of a sudden, this guy or girl—I really couldn't tell which one because whoever it was had long hair and lipstick—approached me. And that was another thing—the guys wore lipstick, and their hair was just as long as the girls. So how do you tell who is a girl and who the fuck ain't! I mean, shit, if I wanted some pussy, this damn sure wouldn't be the spot! So now here's this thing coming towards me with a mouth full of blood. As it came towards me, I gave it this look like just watch what you say muthafucka because I damn sure will reach in my pocket, pull out my pistol and shoot your crazy ass. Now as this thing kept getting closer, I finally realized that it was a damn man—his build told it all. So he came and sat next to me, and asked, "You want some energy?"

I just looked him up and down like he was a lunatic, which he was anyway, and I turned towards Patricia, who was fully engaged in a conversation with this other weird-looking girl. What the conversation was about, I totally didn't know, but I just wanted to act like I was gonna say something to her just to get this fool away from me. Now you would think he walked away, but he didn't. He actually tapped me, and had the nerve to ask me again if I wanted some energy. So I said to myself, 'What the fuck is this energy shit… maybe it is a new drug that I could sell, who knows.' So I asked his dumb ass what the hell this energy shit was. Now I was expecting this dude to pull out a pill or some shit, but he looked at me, smiled, pulled out a razor and cut his pointer finger just a little, so that the blood would come pouring out. And as he moved closer toward me with that bloody finger, he said, "Ya know how much people would pay me right now to suck the energy from my body, here… suck…taste my life." I couldn't believe the nerve of this dude—he told me to taste his life—he actually wanted me to suck the blood from his finger. I looked at his ass with pure disgust, and told him that if he didn't move the fuck away from me, I was gonna blow his goddamn head smooth off. I even pulled out my gun and stared right into his eyes as I pointed that gun right in between his eyes.

"How dare you pull a gun on me! Patricia, who is this human fool you have brought into my cave, who claims he will not dare taste the life that flows in my veins?"

"Yo, dude, I don't know who the fuck you are, but I don't play that shit. So you can call on Patricia's ass all you want, homeboy, but if you don't get up right now and get that bloody-ass finger out my way, I'm gonna shoot your muthafuckin ass. Now you can test me if you want, faggot." Everybody in the room just froze—they couldn't believe that I was pointing a gun at whoever this clown was. I guess he was like some sort of Vampire God, but I didn't care. "All y'all need to be ashamed of yourselves, sittin' up in here suckin' each other's blood and calling' it 'energy.' I hope all y'all get a goddamn disease. You're drinkin' blood—it ain't Kool-Aid, OK, and on that note, I'm leavin', so fuck you very much."

I was on a roll at that point, so while I was at it, as I was leaving the room to go back out into the club, I pulled Summer and Patricia by their arms and told them, "Let's go." They didn't even argue. They both knew that I meant business. It wasn't too often that Patricia had seen me mad but she knew when I grabbed her arm, it was time to go. And it was perfect timing because as soon as we walked out, Rodger and his band came out. And let me tell you, they came out making a whole bunch of fuckin' noise. Screaming at the top of his lungs, 'Life is but an eye blink, then you die'. It was actually one of the very few songs that I kinda liked. It made sense, and that says a lot for Rodger and the rest of those washed-out druggies that he played with.

The song kinda made you think, it was basically about how you go through life with all its ups and downs, then you learn from them, but by the time you are ready to apply what you learned from those things in life to make your life better, you fuckin' die, and it happens all too quickly. Ya see, at this point in time, listening to Rodger's material was crucial for me, especially if I was gonna be his manager and start our label. The crowd in the club was really feeling it too. Heads were nodding back and forth with force as Rodger screamed at the top of his lungs with such expression and rage. It was like Rodger was another person when he was on stage. This total madman would just come out and take over his body. I was really starting to get a good feeling about being his manager, I really was, I mean where could we go wrong with this.

Now I did indeed have a bone to pick with Summer, because of that crazy stunt that she had pulled a couple weeks ago, and the thought of me pickin' that bone came across my mind as I looked at her nod her head to the beat of Rodger's song. For some strange reason, a sense of attraction just hit me—those eyes, her hair, the way she was nodding her head. I was really attracted to her at that moment. So I figured, what the hell! I tapped her on her shoulder and asked her to come with me to the bar to get a drink. And surprisingly, she came, and of course Patricia had to come. I really didn't want Patricia to follow us because there were a couple things I wanted to say to her about how we were getting along, but I said to myself, 'Fuck it. I'll just wait another day'. So I'm standing at the bar, trying to get the bartender's attention, and she was taking entirely too long. What I saw next as the bartender slowly bent down to pick up a dollar she had dropped, almost made my muthafuckin heart stop. My mouth opened, my eyes lit up, I began to shake—it was as if I had just seen somebody who had been dead for ten fuckin' years. It was the girl who was at Fritz's house the night we had robbed him. And we damn sure caught some serious eye contact that even Summer picked up on.

"Shit, Casual, she's pretty but you don't have to look at her like that."

"Yo, we gotta get the fuck outta here right now. Patricia, let's go, I'm gonna get Rodger."

Patricia and Summer were confused and started to get scared by the way I was acting. Patricia kept on asking me what was going on, so I yelled at her and told her to shut the fuck up and that there was no time for games. But by the time I turned back to check if that girl was still there, she wasn't. She had disappeared. Now I was scared because I didn't know where she had gone—she could have called the police and told them that the murderers that killed her boyfriend and that little girl were in the club. I was looking for her throughout the crowd, combing with my eyes to see where she was.

Then I finally spotted her, she was walking towards me with four other dudes that she was with, and they weren't calmly walking over to us either. They were shoving people outta their way to get to me. There was no time to get Rodger. I was too far from the stage. I didn't know if these guys were cops or just some dudes out to get revenge on us. And let me tell ya, by the look on their faces, they sure didn't look like no fuckin' cops. I grabbed Patricia and Summer, and headed towards the back door of the club. The chase was suddenly on—they were right on our ass. As we got to the back door, I tried to open it but it wouldn't open. I started to panic as I kept ramming my shoulder into the door. Now with all this shit going on, I still hadn't told Summer or Patricia what we were running from. They were gaining on us, getting closer, and I still couldn't get the door open. I began to kick as hard as I possibly could to get that door open but it wouldn't budge. As I turned back to see how close they had gotten to me, they damn sure were close enough for me to say, 'fuck it.'

I pulled out my gun and began to shoot. Everybody started to scream and started running back into their direction—just what I wanted. Throughout all the screams and people stampeding, I had time to think about my next sudden move—I knew it had to be quick. I turned to my left, and noticed the women's bathroom door had been open because the girls were running out due to the shots that they had heard. When I looked in the bathroom, I noticed there was a window that was big enough for us to fit through, so I grabbed both girls and dragged both of them into the bathroom. And before I could close the door behind me I heard more gunshots, pop pop pop pop pop pop pop. Now those shots definitely weren't coming from my gun, so I knew they were shooting back. And at that very moment, that's when it clicked in my head that these fuckers were trying to kill my ass. God must have been with us that night because there was a lock on the door.

"Why in the fuck are you two dumb bitches just standing there like assholes. Climb out the fuckin' window now!!"

"Casual, what the hell is going on? Why are they after us?!"

"Patricia, if you don't shut the fuck up and climb out that window..."

I couldn't believe this dumb bitch was actually trying to talk to me while our lives were about to be taken. But they really got a move on when they heard the door being kicked in, and a mean, manly Russian-accented voice yelling out, "You're going to fuckin' pay for this, you bastard, you're not gonna get away." It was then that they started climbing out that fuckin' window. The door was damn near getting ready to be kicked off the hinges but we were all out. But of course, this dumbass bitch, Summer, dropped her pocket book in the bathroom and decided to go back in and get it.

"SUMMER, SUMMER! What the fuck are you doin'? Are you really serious right now? Are you fuckin' serious, Summer?"

"I can't leave my pocket book in there. I have to get it—it has all my shit in there."

So, of course, the stupidass climbed back into the window to get her pocket book. And as she picked it up, my heart just dropped right into my fuckin' shoes. The door finally kicked open—Summer had no chance of getting out—she was fuckin' dead. My heart literally was in my shoes. But somehow she made it to the window. I grabbed her to pull her through but one of those fuckers grabbed her leg and was pulling her back in. It was tug of war, and a matter of who was stronger. And the way things were looking, my ass was getting pulled right in with her. It was over—my life was fuckin' over. I was gonna die in the bathroom of a vampire club. I was pulling and pulling, but this muthafucka was determined to pull her ass in there. Now I don't know how but somehow Summer kicked this dude right in his goddamn balls. And he let go then with no problem at all. And we took off into the night, not even knowing if these guys were gonna go after Rodger. We didn't even look back, we just kept running through the dark New York City streets.

I finally got a call from Rodger as we stopped to catch our breath. He was so excited, he thought somebody had gotten so wild over his music that they had gotten violent and began to fight. "Dude, where the fuck are you? It's fuckin' pandemonium in here, dude. These fuckers are goin' wild over my music. People are getting trampled over and shit. Man, this is the fuckin' shit, man."

"Rodger, I hate to spoil your moment, but those people aren't running because of your music. I mean they are running because of you, trust me, you have a lot to do with why they are running. But that's not important, you just get your ass outta there right fuckin' now, I mean right fuckin' now, Rodger!"

"Dude, for what? I'm like a star in here."

"Yeah, well, I tell you what star—the girl that was in Fritz's house that night when we killed him was in the club. As a matter of fact, she's probably still in there. She was with these dudes, and they tried to kill me. So that stampede that you saw was me—I shot at those muthafuckas and they shot back. She knows us, Rodger, and obviously she's out to get us."

"Dude, are you fuckin' serious? I knew I shoulda killed that bitch."

"Yeah, whatever, Rodger, just get the fuck outta there alright."

We both hung up the phone and we just kept it moving, but of course I had to answer all the questions from Patricia and Summer, who were bending my fuckin' ear off, practically screaming at the top of their lungs wanting to know what the fuck had just happened. So I finally stopped them right where we were in the middle of a crowded city block, because at this point in time, I knew for sure we had lost them.

"Alright listen, both of you, especially you, Patricia, the man that we killed to get that money had some girl in the house, who we probably should have killed, but we didn't. That girl was her, and obviously she wants us dead."

"So what the hell are we gonna do, Casual, run for the rest or our lives?"

"Uh… well, yeah, Patricia, the small price that we are gonna have to pay for now is run, not unless you have any brilliant ideas, which I know you don't, so just chill the fuck out. Trust me like you never trusted me before, and I will get us outta this."

I was just talking shit to the both of them. I really didn't know what the fuck we were gonna have to end up doing. Alls I knew was that I was marked for death by a drug lord's family, and I needed to get us outta Dodge.

# CHAPTER 9

Cameras were flashing everywhere; the paparazzi and tabloid magazines were following our asses ever since we left the motel. The MTV music awards baby! This was the event of all events. To make it, and be nominated for the best hardcore rockband to exist. SUICIDAL! SUICIDAL! SUICIDAL! They all chanted and screamed as we stepped outta that pearl-white stretch Hummer onto the one and only red carpet. And goddamn, was I looking good! Three-piece tailormade suit, and of course, my shades—I had to have my shades on. Now let me tell you about shades something that most celebs won't tell ya. Besides just looking cool, shades are actually a protection from groupie eye contact. Let me explain—ya see, with shades on, I can catch eye contact with the people without them even knowing that I'm looking at them. I could actually stare a person right in their eyes, and they would never know that I'm looking at them. Alls they can say is that I'm looking in their direction. And that's important, you don't want some groupie following you because he or she thinks you looked at them in an inviting manner—groupies can get that way. Alls it takes is a look into their eyes by you and it's like an open invitation to them to walk up to you and hound you. Sounds crazy, I know, but what the hell, that's my philosophy for wearing shades in the night, indoors, and everyplace else that you would have no reason to have shades on.

Rodger and his band were absolutely the shit, and we were gonna prove it by winning every single fuckin' award that we got nominated for. The place was full of rap artists, R&B singers, rock stars, television stars, producers, directors, ghostwriters and all kinds of celebs, all under one roof. And then came the moment we were all waiting for—the announcement for the best new rock group of the year. And the most beautiful woman walking on earth, Alicia Keys, was announcing the winner. She opened up the card and slowly leaned forward toward the mic and said the award goes to… Suicidal.

I couldn't believe it—I mean I knew we were gonna win but it was still a feeling of 'wow, holy shit, I can't believe this is happening'. We all jumped up like wild barbarians pushing and shoving each other. It was like we were making a mosh pit on the way to the fuckin' stage. But of course, I had to fall back and be cool, due to the fact that I had a rep to maintain as a cool, smooth, calm, collected mothafucka. So when we all got on stage, I got hit with a feeling, a high—a high that was like no other, an ultimate rush flowing through my veins. And since I was the mastermind behind this whole thing, Alicia Keys looked right at me and handed me the award. Her eyes were sparkling like they had stars from the night sky in them, and she smiled so bright and wide—like it was the happiest moment in her life just to hand me that award.

As I stared deeper into her eyes, all of a sudden, they turned pitch-black. I was totally immobilized. I felt a sense of sheer evil. I got ice-cold and began to shiver violently. As I looked deeper into her eyes, everyone around me turned to fire. The whole place began to burn, and I heard the faint cry of a little girl, "Mommy, mommy… Where are you, mommy?" Then I heard the sound of a projector, and a snowy screen came up before my eyes, and began counting down from 10.

When it struck zero, I saw my daughter's mother, Lacey, falling from a skyscraper and hitting the concrete. Then it flashed to Patricia in a tub full of blood with her eyes wide open with a newborn in her arms. Both of them were dead. Then I saw Rodger laid out on stage in front of a sold-out crowd with a bullet hole in his head.

I yelled so loudly in terror that I woke myself right up out of my sleep to see four walls around me and a door with a little window. It was all a dream and where I really was, was in a cell, locked up in the county jail, crashing down off of 2 tabs of acid accompanied by some California red devil dust. The only thing that I remember was riding in the back of a cop car and trying to kick out the windows. The floor I was lying on was ice-cold and filthy. Now I never had the experience of being locked up, but I tell ya, they sure as hell don't fuckin' clean in there. And the cops must have really fucked me up because my face felt swollen and my ribs were sore. My mind was in a fog. I couldn't figure out how the fuck I got in this predicament. And before I had another thought in my head, I was getting bailed out.

Rodger had come to bail me out, and the first words out of his mouth were, "Jesus Christ, they fucked you up dude. Holy shit have you seen your fuckin' face, dude."

"No, Rodger. No, I haven't seen my face. I forgot to look in that big, exotic, expensive mirror that they put in the holding cell for inmates. So no, Rodger, I haven't seen my face."

As we got into the car, I looked at myself in the mirror finally, and those cops damn sure did do a number on me. Both my eyes were swollen, and I had a busted lip. I had to know what the fuck happened to me, so I asked Rodger how in the hell I got in this shit, and he just started to laugh.

"Yo Rodger, what the fuck is so damn funny, first of all."

"I'm sorry... I'm sorry, dude. It's just that I can't believe that you don't know what you did to get locked up. It's like how the hell can you not remember what the fuck you did!"

"Oh, will you shut the fuck up already Rodger, and tell me?"

Rodger finally took a deep breath, and began to tell me how I had acted like a fool. We were at a prestigious strip club in California one night. Now I'll get to how we even ended up in Cali in just a few. So we were at this strip club, and we were all fucked-up—it was me, Rodger and his crew. Acid tabs, Agavales gold premium tequila and California red devil dust were the drugs of choice that night. Not angel dust, but red devil dust being inhaled just before we went into the strip joint. We were like animals who broke free from the zoo, and started running the streets. We were throwing money at the girls one minute, and that turned into pouring bottles of beer on them while they were giving lap dances. I mean these girls had probably never seen customers as rowdy and grizzly as we were—we were picking these girls up, swinging them around, pouring beer all over them and throwing money at the same time. I mean I literally gave this one girl a fuckin' beer shower. I ordered like ten fuckin' beers, guzzled down three of them and dumped the rest all over this fuckin' chick, as she just kept riding me and washing her hair as if I was pouring Panteen Pro V shampoo in her hair and all over her body.

Now at this point, something just came over me. I stood up, took my shirt off and started pouring the beer all over myself, and it didn't help that this girl actually grabbed a bottle or two and started pouring beer all over me as I started to strip. All the girls in the club began to crowd around me and cheer me on. 'Take it off! Take it off! Take it off! Take it off!' And that's exactly what the fuck I did. I took off all my fuckin' clothes, and jumped right on the stage on that pole and began to dance. I was down to my boxers, and alls I kept hearing was 'Take it off! Take it off! Take it off!' The strippers were going crazy—it was like I was putting on a show for them. Now two tabs of acid, 100% de agave tequila and some red devil dust mixed with a little bit of Damion De Vos. Shiiiiiiiiiiiit! I took those fuckin' boxers off, and I was ass-naked on stage, swinging my cock for all these strippers. And the tables had turned—all the girls that I was pouring beer on were now pouring beer on me.

I guess the owner of the club wasn't digging this behavior at all because he sent two of his biggest bouncers over to me, and they asked me to get off the stage. Now if you have ever been on devil dust, you can imagine how I was feeling when I saw those two big, muscle-headed bouncers telling me to get off the stage. I already felt invincible and ready to take on the whole world, so as soon as those bouncers asked me to get off the stage, I threw a left hook outta nowhere, hoping to knock one of those bouncers right the fuck out. So I swung as hard as I could and I connected a Mike Tyson-blow right to the jaw of one of the strippers. I missed the bouncer and hit one of the girls, wow... I tell ya, after that I hit the fuckin' ground so hard, it knocked the wind outta me.

According to Rodger, there were cops already outside the club, so it took no time at all for them to respond. I was being beat up by bouncers and cops all at the same time. California cops must like beating up blacks, hell, Rodney King, and now me. Rodger said they were fuckin' me up for hitting that girl. I already started off not liking California, and we'd only been out here but a fuckin' eye blink. Ya see, things were really heating up for us back home in Manhattan. Word in the old neighborhood was that we were marked to be murdered. Turned out, this guy Fritz was a member of a neighborhood gang of enforcers who were already contract killers, and he was well known and respected. It was also told to us that the cops had been paid off very well not to intervene in this whole thing. This whole entire contract killing organization wanted us dead, and that was that. It became a personal vendetta for them to find us; they even put the word out about how they would chop our bodies up and throw us to some wild pigs. So with the money that we took, we flew out to California.

Summer said that she could hook all of us up with a place to stay. She was scared out of her mind due to all the rumors that were flying around about us. It was me, Rodger, his six low-life band members, Patricia and Summer. And low and behold, we ended up doing the same fuckin' thing in California that we were doing in New York—robbing homes, robbing people, getting sky high and doing local shows. The Cali life was so new to us that we just acted like a pack of savage wolves from the deep woods that were dropped off in San Francisco. A couple of bar brawls here, a couple of bar brawls there, we crashed about every party that we heard about, but what was really fun was getting high off shrooms, robbing somebody's house and then burning it to the ground in the middle of the night and watching it. I tell ya, the flames and the fire truck lights had to be some of the most beautiful fuckin' colors mixed together when you're high on shrooms. That became like our thing to do—we got so high one day while watching this club owner's house burn to the ground that we forgot to take the bag of jewelry that we stole from his house. This guy was a real cockface—he wouldn't let us perform at his club because he said that Rodger's music was too violent. The nerve of this fuckin' guy! So we just burned his fuckin' house down. Now here's the spooky thing about it all—everytime we burned down a house, Rodger claimed that there was a man in the fire that would come out and tell him what song to write about. It had to be the sickest thing I ever heard in my life. I tried to tell him, "Yo Rodger, it's the drugs man. It's the fuckin' drugs." But this guy was stuck on the fact that there was really a man in the fire that would come out and tell him what songs to write about. He was really fuckin' serious about this shit too. So, in order for this guy to write a song, he would set a building on fire or even a house. And while innocent families were running out screaming from the blazes, this guy was taking notes on what to write in his next song. We all would sit there and laugh like we were at an Andrew Dice Clay comedy show, watching someone's house burn to the ground while this asshole Rodger was talking to some fuckin' guy in the damn fire that he claimed he saw. You can just imagine how many houses we burned down. It was all over the news and in every newspaper. We were bringing more terror to California than the damn nightstalker—people were afraid that they were next.

It was a Friday night, and everybody had hit the town, except me and Summer. We were all at her condo until Rodger and everybody had decided that they wanted to hit a bar. I really didn't feel like being out and neither did Summer, so we just stayed back and watched DVDs all night. Since Summer and I had both figured out that we were die-hard *Rambo* fans, we popped in one of my favorites, which was the last *Rambo* movie that Sylvester Stallone made. And what made it more interesting was that we both had a whole plate of coke to sniff to ourselves.

We were actually having a nice time, and a really great conversation until Summer giggled, and said, "Ya know, I think he is so fuckin' sexy. Oh my God, just look at his body."

"What!!! What!!!" I shouted, "What the fuck did you just say, Summer? Are you serious? Sylvester Stallone! Sylvester Stallone? Isn't he half fuckin' retarded? There is nothing sexy about that dude. I mean, come on, his name is Sylvester, for Christ's sake!"

"Well damn, Casual, I wouldn't expect you to think he's sexy. You're a guy. You're not supposed to think he's sexy. I swear, you fuckin' men can never give credit to another good looking man!"

As soon as the movie was over, I turned off the DVD player, and put regular television on, and sure enough, the Lakers and the Celtics were playing. It was a close game, 80 to 78, and it was the last quarter with one minute to play. Now my favorite team were the Knicks but I still loved a good game of basketball. And this game was getting intense—the Lakers were ahead by two and the Celtics came down the court and hit a clutch 3 pointer. Now the score was 81 to 80, the Celtics were up with only a minute to play and the Lakers had the ball. Bringing the ball up the court was last year's MVP Kevin Roberson, who was an absolute magnificent point guard. They worked the ball around looking for an open shot, finally, their star center was open in the lane for a pass but it got intercepted by the Celtics. It was a fast break and the clock was going down to the last seconds. But the Celtics lost the ball. It hit off the small forward's foot and the ball went out of bounds. Now the ball belonged to the Lakers again, with Kevin Roberson pushing the ball up court. The clock was at 10, 9, 8, 7… the crowd was on its feet. It was absolute pandemonium… 6, 5, 4, 3… Kevin Roberson then took the final 3 point shot 2, 1… the ball went up, came down, and bounced off the rim—he missed the shot. "Goddammit, Kevin, you fuckin' suck, you fuckin' suck, you bum all the money they pay you, and you can't hit that fuckin' shot. Somebody trade this dickhead!" I shouted out. I was furious. I mean I couldn't believe this fuckin' guy had missed a wide open jump shot off the screen.

As I was ranting and raving about this Kevin Roberson character, I looked over at Summer, who had this wide grin on her face—as if she was glad that the Lakers had lost. I politely asked her what the fuck she was grinning about. She leaned over and before she answered me, she took her pinky fingernail, dipped it in the coke, and took a cute little lady-like snort. And in a real subtle voice, she said, "I totally hate that fucker. Oh my God."

I was a bit shocked to hear that comment coming from her mouth because she made that statement like she actually followed pro basketball or some shit. "Hey, Summer, now I gotta ask you. Please tell me why you hate Kevin Roberson? I mean I don't like the guy at this moment only because of the simple fact that I hate the Celtics and that bastard missed a very important game-winning shot that he damn sure should have made. You sittin' up here talkin' shit about this guy like you follow basketball—I mean fuckin' really, Summer."

I was not expecting her to say anything back, but in response, she cocked her head to the side, and said, "I know way more about those basketball players than you, Casual—that's for sure."

I burst out laughing, "Are you kiddin' me right now, Summer? I follow basketball like nobody else that you know OK! You absolutely do not know more about these dudes than me. Conversation closed. There is no need for us to even be talkin' about this any more. This is fuckin' foolish. I eat sleep and shit basketball, Summer."

"Oh yeah oh yeah," she said, with a snotty attitude, being the bitch that she really knew how to be. "Well, let me tell you something Mr. Fuckin'. I follow basketball. Let me tell you what he drinks at parties—white Russian on the rocks, extra strong, his favorite food is porkchops and applesauce. And he absolutely loves to eat sushi."

"Summer, I don't give a fuck about that tabloid shit you be reading about these guys in the magazine. I'm talking about points, assists, rebounds, stats, girl, stats. I couldn't care less about what the fuck Kevin Roberson eats or drinks. So what are you really saying here, Summer? Oh wait wait, let me guess. He's arrogant, he's a dog and he cheats on his wife too right? Well, I got news for you, Summer. You don't need a magazine to tell you that—all those muthafuckas cheat on their wives. So now what are you going to say?"

I tell ya, she didn't have to say shit after that because the bitch started to fuckin' cry—she actually started to really cry. I said to myself, 'What the hell is wrong with this crazy bitch? First she says Sylvester Stallone is sexy, now she's crying because I said she doesn't know more about basketball than me. Maybe it was the coke...' But coke don't make muthafuckas get emotional, and to tell you the truth, the coke wasn't that damn good anyway.

"Yo Summer, why in the hell are you crying? It's only basketball—it's really not that serious. Just take a deep breath OK? In and out. In and out."

"Oh, will you shut the fuck up! Shut the fuck up!" she shouted. I jumped back as soon as she shouted it. Her face was all red and full of tears, and her hair was a total mess. This bitch was really starting to spook me the fuck out. "OK, Summer, cool dude, I tell you what, I'll never ever watch another basketball game with your ass again, especially when this guy, Kevin Roberson, is playin'. I mean, damn, you act like this guy raped you or some shit!" And with a stony look on her face, she looked up at me, and said, "For your information, I was raped by that son of a bitch, you asshole." Immediately, I started to laugh out loud—like she had just told me a fuckin' joke, "Yeah right, Summer! Are you serious? Get the fuck outta here. Kevin Roberson raped you—no fuckin' way!" Summer wiped the tears that were running down her face, and didn't say anything. We both just sat there looking at each other for about ten seconds until she broke the silence and said, "You don't believe me, do you?" And she was absolutely right at first, I didn't know what to think.

She sat on the couch Indian-style, pulled her hair back, put it into a ponytail, and took a deep breath. "Look, Casual, I don't know why I'm telling you this, but I guess I owe you some sort of an explanation for sitting here and crying in front of you like this. For a long time I was a Dallas Cowboys Cheerleader, and what a life that was, let me tell ya. I can tell you about every single one of those bastards on that football team, hell, I can tell you about half the guys in the entire NFL, including some of the owners. And none of those fuckers are faithful husbands—well, the ones that are married anyway. And if you ask me how I know this, I will gladly, without any shame, tell you I know—because I slept with 80 percent of them. And the ones I didn't sleep with were sleeping with my friends."

"OK hold up here, Summer," I interrupted, "So what does you being a Dallas Cowboys Cheerleader have to do with Kevin raping you? These are two whole different sports here, Summer."

"Well, if you stop interrupting me while I'm telling you, you would know what the hell that asshole has to do with the whole thing."

I immediately closed my fuckin' mouth, and promised not to interrupt her again, because this shit was actually getting kind of good, and I wanted to know how why and when this dude raped her. So she began telling me how she was good friends with the running back from the Dallas Cowboys, and that they would always hangout. This guy turned out to be good friends with Kevin Roberson and that's how they hooked up. She kept going on and on about how kevin was a raging alcoholic and one night, they went back to the hotel, and he started forcing himself on her. She wouldn't give in and give him any pussy, so he raped her. Now according to Summer, he didn't just rape her ass, he fuckin' beat the shit out of her. The story was getting kind of long and boring, so I just said, "Well, it happened. It's over, and I think that you should move on from this."

It wasn't that I didn't care—I just didn't want to hear it anymore, I felt like I was in a soap opera or some shit. I must have really pissed her off when I made that comment because she threw her drink in my face, and then had the nerve to throw the whole bowl of coke in my face on top of that, and ran straight to her room and slammed the door. So there I was sitting on the couch with coke stuck to my face, and as I turned to look at the TV, who was on talking to the sports commentator—Kevin muthafuckin Roberson. I burst out laughing.

# CHAPTER 10

I was sleeping peacefully. It was a warm, sunny California morning, and I was gathering up some really good rest… until Rodger barged into the room, and jumped on me. His breath reeked of rum, as if he had just gargled with a bottle of overproof. On top of that, he not only smelled like heavy overproof rum, he fuckin' spilled it on me, because he was holding the bottle in his hands.

"Duude, we gotta go right now. Wake the hell up—we gotta go."

I was so pissed, I said, "Rodger, if you don't get the fuck off me right now, and let me sleep, I swear I'm gonna shoot you. And your fuckin' breath stinks, Rodger, MOVE!" Rodger was so excited that he totally ignored my frustration, and continued to jump on me.

"Duude, dude, we're gonna be rich—you have no fuckin' idea, dude—we're gonna be so fuckin' rich and famous. Wake the fuck up, dude!"

"Yo, Rodger, it's early in the morning, OK, and you know what else, what if I had a bitch in the bed right now, what the fuck would you say then huh?"

"I couldn't care less if you had some whore in here. Do you realize who I spoke to, Duude?" Rodger was so damn excited about whoever it was that he had spoken to that his consideration for me getting any kind of sleep went out the fuckin' window. I peeled the covers off of me, sat up in the bed with my gun in my hand, and put it right to Rodger's lips.

"Look, Rodger, I don't care who you spoke to, OK! Alls I wanna do is sleep. Haven't you learned anything from having a black friend? Don't fuck with my money, my food, and my sleep, OK, Rodger?

"Sam Hatchett," Rodger shouted, "I just spoke to Sam Hatchett—he heard one of my old demos and he loved it."

I didn't even answer Rodger. I just laid right back down, threw my gun on the floor, and pulled the covers over my face.

"Casual, I'm talking about Sam Hatchett—Sam Hatchett from Space Boy Records. He wants to sign me."

For a minute I said to myself, 'Oh my God, I wished he would just shut the fuck up.' But then, I said that name to myself... Sam Hatchett, Sam Hatchett, Sam Hatchett... Then it dawned on me—Sam Hatchett from Space Boy Records—he's a fuckin' legend. I sat straight up in the bed, and shouted, "Sam from Space Boy Records! Ohhh shit! What did he say!"

"Duude! Duude! I totally blanked out, dude. So I told him that I was Rodger's brother and that I was out on a underground tour."

I couldn't believe this fuckin' asshole. I could not believe what just came outta Rodger's mouth. Here he gets a call from the one and only Sam Hatchett, I mean this guy was like the Russel Simmons of hardcore rock, and this fool tells him that he's his brother and he's out on a underground tour! I was absolutely on fire—you probably could have seen smoke coming from my ears if you looked close enough.

"So Rodger, I'm gonna give you a moment to show me that you do have some intelligence. Here's your moment to shine, Rodger. Because Lord knows you haven't had many intelligent moments in your life. Did you at least get his number, please tell me that you at least got his number?."

Rodger sat there with this dumbass look on his face. And that alone gave me the answer that I wanted. I felt like picking my gun back up and shooting him right in his face. So he finally answered me—all slow and retarded—saying, "Ohhhh shit, dude, I didn't even think to ask him that."

I blew up at this point—I mean I blew my top, I cursed him out so bad. "Rodger, why the fuck are you so damn dumb? Why would you tell that man that you are not you and that you are your brother and that you are on tour? Why would you say some shit like that?

"Uhhh… duhh… Hello, Casual, I did it so that he would think that I'm famous. Come on, think Duude!"

"Think? Think! You want me to think, Rodger? Yeah, I think you're a dumbass, that's what I think. You wanted him to think that you were famous. Come the fuck on, Rodger. He knows you ain't fuckin' famous. He's famous, Rodger. Famous people are on TV, Rodger. Famous people know famous people because first of all, they're famous, Rodger. You came in this fuckin' room to wake me up outta my fuckin' sleep to tell me that you told Sam Hatchett that you were Rodger's brother and that you were on tour. You could have waited until I got up for that dumb shit. As a matter of fact, you shouldn't have told me that in the first fuckin' place."

Rodger left the room and I tried like hell to go back to sleep. But no matter how hard I tried, it wasn't gonna happen. I just couldn't believe that Rodger had told this guy what he told him. Since I couldn't go back to sleep, I decided to just get up. I was definitely hungry, so I went into the kitchen to find something to hold me over. Now who do

I see when I get into the kitchen—Rodger's dumb ass accompanied by his even dumber friends that all played in the band smoking dust. As if Rodger wasn't dumb enough already, and now here he was getting dumber and dumber with each puff of that California devil dust. He was just smoking up the little bit of sense that he did have, which amounted to what God has given a fuckin' billy goat. Of course, there was nothing to eat but some cereal, so I had no other choice but to eat it. And hell yeah, I ate the whole fuckin' box with no necessary respect for anyone in the house who might want some.

My mind was just racing back and forth, and for some strange reason, Lacey came to my mind, then it came to me. Yeah, I could call Lacey. Lacey mingles with the movers and shakers on a daily basis. Rappers, rock stars, singers, actors, and those types. The thing was that I knew that even if she didn't know him, she definitely knew somebody that did, and that's for damn sure. I figured I'd call her to see if she could get me in contact with Sam Hatchett—and that's right, I said 'me' because if something were going to professionally happen eventually, I couldn't depend on Rodger. So I figured I definitely am gonna drive this bus. And now is definitely a good time to get back into Lacey's life. She had just landed a super big role—the lead in the upcoming film, *Wonder Woman*. This was super huge for Lacey's career, and just as big for me, if I played my hand correctly. Don't get me wrong, I didn't want Lacey back, but I sure as fuck was going to try and be a better father to my daughter—that's all I needed to do. Right after I finished my cereal, I gave her a ring. For Christ's sake, I hadn't even called my daughter, so this was going to be something. With me being on the run, and Lacey being a movie star, our daughter was bound to be a pole dancer when she gets of age. After a few rings Lacey picked up.

"Hello"

"Hey, Lacey, its me, Casual, how ya been?"

"Oh my God, Casual, is that you? Oh my God, where are you? No, wait a minute, hold on, why am I being nice to you? Where the fuck are you, Casual? I haven't heard from you in I don't know how long."

"Well, thanks for asking, Lacey, I'm doing great. I have to say that I can't complain about a thing."

"Ya know, Casual, I almost thought you were dead. Why haven't you called?"

Now I knew that I had to be as polite as possible towards Lacey because I was fixin' to say 'Lacey, this is nothing new. I never fuckin' call you so please spare me.' But I just told her that I had gotten into some trouble, and that I needed to get away for a while. I also told her, "Hell, don't feel bad because I haven't even called my parents." Lacey always had a soft spot for me, so she immediately asked me where I was. I wasn't about to even tell her that nor why I was where I was, so instead, I just got right into why I called her in the first place.

"Hey, Lacey, check it out. Do you know Sam Hatchett from Space Boy Records?"

And of course, she gave me the answer that I was not only looking for but also the answer I knew anyway.

"Sam! Sam Hatchett! Of course, I know him," Lacey responded, as if she was excited to hear his damn name. Now just by the way she said his name—like she was all fuckin' happy—I knew she knew this guy real well, which also probably meant that she had sucked his fuckin' cock a couple times. So, of course, I teased her, "What do you mean, Sam!" I repeated his name just how she said it. So she gives me this little slutty-ass chuckle, like I'm some stupid clown, and says, "I like Sam. I think he's awesome. He's such a fun guy to be around."

So I chuckled back at her in a sarcastic manner mimicking her, "Ha ha ha ha ha ha! He's such a fun guy to be around. I love it when he jams his cock down my throat."

"Oh, shut the fuck up, Casual, what do you want with him anyway?"

"Yo, check this out, Lacey. You ain't gonna believe this crazy shit. Somehow this guy Sam got Rodger's number, probably off of the back of one of his demo CDs, and he actually called him. Now why I need his number after he already spoke to Rodger is a different story, and no, I'm not getting into it. So what I need from you is his contact information."

Asking Lacey for his information was almost as easy as breathing. She came right out and said, "OK, give me about twenty minutes and I'll call you back with his info." And just like clockwork twenty minutes went by and she called right back.

"Ok, listen, Casual, I just got off the phone with Sam. He's having a huge party at his house in Laguna beach for his birthday. He said I can bring you guys, well, as a matter of fact, he wants to know if you guys want to perform. So can you guys get out to California?"

The way this whole thing was playing out was almost incredible—it seemed like everything was falling right into place. And the fact that he wanted us to perform at his house out here in California, where we already were—wow, how perfect could a situation get! I didn't want Lacey to know that I was in Cali so I told her to just get me the address his place, and we would meet her there.

"So are you going to tell Rodger to perform? Oh my God, I fuckin' love it when Rodger performs and gets all crazy."

"Yeah, yeah, yeah, yeah… Lacey, don't even worry. I'm gonna tell him to perform. Keep your fuckin' panties on, girl."

"Don't yeah-yeah-yeah me, Casual. You know this could be a good opportunity for you guys. The party is next week, so please make sure you guys show up. Plus I want to see you."

"Trust me, Lacey, we will be there, trust me. But listen, I gotta go, so please kiss my daughter the next time you see her, and when we hang up, just text me Sam's address and all that shit. I'll see you there. Gotta go. Bye."

I had to hurry and hang up because as fucked-up as it sounds, I knew she was going to get into a conversation about our daughter after I said, 'Kiss her for me.' So I hung up real quick. One week flew by with wings on its back. Before I knew it, we were on the road to meet this Sam Hatchett cat, and we rented a nice smooth RV to get us there, so that we would all ride in comfort. It was me, Rodger, Bulldog the drummer, Skeet, who played the shit out of the electric guitar, Animal man, who was fresh out of prison a year ago for being convicted for manslaughter. He did fifteen years for killing some guy in a bar fight. But he could play the electric guitar like a muthafucka. Then there was Frenchy, he was cool as a fan, who also did some backup singing with Rodger, as well as played the guitar. We were a moving violation on the fuckin' road—with cocaine, dust, and bottles of tequila, which we chased down with beer. It was just a city thing that we did—drink tequila and chase it with beer—we called it 2killya. It was our own way of saying 'tequila', but since we added the beer with it, we called it '2killya'.

So here was our plan. Since this Sam dude told Lacey that he wanted us to perform, I knew we had to rock this fuckin' place, not to mention all those superstar bands down with Sam's label would be there as well. There was Bad Intentions, with a number one on the charts, and Dirty Bars of Soap, who also had some big hits. Now Rodger and his crew had no respect for both of these bands. Me, well, hell, I didn't like rock music any fuckin' way, so these fuckin' bands were nobody to me. I mean who the hell calls themselves 'Dirty Bars of Soap'—I mean, fuckin' really. So with all that in mind, we really wanted to rock this joint. I had Rodger and his band wear the Michael Myers mask, and I had them all dress in black—black jeans with black hoodies, and we all had guns. The plan was to kidnap Sam, hold a gun to his head, bring him out on stage, and make him announce the new number one group that he was about to sign. It was the perfect plan, and what made it even more exciting was the fact that this dude Sam had no fuckin' clue that we were about to kidnap his fuckin' ass, and hold a gun to his head.

We were already late as hell. Lacey was ringing my phone off the hook, leaving messages saying, "Casual, where the fuck are you? Don't embarrass me. You better not embarrass me, Casual." I mean Lacey was blowing me up—every two seconds, she would call and leave nasty messages about how I ain't shit and that she's never going to stick her neck out for me ever again. Like she really had to go out of her way to get in contact with this Sam cat. She probably had him on fuckin' speed dial, for Christ's sake, and like I said, she was probably giving him head whenever she could.

We had finally arrived at the house. There were BMWs, Mercedes, Ferraris, Porches, Hummers, and all kinds of high-roller cars parked out front. I called Lacey to tell her that we had just pulled up. She told me that he was on the upper deck of the house, and to go introduce ourselves. So here we go—we darted out of the RV and ran into this dude's house, guns drawn. You shoulda seen the look on these people's faces when we hopped out. We were knocking people down and pushing them out the way from the outside of the house all the way into this guy's house. It was like we were on a recon mission for the Marines. We searched all through the house until we got to the upper deck, which was a balcony. And there stood this little blonde-haired punk-ass lookin' muthafucka, who I just knew was Sam. I just had that gut feeling that it was him. We ran up on that fucker so hard, he damn near shit his fuckin' pants.

"Are you Sam? Are you Sam, you muthafucka?"

"Yes, yes, I'm Sam," he replied, all scared and shaky, like the little bitch that he probably was—the look on his face was absolutely priceless. I had my pistol right in between his eyes, and it wasn't only my gun. This guy had six fuckin' guns in his face—six fuckin' guns pointed at one little, scrawny, rich, punk-ass Sam Hatchett, CEO of Space Boy records. Now Skeet was so fuckin' wired up off coke that he was yelling at the top of his lungs at this guy.

"Put your fuckin' hands in the air, you fuckin' faggot, you faggot. How does it feel, huh? How does it feel to look down the barrel of this gun, faggot? Huh? How does it feel? Answer me, you fuck," Skeet shouted in rage.

He started waving his gun back and forth in Sam's face, and I'm sayin to myself, 'What the fuck is wrong with this asshole?' I was about to tell him to shut the fuck up and then the unbelievable happened. POP! Skeet's gun went off. And not only did his fuckin' gun go off, the bullet hit Sam in his left shoulder. And let me tell ya, you shoulda heard the scream this fuckin' guy let out. I just put my head down, and said to myself, 'We fucked up again. Once again, we fucked up a good opportunity.' The one chance we get to make it big with Sam Hatchett, we shoot the guy in his own house. Before I knew it, Lacey came in—I guess she must have heard Sam's scream as she was making her way to where Sam was.

"Please take what you want. Take whatever you want. Please just don't kill me," Sam screamed out in complete horror. This guy, Sam, thought we were really going to kill his ass—he had no idea that we were staging this whole thing. Then, of course, to make things worse, Lacey came in screaming, "Oh my God, Sam, are you OK?" Which made me think even more that she was definitely sucking this guy's cock. When she saw the blood coming from his arm, she started to freak out. I immediately put my hand on Lacey's shoulder and began telling her that it was an accident.

"Lacey, you know these criminals? They tried to kill me," Sam shouted out in fear.

"Oh shut up! Shut the fuck up! If we wanted you dead, we would have killed you already muthafucka," I screamed out. I was already pissed that Skeet had shot Sam, so I was on ten—I was steaming. I wasn't even worried about what the hell Lacey was gonna say because Lacey would believe me over Jesus Christ himself. So I grabbed Lacey by the back of her neck and took her to the corner of the hallway. "Listen Lacey, this whole thing is a fuckin' accident. It was supposed to be all staged. Trust me, Lacey, you know I would never just come out here and deliberately do some dumb shit like this," I told her. It was kind of fucked-up because Lacey was high out of her mind, and she started laughing almost hysterically. She actually started to fuckin' spook me out a little bit because she was laughing like an evil, nasty witch.

"Lacey, what the fuck is wrong with you—I mean, I know coke makes you real stupid and silly, but goddamn girl!"

"Shhhhhhhhhhhhhhh..." Lacey said, putting her finger on her lips, "I don't want them to think that I think this is funny."

"Excuse me, Lacey, but I think it's a bit too late to worry about that. I think they know that you think this is funny because for you're fuckin' laughing like a goddamn hyena. I know that's not just coke too, Lacey, what the fuck are you on?"

She tried to keep a straight face but she just couldn't do it. She whispered in my ear that Sam had given her some awesome shrooms. "I've never had shrooms like this. Holy shit, I'm so fuckin' ripped right now, Casual," Lacey said, with a smile from cheek to cheek.

"Goddammit, Lacey, goddammit! What the fuck is wrong with you? Why didn't you say something? Now you know I love shrooms, girl, can you get some more?"

Now here's the fucked-up thing. While all this shit was going on, Sam was lying on the floor, crying like a bitch, holding his bullet wound. And everyone was standing around as if they were waiting for me and Lacey to make a decision. And here we were, Lacey and I, discussing whether or not she can get me some shrooms. Not to mention the fact everyone heard her laughing hysterically, as if what just happened was comical. It was as if we fuckin' forgot this guy even got shot, boy, I tell ya, between us both that's what the fuck being on drugs will do to you.

"Listen, Lacey, I gotta break the fuck outta here, OK, because you gotta get this guy some medical attention, and I can't be here when they come."

"Casual, what are you talkin' about? Now you're starting to scare me. Why can't you be here when they get here?" I cut Lacey right off.

"Look, Lacey, don't ask me any fuckin' questions. I have to go. Call an ambulance for him, and please tell him that I didn't mean for this to happen, and also tell him I know it's not a lot but I'm gonna send him ten thousand dollars for all this madness." I figured I had to at least try and make some right out of a whole bunch of wrong. So I felt like we had to at least pay him, from some of the money we took from Fritz. Hey, he probably thought we were bottom-shelf humans anyway, compared to him. To him, ten thousand dollars was nothing. I mean it wouldn't have made a dent in the bags of money that we had stolen anyway, but Sam didn't know we had some cash. So to him, this gesture would be like taking a penny from a bum. Because I was also going to write him a letter stating that we were a struggling band, just trying to get by. I would explain that we got paid from little underground shows that we performed at. So with the money that we earned from these shows, I felt it was only right that we give Sam this money, as an act of saying sorry. I had it all planned out smoothly.

"Everybody, let's go," I shouted. "Let's go now." I kissed Lacey on her forehead and we raced out of there.

# CHAPTER 11

The underground of California was now Suicidal. Every skinhead, every skate boarder, every felon, jailbird, plus people of the night, crooks, and druggies of all kinds, were all now die-hard Suicidal fans. These people fuckin' loved Rodger and his band. They were the new street wave in California in the underground spotlight. And we made it known that we were from New York. Everytime we performed, we made it known that we were straight out of New York. The whole California night scene had Suicidal rocking loud through the streets. We rocked and socked every underground bar that existed all up and down California. We eventually got way too big for the underground scene. We were packing bars so much that it was against the fire code in the building. We exceeded the capacity in every underground bar. It was sick—we started then doing regular night clubs instead of hole-in-the-wall bars. And let me tell

Ya, we packed that muthafucka up as well.

I had gotten an idea one day while we were out at this dangerous underground bar called The Fight Club. This club was known for having brawls all the time, and big-time fights always broke out there. And we were also known to go out and kick ass as well. I mean that's basically how we got so hot in California. We were brawling out at these spots—people started to respect us. The underground hardcore Megadeath scene began to give us our respect. If you asked me, we took it, but we were known not to back down from nobody. They all knew that Suicidal was known for tearing a fuckin' bar down. Me, Rodger, Skeet, Bulldog, Animal, and Frenchy. And how can I forget Patricia and Summer! Let me tell ya, between us and a couple of pals we met while touring the underground night life, we were a bunch of fuckin' head crushers. We got drunk, partied hard, and got violent. We would start shit for the fuck of it, so imagine what we were like if you popped off some shit with us.

We were at The Fight Club, and Rodger and his crew had just finished performing. It was absolutely packed in there. There were people screaming and chanting 'Suicidal, Suicidal, Suicidal'. But when we got outside, some dickhead felt brave, and decided he was going to toss an empty beer bottle at Patricia. It got real ugly after that. Patricia was going crazy because first of all, it wouldn't be like her if she didn't go crazy. Then, of course Rodger got crazy, and after that, it was a ripple effect—everyone got crazy.

After that situation happened, I got this great idea that we should get pit bulls—at least two of them. While Rodger performed, he could have the dog on a leash, and Frenchy could have the other one. We would be the only rock band that ever did that. I thought it would be a perfect protection for us as well as a good publicity thing. So whenever Rogder and his crew performed, they had two pit bulls on stage with them, and they were some mean sons of bitches, let me tell ya. Rocky and Apollo were their names—and even the dogs were becoming a hot commodity. We were known as the band that performed on stage with two mean-ass pit bulls. Alls they did was bark, growl and show their teeth, and the crowd reaching up and trying to touch Rodger didn't make it no better.

Let me not forget about the whole Sam Hatchett situation. Well, that didn't go so well at all. Can you believe this fuckin' guy went and told the press and all the tabloids that he got into an altercation with a black gang member, and he ended up getting shot? I mean the story was great—I couldn't have asked for a better lie. After all, the better the lie, the more it protected our freedom. Amazingly, the story that he put out actually made him more famous. Everybody wanted to interview him to find out what the news was on how and why he got shot.

But he fucked up when he told Lacey that our music wasn't good enough for his label, and that he didn't think that we could bring in enough revenue with what we were capable of. The nerve of this guy! He was just mad that Skeet shot his ass, and we showed no fuckin' remorse for our actions. So we decided to do Sam a favor—if it was exposure he wanted, it was exposure he was going to get. Rodger put out a song dissing all of Sam's groups that were signed under his label, saying that they are full of bubble gum music and that they are way too scared to show up on the streets of California and hit up the night life. We leaked that song all throughout the streets of California for everybody to hear.

Now here's the thing, ya see, a guy like Sam is not really going to get touchy about the song because he doesn't want the real truth to come out about how he had gotten shot. Not like we were going to say anything anyway, but that would have made him look really stupid. But what one of his groups signed under his label did was answer back— they made a song about us. And that was exactly what we wanted them to do—mention our name. And as soon as they did that, we became a household name. Ya see one of Sam's groups—Dirty Bars of Soap— was a popular group. I mean they were a serious household name who performed tours all over the world. And now they were mentioning the name Suicidal in their music. They couldn't have helped us out any better. The buzz that we got just from them mentioning the name 'Suicidal' in their music was out of this world. Not only were we the talk of California's underground nightclub scene, we were now talked about by those who had no idea who we were as well. Simply because if you were a fan of the Dirty Bars of Soap, you now wanted to know who they were referring to in their song that was bashing us.

On the other side of things, I had gotten news that my parents had posted a 'Missing Persons' award for me back in New York. My father was already a fuckin' cop, so that turned things up just a tad bit more. I had gotten the news from Lacey—she called me from New York and told me that she was staring at a 'Missing Persons' poster of me against a local store in Manhattan. I started to laugh hysterically as soon as she said it. As serious as this was, I seemed to find it somewhat amusing. Lacey had said that she couldn't keep it a secret from my parents any longer so she went to my parents' house and told them that I was OK. I felt it was only right to give them a call, so that's what I did. I knew my mom was worried sick. When I called, of course, they weren't at home, so I left a long detailed message saying I was OK and for them not to worry about me.

I knew that contacting my parents was important, but doing so was farthest from my mind. What was really on my mind was managing Rodger's band and taking them to the top, and getting us some real fuckin' money. Because living like this was just not cutting it for me at all. I was tired of sitting around, getting high, robbing innocent people of their money, and just being a bum, period. So, as I sat on the couch, turning my tequila bottle upside down, getting every single last drop out, something popped into my mind out of nowhere. It was like a light bulb with a thousand watts just flicked on inside my brain. The idea came from a movie that I was watching about this guy who was blackmailing people for money, and he actually got rich off of it.

I kept thinking to myself, what if Summer had told Kevin Roberson that if he didn't pay her she was going to go to the police and the press. I know for a fact he would have given up a little money just to keep that hushed up. He damn sure wouldn't want that kind of publicity, so I knew he would have coughed up some cash to give her. I don't know whether it was the tequila talking to me or whether it was the movie that planted the seed. But I was feeling real strong about having Summer get back with this Kevin Roberson character, dick-tease him, and have him do to her what he did before, but only this time, it would be recorded, and we would blackmail his fuckin' ass for everything he's got. I said to myself, 'Yeah, that's it! That's it! That's what I was gonna do. I was gonna be the mastermind of a blackmailing operation. And Summer was up for hire. And once I got the money that I wanted, I'd start up my own label, and send Rodger's band right to the top. The only obstacle was convincing Summer to get down with my master plan. We seemed to be getting along pretty well, so I figured I'd just take her out for a bite to eat, sit her down, and lay my blueprint out. The worst thing that she could say was 'no', but hell, I would never know unless I asked.

# CHAPTER 12

"So do you mind telling me why the hell you brought me to this fancy-ass restaurant, Casual? Is this a date leading up to you wanting to get in my pants? Because this is really not you at all. And those shades, Casual, why the fuck do you have shades on inside a restaurant—not to mention when the moon is out? And you're dressed like you're going to a damn job interview. What the hell is going on with you, boy?"

What Summer was referring to was the way that I was overly dressed, well, in her opinion anyway. Ya see, I had made up my mind that from now on, I was a stone-cold businessman, who was bound to get shit done. And blackmailing muthafuckaz was my forte. The arrogance coming off my character was reeking like bad cologne as I laid my blueprint out to Summer.

"So here's why we are here, Summer. I'm tired of being broke."

I guess Summer was waiting for me to say a lot more than I did, because she shrugged her shoulders and replied, "Ohhhhhkaaaaaaay, and soooooooo that's it, you got all dressed up and took me to this fancy restaurant to tell me that you're tired of being broke, Casual, are you high?"

"No, I'm not fuckin' high, OK. I mean… well, I did sniff up a couple lines before I came but I know exactly what I'm saying. I'm saying I'm tired of being broke and just lying around, getting high and watchin Rodger fuckin' perform. I'm sick of it."

"So if you're tired of being broke, Casual, why don't you get a fuckin' job. That's what most normal people do when they want money," Summer sarcastically responded.

"Well, ya see, babygirl, I already have my own enterprise, and to top it all off, I have a position to offer you. So I guess you can say that you are at your first interview with me. Let's start this off the correct way. Hi, my name is Damion Devoh and I am the owner and creator of D&D enterprises. Nice to meet you."

Right away, Summer took me for a fuckin' joke and she laughed right in my face. "Casual, how in the fuck are you going to offer me a job? You just sat there and told me you are broke. So how in the hell would you be expecting to pay me?"

As I took a sip of water, I chuckled because Summer had no idea what I was bringing to the table. I wasn't going to waste anymore time with it—I shot it straight at her. "Hey, ya know what I'm about to tell you may be very hard for you to swallow, Summer. But you have to believe that whatever I tell you is for our best benefit. I really need for you to trust me on this because this can be extremely dangerous."

I guess the anticipation was eating Summer alive because she slammed her hand on the table, and shouted, "Dammit, Casual, will you just spit it out—I mean fuckin' really!" So since she was so eager to hear what I had to say, I laid it right on the table for her. "OK, Summer, check it out, I want you to get back with Kevin Roberson, flirt with him, go out with him, do whatever you have to do to get back with him. And when you get back with that cocksuckin muthafucka, I want you to lure his ass back to a hotel, act like you want to give him some pussy but then at the last minute, change your mind. Make him rape you all over again. But only this time, we are gonna record the shit on videotape. Now a couple weeks later, he's gonna think that he got away with it. But we are gonna blackmail that son of a bitch. We're gonna tell him that if he doesn't pay up 800,000,000 dollars in cash, we're gonna leak the tape out to the media, and send his black ass to jail."

There was nothing but silence at the table. The shock that was on her face was worth a picture. She stared at me as if I was totally insane. "Casual, are you stupid or just plain outright crazy? I mean who the fuck comes up with an idea like that? Is something wrong with you, Casual, seriously?"

"Ain't shit wrong with me, girl. It's what's right with me. This could really work, Summer, with all the sports celebs that you know. Are you kidding me!"

"No, it won't work, Casual, because I'm not doing it. You expect me to get raped on tape for money!?"

"Hell, yeah," I responded, in a loud tone, "Hell, yeah! That's exactly what it's gonna take. I'm telling you, Summer, we can really make this shit happen. How can you even consider passing up an opportunity like this?"

At this point, I felt like I was giving a speech—almost like I was campaigning to be the president of the United States. Only I was trying to win Summer's mind. I needed to corrupt her mind into thinking that this was OK. I had presidential music going off in my head. It was hit or miss for me in the 9th inning. So, of course, what did I do—I immediately attacked by bringing up Summer's troubled past of being raped by Kevin Roberson—so subtle and so calm, I ripped her a new asshole. Hands folded in the middle of the table, I continued to inject my poison with that famous presidential music going off in the back of my head.

"Summer, Summer, Summer, you're a pretty girl, I mean look at you. But to be honest, you have been demoted down to a 5 from a perfect 10 because of the defense mechanism you've obtained from being physically as well as mentally disrespected by this egotistical grandiose bastard. So now you're just a cold, lonely bitch, who hates men who are successful because a man of that caliber stole your womanhood from you, and you can't get it back." That presidential music was getting louder and louder in my head.

Summer smiled, and with a charming voice, she seductively placed her tongue on her top lip, and said, "First of all, who the hell do you think you are—some fuckin' great debator? Second of all, you are so wrong about me. Thank God, I'm not paying you to be my psyc doctor. Third of all, you look so ridiculous with those goddamn shades on, I can't even bring myself to even take you as a joke—you look like a fuckin' mental case, Casual."

Immediately, I cut her ass right off in the middle of her little statement, which meant peanuts to me because I knew it was all bullshit.

"Shut the fuck up, Summer, please, OK! This is not about me here."

"Well, then who is it about, huh? Tell me who the hell is it all about 'Mr. I have this great fuckin' idea to have me get raped on tape'. Don't give me this fuckin' pimp talk shit, Casual. I'm not getting raped on tape, not for you or anybody else. Please I can't figure out who's worse—Kevin Roberson for doing what he did or you for wanting him to do it again and put it on tape!"

"Hey, hey, don't forget, we are going to get paid for it as well after we blackmail him," I added sarcastically. Now, of course, I knew Summer was not going to say 'yes' right away. This was just the introduction to it all—I knew it was going to take some time. So let's just say, that night didn't go so well. Summer actually got pissed off, threw her drink in my face, and stormed out of the restaurant. This was a tough thing for any female to get involved in, no matter how thorough they were. To get raped on tape and let some guy humiliate her—possibly even beat her up really bad or rip her insides out… Something like this takes a soldier-type of girl.

Three months had passed by, Summer and I were hanging out everyday, and we were starting to become real cool with each other. I would even go shopping with her at times, and watch her try on all kinds of stupid fuckin' outfits. It was almost as if we were spending every waking moment together. I was really starting to dig Summer the more I got to know her. And to top it all off, she was beginning to understand who I was, and why I did the things I did and said the things that I said. My arrogance and my I-dont-give-a-fuck ways were starting to grow on her.

One night, we got so fuckin' trashed that we started arguing about who sniffed up the last line of cocaine. Now the argument got so heated and intense that she got mad and slapped the shit out of me. I couldn't believe this fuckin' girl actually slapped me as hard as she did. So I slapped her right back, and I didn't use the front of my hand—I used the back of my hand to slap her ass. I guess a mixture of my attitude, her attitude, a bottle of whiskey and some cocaine, was not a very good combination. We actually started fighting to the point where I had to pin her down to the ground, so she couldn't get back up. As I held her pinned to the floor, there was a moment of sexual clarity that came between us. I stared into her eyes, and she stared right back into mine, both of us breathing heavily from being out of breath.

I went for it—I went straight in and kissed her. One thing led to another another, and the next thing I knew, we were fucking like some wild jungle animals—biting each other, scratching each other and hitting each other. This girl was indeed a fuckin' rock star in bed. She started to bite my chest while we were fuckin' and all of a sudden, this bitch bit me so damn hard that when I pulled her off, she had a mouth full of blood. She must have tore right through my flesh—blood was all over her mouth and was beginning to drip down her chin. The lust that was runnin through my veins had me on fire. And even with all my blood dripping from her lips, I continued to kiss her. The Devil was in the room that night, and he was applauding me as I continued to excel in his work.

Here we were, about another 3 months after more jungled-out drug sex, on top of me injecting more of my poison into her head. And you know fuckin' what! The shit was working. Every fuckin' day, she was getting more used to me and understanding my vision. One night, she just came out and said that she was going to take me up on my offer. I mean for crying out loud, that was all I fuckin' talked about. Blueprint after blueprint after blueprint… I drilled my master plan into Summer's head. I needed everything to go exactly according to my plan, and I wasn't going to settle for less. And since Summer had connections everywhere, I took full advantage of them. I needed cameras—hi-tech cameras—those little, tiny-ass cameras that couldn't be spotted while the rape was going on. It just so happened that Summer used to date this FBI agent, who was also a private detective as well as everything else that had to do with spying on a muthafucka. He told us where we needed to go and that's exactly what we did. I brought so much hi-tech equipment and all types of monitors with the leftover money we had from the Fritz's robbery. I also had to buy a van, so that I could hear what was going on while Summer was getting raped. Just in case shit got outta control, I would have to shoot someone. The sick shit about it was I really didn't care too much about if Summer got hurt. Alls I cared about was the operation at hand. It's just the simple fact that she was part of my operation—a big fuckin' part at that.

I would be the first dude in American history that thought of an idea such as this and actually went through with it. It was so easy—I mean Summer was a knockout beautiful girl with a super banging body. What guy wouldn't want her. But my aim was basketball stars, football stars, actors, and anyone else who was prestigious super star on television, and I wanted them to be married—that was the icing on the cake. Breaking news: Basketball star Kevin Roberson has been charged with the rape of a 25-year-old girl, a video tape was givin to police and now Kevin Roberson could face years in prison. Now you tell me what star in their right mind wants that shit to leak out, on top of all that their wife and kids now know because it's all over the news and tabloids. He will be at my fuckin' mercy when it comes down to coughing up some money.

And it wasn't just gonna stop at Kevin Roberson—I had my mind on politicians and people working with important titles because they damn sure like to fuck behind their wives' backs with all kinds of prostitutes. They can't afford for that shit to leak but they sure can afford to pay off a blackmailer, and I knew that for sure. I had everything I needed equipment-wise, plus a down-ass girl to make it all happen. The only thing left to do was to start blackmailing muthafuckas, and I couldn't wait.

# CHAPTER 13

It was a Friday night, and the rain was falling from the sky and hitting the ground so hard, you could feel it. Rodger and I were out on a sextacy run for Patricia—sextacy was our way of saying ecstacy because of course, she needed to get high in order to function. Plus she told Rodger that if he went out to get it, she would give him some of that good ol' sextacy love. The reason I went with Rodger was because I was the only one with bullets left in my gun. Rodger and his dumbass crew wasted all their fuckin' bullets shooting at random targets, like the tires on parked cop cars. One night, they shot out the tires of an ambulance while it was going at full-speed responding to a call somewhere. We sat and watched it flip over 3 times just because we wanted to know how fast they would send an ambulance to an ambulance accident. These are the things that hardcore drugs on the brains of people who don't use their brains will do. So we got back to Summer's place, and immediately, Patricia jumped up asking, "Did you get it? Did you get it?" Rodger pulled out the bag and showed her the pills, and the next moment, they were tongue-kissing in front of everyone. It was so disgusting and sloppy, I couldn't take it any more. So I said, "Yo, can y'all please take that shit elsewhere—nobody wants to see that."

"Oh, shut the fuck up, Casual," Patricia snapped back. "Don't get mad because Rodger knows how to treat a lady." They were all in each other's mouth, swapping spit, and you could actually hear their lips and tongues coming together. It was the nastiest thing ever—both of them had rotten, fucked-up teeth, and they both smoked cigarettes like a damn chimney.

"Yeah, Patricia, you really gotta smooth mothafuckin' man," I said, with a smirk. "I just wish I had a relationship with such love like you guys have—the both of you make me wanna fuckin' throw up everything I ate today." Of course, neither of them paid any attention to me, as Rodger then lifted up Patricia's shirt, and started stroking the little bit of titties that she did have, in front of me, Summer and the rest of Rodger's crew. Patricia was so skinny that you could see her fuckin' ribs—it was getting to the point where I was actually getting pissed the fuck off. We were all sitting around listening to 89.9 Rock FM, which was Rodger's favorite rock station ever since we had been in California. Every Friday night, the air jockey would play a new song from an unheard-of band, and after the song was over, they would take calls from the listeners and let them decide whether to trash it or cash it.

"Yes, yes, yes, fans, you're listening to 89.9 rock radio, and I'm your air jockey Peter Bradshaw. It's Friday, folks, so you know what that means—it's 'trash it or cash it' time, where we play you a new song from a local unheard-of band. And we gotta new one for you fans— here's *Bloody Guitar* by Suicidal." We all just fuckin' froze—it was almost like we were on TV, and somebody just pressed pause. I held my whiskey bottle in mid-air, in pure shock. That heavy guitar kicked in, followed by a mild electric guitar in the background. Then came the lyrics. 'I have nightmares with my eyes open'—Rodger screamed into the microphone. It sounded like magic to my ears coming from the speaker. The song was actually about how many times Rodger had contemplated suicide and how he hates life. Now you gotta understand this wasn't just a song. This was how Rodger really felt about life, and that was no joke. It was impossible not to like Rodger's stuff, even if you weren't a fan. His music was real; it was sincere, genuine; every line he sang and every song he put out was based on his suicidal, drug-addicted life. After the song was done, we all tuned in even closer to the speaker, so we could hear if they trashed or cashed his song.

The air jockey went right into it. "OK. OK. OK, fans, you heard it first here. We got the phone lines lighting up, and here we go—let's take the first caller."

"89.9. You're on the air—trash it or cash it?"

"Yeah, Pete, what's up bro! This is Chris from San Diego."

"What's up, Chris from San Diego. Are you trashin' or cashin', dude?"

"Dude, I'm gonna cash that one. That was solid, dude, totally solid."

"OK. OK. OK. That was the first caller, and he said 'cash it.' We're gonna take the next caller. Hello 89.9. You're on the air."

"Hey, what's goin' on, Pete. My name is Jimmy, and I'm gonna cash that one. Those guys rock. I actually heard about them before but this is my first time hearing them. I liked what I hear from them, Pete. I'm definitely cashin' that one."

The air jockey from 89.9 took about 7 more callers, and they all said 'cash it'. We were all fuckin' shocked. I mean we just got hit blindsided with that feedback. Now it was real to all of us. Now we knew that people knew that we were the real thing. I was just shocked and sitting there absorbing all this shit. I had my operation with Summer about to lift off the ground, and now Rodger and his band were becoming a hot commodity. I said to myself if this all works out in my favor the way I planned, we could be a big fuckin' deal.

Now two weeks had gone by, and we got phonecall after phone call. Ya see, Rodger had left his phone number on the back of the CDs he had been giving out everywhere he went. Just our luck, this big-time magazine called *Rolling Star* got hold of Rodger's number. So of course we went because it wasn't like it was far—they were based right in California. We took a couple of pictures, and told them how we came up.

The interesting thing about this whole interview was that somehow these nosey pricks knew that I had a child with Lacey. I mean these magazine tabloid fucks must really dig and do their homework—how they even knew that shit amazed me. So, of course, I threw a spike in the drink, and told them that yes, I had a little girl with Lacey, and I also told them that we were still together. I knew that if I said that to them, they would treat me in the same fuckin' royal manner in which they treated Lacey. And let me tell ya, Lacey was a household name for real—a knockout superstar—every fuckin' where she went, cameras were around. That's what we needed—that was what the fuck we needed. I was gonna ride Lacey's back right into the world of fortune and fame.

The celebrity world was in for a real fuckin' ride, because in my mind, I was already a superstar. I told the magazine that I was the CEO of Suicidal Records, and I was lying my ass off. In the back of my head, I'm saying to myself, 'These fuckin' people are really, really, really stupid'. I considered myself what I like to call 'an enterpriser'— the mastermind behind a serious blackmail heist, and the CEO of a rock band—now that will make you laugh.

By the time spring came back around the calendar, we found ourselves opening up sold-out concerts for some big named artists and rock bands. We even got invited to perform at a couple of award shows, attended some private parties for some celebs, and stayed in the limelight. And if you're wondering how we got around to all these events, it was, of course, Lacey. And why wouldn't she, with all the fuckin' money she made, who else better to share all that with than me? I mean we did get paid from the show organizers for performing but we had to pay for our room and board. To tell you the truth, she didn't mind anyway. She was actually kind of proud to see me doing something with myself.

But here's what really put us on the wheels of fortune and fame—we were opening up at this sold-out concert in London for a band called Shotgun Shells. Now we overheard from a lot of people that the lead singer of this particular rock band would put all types of fake blood on his guitar, signifying that his guitar was bloody. His name was Bobby Mcgrath, and word was, he was supposed to be no one to fuck with—to me, it was all a gimmick but anyway, back to the story. When Rodger found out about this shit, he went bananas. I mean everytime Rodger would hear his name, it was like nails on a chalkboard.

Ya see, don't forget Rodger's single as his introduction to the music world was called *Bloody Guitar*. Now the difference here was that this Bobby dude had a nice, cute, little gimmick of being a maniac and a bar brawler, but Rodger's issues were no gimmick at all—he was really a genuine fuckin' maniac. This guy Bobby painted blood on his guitar; Rodger actually tried to kill himself one night by slitting his wrist. And he almost succeeded at it because he cut both wrists bone fuckin' deep, I still ask myself till this day, how in the hell was this dude still living because those cuts were so deep. Luckily, I came to his house that night because I wanted to get high. I knocked on the door and he wouldn't answer, so something told me to walk in and there he was, slumped over his guitar, bleeding heavily from his wrists. It was all because Patricia and he had gotten into a huge fight, and she had decided to leave him. And boy, while she did that, Rodger slipped into a state of darkness and began to fade away. I mean Patricia was everything to this guy—she was the only reason that he continued to live. Now the blood from his wrist that stained the guitar was all over, and Rodger never washed it off, and he had no intention of doing so.

So now, we're in this packed arena in London, and Rodger was not himself—he had that maniac look in his eyes, and I knew what it was that was bothering him. I even tried to talk some sense into this crazy-ass mothafucka, to just let it all go but Rodger wasn't hearing me at all.

While laughing, I said to Rodger, "Rodger, you need to chill out. I mean it's not that serious; it's only a guitar."

"The hell with you, Casual. Fuck you, and fuck him too. He stole my identity. Look at him. Look at that son of a bitch on stage." And so it was, I turned to look at this Bobby character, and damn sure, he had painted blood on his guitar. Now we were standing right backstage behind the wall, so they were performing right next to us. I laughed because I thought it was funny. I turned to start joking with Rodger, but by the time I turned around, he had already run right by me and security, on to the stage, and was kicking this dude's ass all over the stage. I, along with the rest of Rodger's band, ran on to the stage. It was a disaster. We were all fighting on stage in London that night.

The very next day it was all over the tabloids, and all over the radio stations. We were the talk of every rock and pop station that existed. Like I said, Bobby and the Shotgun Shells were supposed to be known for being brawlers, but now it was move the fuck over Bobby, there's a new band full of real badasses on the scene. And that's how we were publicized all over as the new badasses. Big-time labels wanted to sign and get us on board, and were doing anything to try and get us on board. And you're goddamn right, I told those greedy bastards, 'hell no'. Why the hell should I split the pie with those fuckers? Hell no, I wasn't gonna give them a dime. Fuck them. They can go live off somebody else and leech off of them, but not us. And plus I had my own plans—I was gonna be the first black rock n' roll CEO in history.

That was my goal—it might as well have been I mean hell this is what I've lived for the longest, Sex, drugs, rock n roll, and more of it. And the best thing about it was that I didn't even like rock music.

To top it all off, I had made up a lie that I was still with Lacey. The only thing that was fuckin' that up was the fact that she was fucking at least 5 to 6 guys, who the tabloids were already on top of and knew about. So it looked like she was cheating on me all over the tabloids and TV shows. In those people's minds, I was a clown, but they had no idea it was a fuckin' lie just to get me in the door. It was great because wherever Lacey went, she co-signed that we were together as well. Even to the guys that she was fuckin'—she told them that we were together. So you can imagine what they were saying about me. They probably thought my little heart was being crushed and walked on by Lacey. But like I said, they had no fuckin' idea of my masterplan.

Now with Lacey playing the star role as Wonder Woman, this was big. As long as she was being followed, I was being followed, and I made sure that I was fuckin' seen everywhere with her. And every time we were out, and those nosey fuckin' paparazzi faggots asked how our relationship was going, I just acted like I never knew what was being said about us. It was easy because I really didn't give a fuck. I would grab her ass and smack it in front of all those cameras. I was labeled as Lacey's bad boy, who was bound to bring her life and her career down the toilet.

One night, we were at the Emmy Awards, and while we were stopping to pose for pictures, I decided I was gonna give them a real fuckin' show. I grabbed Lacey by her neck and shoved my tongue down her throat. And just like I thought, they were talking about us day in and day out. You had Ike and Tina, Bobby and Whitney, and now there was Damion 'Casual' Devoh and Lacey. Lacey became even bigger after this *Wonder Woman* movie—it was a box-office hit. I even liked the movie, and I wasn't a real big Wonder Woman fan, but it was a great fuckin' movie.

As time went on, ya see, Lacey was partying hard with big-time celebs, and was getting hooked on all kinds of drugs. Just as fast as she was up on top of the world, she was coming crashing down, and it wasn't because of me this time. Her fuckin' name was being kicked around as being in love with this big-time actor, and the actor was not in love with her. I guess what had happened was Lacey caught this guy sleeping around with some other fuckin' actor, and it wasn't no fuckin' woman either. She was fuckin' crushed, but we all seemed to think it was funny (me, Summer and the rest of us) because we always used to tell her that guy seemed a little funny. But she didn't fuckin' listen—so what does she do—she keeps on chasing this fuckin' loser. It was a fuckin' disaster. Lacey's life was becoming a wreck right before my eyes.

One night, can you believe, she actually was out at some club that all these big-time celebs hang in, and who did she see in there—her boyfriend's faggot lover. So they actually started to fistfight, and Lacey got beat the fuck up. It was all over the magazines—it was on every radio station, and on every fuckin' TV show. It got to the point where I started to feel sorry for her. But what I did was the smartest thing anyone could have done. I took full advantage of Lacey's fuck-ups and I capitalized on them. I was doing interviews all over the place for top dollar. People wanted to know what was going on with Lacey, and they weren't getting that info from her or her faggot lover. So they contacted me because they figured I would know. I told them, 'Hey, you wanna know what the fuck is going on? Hell, if you want to know from me, you better cough up some fuckin' cash, and some real fuckin' cash too.' Of course, these people wanted to know so they paid me to come on their little fuckin' show. I only did it for two reasons—one to get my name out there so that I could promote Rodger's band, and two, so I could get some fuckin' money.

These interviews were so big because ya see, not only did they want to know about Lacey's love life with this loser, but there was a rumor flying around that Lacey had caught HIV from this guy. That was what they really wanted to know. So when they asked me, I just beat around the question like it wasn't even asked. I bet all the viewers were getting pissed. I mean I went on at least 3 different interviews on three different fuckin' shows. And on all three shows, none of them got the real fuckin' info they wanted. But I sure as hell did get the cash for doing them. And the answer to the rumor was that it wasn't a rumor— Lacey did in fact have HIV. I was the first person she told. And let me tell ya, she cried in my fuckin' arms like a baby. Her life was over. The tabloids kicked dirt on her name so much that it was impossible for to make a comeback. And after they confirmed the fact that she had HIV, it was really over for her. Here was an actress who had turned into a trashy drug addict, and who was constantly in the news and in magazines for making a fool of herself. And on top of all that, she had HIV—the world came crashing down on Lacey's head. That same world that she had in the palm of her hands was now weighing her down.

# CHAPTER 14

"OK, Summer, now I'm not gonna ask you if you're ready to do this because if you wasn't ready we wouldn't be here doing this. So, are you ready?"

"Casual, what the fuck! You just told me that you weren't gonna ask me if I was ready."

"I know. I know. I know. I'm just checkin'. I'm just double checkin'. Do you realize what we are involved in, Summer? This could really be big for us, remember."

Tonight was the night that all my planning and blueprinting was gonna come to life. Eveything was in place, and we were ready to roll. We were gonna rob Kevin Roberson blind, and the fucked-up shit about the whole thing was that he was gonna think that it was all his fuckin' fault. The heist of the century was what I was calling it—the plan was pure genius. I mean, I had this blackmail thing down and ready. While most fuckin' criminals were out strong-arming banks and other shit like that, I, on the other hand, was gonna blackmail my way into the American dream, by being America's worst nightmare. And I loved it so much because nobody was gonna know who the fuck I was.

Ya see, Summer knew where Kevin hung out at, and can you believe that when we went out to this bar that was in Hollywood called the Thirsty Fish, this fuckin' guy was actually in there. It was almost too good to be true how this was all going so easy already. I mean what were the fuckin' odds of this guy actually being there. So here I was, in this expensive-ass bar in the middle of Hollywood. I acted as if I was just a friend of hers from New York, who was looking for a nice time. She introduced him to me like that because I didn't want him thinking we were together. Because if he thought that then he wouldn't bite my bait—he wouldn't go with Summer back to the hotel room that we already had purchased with all the microphone shit set up. I was so on top of my fuckin' scam, I could have done it all reverse, and still came off with a smooth robbery. I was acting like a real cockrider too—like I was really a fan, and how I thought he was one the top ten best players in my opinion in the NBA. This guy was so arrogant that he actually told me to shut the fuck up—I mean I was really acting outta character—as if I really gave a fuck about him. This guy thought I was the cornball of all cornballs. I know he was probably wondering why Summer was even with me. So as soon as I saw him and Summer chit-chatting, I slid off to the bar and let her work her magic.

It took three whole fuckin' hours of waiting at the bar for Summer to wheel this bastard back to the hotel. As I saw them leave the bar, I ran to the van that had all the recording equipment inside, and I drove to the hotel. I got there before they did, and let me tell ya, it didn't take long for them to pull up in the parking lot behind me. It was working. It was actually working. This muthafucka had no idea that he was getting ready to get robbed for everything he fuckin' had. I had microphones hidden all over that fuckin' hotel room—he was so done, you could stick a fork in his ass. As they entered the hotel room, I could hear the whole conversation. Summer had already told me that he didn't like to fuck with a rubber. So that was what was going to spark it all off. Summer was gonna get him so hot and ready to fuck her brains out, then she was gonna stop him and say, 'Do you have a condom?' And knowing damn well he doesn't, that's where all my dreams were gonna come true.

Sounds sick in the head, but I was destined to pull off this heist. I could hear them kissing and breathing hard over the speakers I had in the van. It was getting real intense in that room. Ya see, technically, I already had this guy in the palm of my hands. He didn't even have to rape Summer. I had enough on this guy already, just because of the fact that he had just gotten married last year. Alls I really needed was to threaten him that I had a tape of him fuckin' Summer—I had little hidden cameras in the room that were recording my dream come true. That alone would make him pay up some cash. But it wouldn't make him pay up at damn near everything he had and more. I knew if I had him on tape raping Summer, he would not only be paying me to save his marriage and the embarrassment that the NBA would put him through, he would also be paying for his fuckin' freedom.

So now, here I was, in this van, listening to Summer cocktease this fuckin' guy to death. If you ask me, I think she really put on a show—she could have won an Academy Award for the act she put on in that room. I actually was starting to get turned on because she layed down on the bed and started playing with her pussy in front of this guy, and when he was ready, she told him to wait. She wanted him to watch her play with her pussy. I said to myself, 'Holy shit, this fuckin' bitch is hot.' My cock got so fuckin' hard, I actually pulled it out of my pants and started jerking the fuck off. It was as if I was listening to a porn flick of some hot girl playing with her pussy and talking super dirty. Now when you're outside a door, listening to a girl who you find amazingly sexy talk dirty to someone, your mind begins to go berserk.

## A SUICIDE STORY

"I want that fuckin' cock in my pussy so bad," Summer softly whispered to this guy. "You want me, you motherfucker, huh—you want this wet pussy," she said. I nutted all over my hand and my pants. It was crazy. Here I was, recording a heist trying to rob this muthafucka for everything he has. And I'm in this fuckin' van jerking my cock off to Summer as she plays with her pussy trying to bait this guy. I had to clean my hand off and get back to business because if it got too out of control in that hotel room, I was gonna have to go in there and kick his fuckin' ass. The heist was damn near in the bag, but it wasn't what I wanted. I could have pulled the plug on the whole damn thing but that wasn't what I wanted. I needed to have his whole entire life in the palm of my hands. I wanted him to make that mistake and rape Summer. And by the time I said to myself, 'This shit is taking forever,' I heard Summer say to him, 'Wait… wait… Kevin, we forgot to get a condom.' I was fuckin' shocked by what happened next. This cocksucker had a condom, so now Summer was going to have to come up with a plan to get this guy to rape her.

I don't know what kind of plan Summer was working with but the next thing I know I was listening to the both of them fuckin' each other. I didn't know what the hell was going on. Summer was fuckin' this guy's brains out and by the sound of things, she seemed like she was fuckin' enjoying it. So now I'm listening and I'm saying to myself, 'What in the hell is this bitch doin?' I couldn't fuckin' believe what I was hearing—if I wanted to hear Summer fuckin', I woulda fucked her myself and recorded it and then watched it afterwards while I sniffed up a couple lines. I was confused, nervous, and pissed off at the same time, until I heard Summer say, "Wait! Oh no, the condom broke. I can feel it."

I don't know if this fuckin' guy heard her or not, but she said it again and again telling him to stop.

"Wait. Stop! Stop! Kevin… Stop, stop!"

"Shut the fuck up bitch, and take this dick. Shut the fuck up!"

"No! Kevin, no. Kevin, Stop, stop, stop, stop!"

"Bitch if you don't shut the fuck up, shut up, I ain't playin wit your little stupid ass shut the fuck up, you ain't notin but a fuckin' slut you know that".

Summer began trying to fight this guy off by screaming and kicking but he wasn't budging. It sounded like he was starting to choke her. It was working—it was fuckin' working. I had never been more excited in my whole damn life—it was the sickest thing that a man could fathom. Before I could blink my eyes and swallow my spit, Kevin Roberson began beating Summer's ass. I actually heard him slap her at least 5 times, not to mention he had his hands wrapped around her throat tighter than a boa constrictor with its prey because I heard her gagging and gasping for air. I can't imagine how a man can get turned on by getting pussy from a woman who is screaming at the top of her lungs for you to stop. But the excitement of me knowing that this guy was going to be robbed blind for what he was doing at that very moment, made my cock hard once again. And my cock wasn't hard because I was turned on from him fuckin' the shit out of her and beating her up. It was hard because I was gonna be a rich muthafucka because of this shit. It was like a rush that I never felt in my whole life, better than any drug I ever tried. More exciting and thrilling than any house I ever burglarized. Here I was, listening to this guy choke the shit out of Summer in that hotel room while he continued to rape her and I was loving every minute of it.

But as the next two minutes passed by, things started to get a little out of control. Ya see, Summer had clocked this asshole over the head with the telephone that was in the hotel room and I heard that shit go right upside his damn head. The blow to his head was so fuckin' hard, it got him off of her. But then it got ugly in there. It went from him raping her to them now engaging in an all-out fight inside the room. I knew

I had to do something. So I ran out of the van towards the room. My thoughts were all over the place. I even left my gun inside the van but I knew I couldn't go back for it. I had to get Summer out of that room somehow. I didn't want to barge in, so I just knocked on the door, and said, "Hotel security. Is everything OK in there?"

"Yeah. Everything is OK. Don't worry," Kevin shouted back from behind the door.

"Well, I'm gonna have to have you open the door, Sir. I gotta call saying there was a fight in there, so I'm gonna have to ask you to open the door."

"Look, asshole, I told you everything was OK in here."

"Sir, I'm sorry, if you don't open the door, I'm gonna be forced to call the authorities. I need you to open the door."

It got quiet after I made that threat to call the police. Then I heard footsteps coming toward the door. My heart was pumping so fuckin' fast, I thought I was gonna pass out. Sweat was pouring down my face, and I was shaking like crazy. The door opened and it was Kevin. I didn't hesitate at all when he came to the door. I kicked him right in his balls as hard as I could, and told Summer to get the hell out of there. Alls she had was a sheet to cover herself, but we both ran out of there, and hopped into the van leaving Kevin lying there on the ground holding his testicles. We waited in the van for him to finally get in his fancy-ass car and peel out of there because I needed to go inside and retrieve all the little cameras and mini-microphones I had in there.

"Oh my God, Casual, you're a fuckin' genius. I did it, I did it!" Summer shouted with blood coming from her nose as we drove off and headed back to her house.

"Wait a fuckin' minute here. What the hell do you mean 'you' did it, dammit! We did this shit. This is not an individual achievement, Summer."

"That was fuckin' fun. Oh my God, what a fuckin' rush, baby, what a fuckin' rush. I need a fuckin' cigarette right now!"

Summer was so excited that it was spooky to me. I mean that shit that I had just pulled off was pure fuckin' evil. This was a different side of Summer—it was almost like she was possessed with lust for this whole thing. She had gotten a rush from the shit. I mean normally someone would be just a bit fuckin' traumatised after some shit like that, but not Summer. It was as if she got turned on by it—it was like she was sexually driven by it. She wouldn't shut the fuck up the whole way home. She was smacking me while I was driving, and jumping all over me like a kid who had too much sugar at night.

"Wow, oh my fuckin' God, I can't believe I just pulled that off, I bashed that fucker in the head with the phone—that felt so fuckin' hot to me. Oh my God!"

"You need to calm your ass down, Summer. That's what you need to do. We didn't even get the goddamn money yet and look how the fuck your actin'. And while we are sittin' here talkin' about the whole thing, you were in there fuckin' that cat like you were enjoyin' it. Let's talk about that, huh."

"Awwwww... Is someone a little jealous? Well, look at this, would ya! Casual, are you a little jealous? I bet you were in this fuckin' van jerkin your little pecker weren't you?"

"No, bitch, I wasn't, OK!"

I was lying about that because I damn sure did jerk the fuck off but I sure wasn't gonna let her know. "No, I wasn't jerkin' off for your information, Summer. And please tell me why I would even get a little jealous of that muthafucka. For Christ's sake, he had to rape you in order to get you the first time he fucked you. And the second time, he got set-up because he wanted to fuck you again, not knowin' we were gonna blackmail his dumb ass. And by the way, was he uncircumsized—I thought I heard you say pull that skin back—so on top of all that, this guy has an ant eater attached to him."

A couple of weeks passed by, and I already had this thing burnt down to DVD, and had crazy copies of it. I had Kevin's home address and his phone number. I had gone the whole nine yards—I even had information on his wife. Lacey knew her because his wife was this actress named Aliviah Mendez, and she was fuckin' hot, let me tell ya. I even had her agent's information. I had every body in the bag. But I was gonna do justice with these heists that I was pullin'. Ya see, I figured that because I was already doing fucked-up shit with my life, and had done fucked-up shit, and was still doing fucked-up shit, I could at least be like a vigilante to every scum of the earth, like Kevin Roberson, who likes to rape woman. Because to tell ya the truth, it turned out this guy didn't just rape Summer. He was notorious for the shit—he actually had 3 other woman under his belt. And I got that information from Summer and Lacey.

Now I really had this faggot by the balls—he couldn't afford to have that out there because if he didn't fuckin' pay me, I was gonna have Summer come out with it and have the shit all over the media. And not just her, I was gonna convince the other bitches that he fuckin' raped to do the same damn thing. Because oh yeah, I had all their contact information as well. So I guess you can say, I was lookin at a real fuckin' payday. I had mailed the DVD to Kevin's house with a little note saying, 'Check this porn flick out—I bet you'll pay a fortune just for a copy.' And I had Summer put some kiss marks on it. The kiss marks were my trademark for this new business that I was involved in. That meant if you seen 'em somewhere, if you got them kiss marks in the mail attached to a note with a DVD, your bank account was now mine. You would totally be my fuckin' economic slave; your finances would now become mine; call me the new fuckin' Uncle Sam, taking a chunk of fuckin' money outta you rich muthafuckas' pockets. So here

I am, day after day, just waiting for this guy to call me because I left my phone number on the note.

One night, Rodger and I stayed up shooting the breeze about this whole operation I had going on, and he agreed that I was a fuckin' nutcase. We were on Summer's balcony, drinking 2killya and smoking on some good ol' California red devil dust when my phone rang.

"Hello, this is Casual, CEO of the Manhattan Project. How may I be at your services?"

There was complete silence on the other end of the line, so I just repeated myself.

"What the hell is goin' on here? I got this fuckin' DVD with a note in the mail, and it told me to dial this number. Who the hell are you?"

"Ohhhhhhhhhhh now, Kevin, Kevin, Kevin, does it really matter who I am? I mean, dude, are you really sitting over there wondering who I am? Come on, Kevin, after looking at yourself on that DVD, you're gonna tell me that the first thing that came to your mind was who am I? Because quite frankly, Mr Roberson, you have a lot more to worry about than just who the hell I am."

"You sick muthafucka, I don't know who the hell you are or what the hell you're trying to do but if I track you down, I swear to God, you're a deadman. I've got the best lawyers money can buy, so I don't know what the hell you're trying to do—whatever it is, it won't work."

"Ohhhhhhhhhh! Now, Kevin, Kevin, Kevin, don't get all worked up about this, please. You're making this more complicated than it has to be. Now you can do two things—you can listen to what I have to say. Or you can go to your lawyer and tell him that you received a DVD in the mail from an anonymous person with you beating and raping some girl on it. Dude, Jesus Christ couldn't defend you in a court room on this one—just listen to what I have to say and everything will work out. Trust me, Kevin, I'm a professional at this."

"What the hell do you want from me? I don't know who this is but this is absolutely crazy. You send me this DVD with this note attached but I have no idea what it is you want from me."

"Kevin, now look, you're a smart guy. Why would someone send you a DVD of yourself raping an innocent woman—an innocent white woman at that? And you're a pretty dark dude, so this wouldn't look good to white America, if you know what I mean. A poor little white woman was raped and beaten by you, dude, and it's on fuckin' cam, dude. Not to mention I know about the other girls that you stole pussy from. Not only do I know that you stole pussy from them, I know all their info, dude, so think about what you're saying. Now you can be arrogant and stubborn, and think that I'm a joke, if you want—you'll wake up tomorrow with your name all over the tabloids and on every single eyewitness news channel. And they will all be bashing you once they see this shit OK. Trust me on this one, Kevin, you don't need this in your life. Alls I'm asking for is 10 million dollars in cash by next week, and we can keep this our little secret, how's that sound."

"10 million!" Kevin shouted out in total shock, as if he had never seen that much money in his fuckin' life. You want me to pay you 10 million dollars? Are you fuckin' crazy?"

"No, Kevin, I'm not crazy. But you sure would be crazy if you don't pay it. Look, Kevin, I'm not gonna sit on this phone and debate this with you. You either pay me 10 million dollars or I'm sendin' this DVD to every TMZ, and every fuckin' tabloid paparazzi that exists in showbiz. Please don't fuck with me, dude."

It was like snatching candy from a baby. Summer and I had a joint account so I gave him all the info that he needed to wire me my fuckin' cash. And that he did—the next day, I had 10 million in cash in my account. And this was just the beginning. I was going to suck the celebrity world dry of finance until I had so much fuckin' money, I could start up a licensed lending company—basically a legal loan shark muthafucka.

## CHAPTER 15

Kevin Roberson from the LA Lakers, Steven Lorenz from the Dallas Cowboys, Sebastian Letterman from the Late Night Show on Fox 5, knockout artist Nicholous Clayman, the heavyweight champion of the world, and rap artist Dollar Bill, who has been the number one top-selling rap artist so far in the hip hop industry. All victims of my Manhattan Project. All victims of the beautiful hot pink kiss marks with that special DVD attached to it. It was the kiss of financial death. The dangerous but sexy and seductive walk and talk of Summer crept quietly like a thief in the red-light district, warning all celebs and stars from all walks of the entertainment life, keep your dick in your pants, and a tight hold on your bank account. She comes out at night like a streetlight that shines over the neighborhood, sweet honey in her mouth but a bitter stinger at her tail. The Torah describes her as the strange woman—a harlot with a perverted tongue that's whispers sugar-coated words during pillow talk. Her victims have suffered a tramatizing loss in their bank account and a serious case of sleep deprivation. This whole plan of mine was working just the way I had planned it.

I guess a man just doesn't know what the word 'no' means. Ya see, I called it a project for a reason. Think about it like this. Here you have a sexy woman willing to fulfill your nastiest fantasies in front of you, whispering in your ear, rubbing your cock until it's rock hard, putting her hot, wet mouth all over it as she caresses your balls, spitting on it and licking it off, telling you that she wants to fuck your brains out as she lets you shove your cock down her throat only for a second just to get you so worked up that psychologically, your brain has let go of all inhabitions that it possesses. You're ready to fuck her; you're ready to release and explode inside of her. She then lets you put your cock inside of her tight pussy, only to tell you to get off of her because she doesn't feel right and she wants to leave. The average man can't let that happen. Suddenly when the word 'no' gets thrown around, its like it's a foreign language to him. A little fight, a little push, a little shove, a couple of screams, and suddenly RAPE is born.

I was 50 million dollars richer. I purchased a house on the beach for me and Summer, and of course, I purchased a house for Rodger and Patricia and his crew because he damn sure wasn't gonna stay with me. Nothing at all changed though, we all were still some hardcore drug addicts—cocaine, speed, dust, alcohol, weed, LSD—you name it, we were high on it.

Lacey was staying with me. I was supposed to be 'taking care' of her because she was an absolute mess. She was such a fuckin' mess that the tabloids didn't even mention her name anymore when they saw her out acting like she didn't have any sense. But what they did do was follow our daughter around because she was growing up to be a beautiful little girl. Lacey's parents had taken our rights to see our daughter due to us being such fuck-ups. Lacey still had enough money to go around, so she had medication for her sickness.

Things were actually going pretty well though. Rodger and his crew were still doing shows all around the world. He actually was asked to star in a couple of movies but that wasn't Rodger's style. He played in a little role in this mafia movie that came out. Lacey knew a producer that was a die-hard fan of Rodger, and offered him a small part. If you ask me, it wasn't a small part at all—it was actually kind of big. Rodger didn't want to do it but I persuaded him to do it just to get exposure for himself. The whole band got exposure, actually—their role was to be this band that this mafia guy's son took a liking to. So Rodger and his band actually got to play a song in this movie. It was all good for publicity, so Rodger decided to do it.

Things at the time were really smooth, except for Lacey who was extremely depressed. She just fell into a deep state of depression, and the only thing that made her come alive was hardcore drugs. I remember one night Summer and she had a big fight because we had found out that Lacey did the most shocking shit ever. She was going out and sleeping with random guys and not using protection—so she was actually spreading this fuckin' disease to guys she was sleeping with.

One night, Summer's cousin came to stay with us. He was a regular kid, who just liked to party and not listen to his parents, but he was a cool kid. Now when I say it was her cousin, I'm not talking about some 4th or 5th cousin down the blood line. This was Summer's mom's sister's son. So he was also actually Patricia's cousin as well, because Summer's mom andPatricia's dad were brother and sister. So Summer, Patricia and this kid were all related. Now why this kid decided to get high on coke and drunk out of his mind and stick his dick inside of Lacey was beyond me. He wore a condom but the fucked-up part was that the damn thing apparently broke. When Summer found out about this shit, boy, did she flip the fuck out, and when he got tested, she flipped out even more because he did indeed come up with the HIV virus. There was a bunch of arguing and screaming, and it was getting out of control. I wouldn't let Summer get to her, so she finally calmed the hell down and went into the back room. Now I wasn't paying attention to where she went—I was just trying to hold back Lacey at this point. I turned to see Summer running toward us with my fuckin' gun in her hand and alls I heard next was gunshots. Luckily, Summer couldn't shoot to save her life because she fired off three fuckin' shots and they all missed Lacey. Rodger dove across the table, and tackled her onto the floor. She was fuckin' pissed, let me tell ya.

Now here was the fucked-up thing. Summer was pissed off at me because I was trying to play the middle man in the whole situation. She told me that if I don't kick Lacey out that she was going to leave, and that I could forget about this whole thing that she and I had going. So here I was, thinking to myself, 'Damn, what do I do? Keep my child's mother here to keep an eye on her. Or keep my operation going on with Summer, and let me tell ya, it wasn't a very hard fuckin' decision to make. Lacey was gonna have to pack her shit up and get out. The cool thing was that Lacey totally understood my position. She didn't get mad at all—she just packed her shit and moved out. I actually sat and thought about how crazy this shit was one night. My child's mom, whose life was going straight down the toilet, was having sex with Summer's cousin under my roof, and had given him HIV. How crazy was that! I mean shit like that doesn't just happen to everybody.

Lacey still continued to hang out with me, Rodger and his crew, when they performed and when we went out to parties. I mean I just wasn't gonna cut her out of my life—she was my daughter's mother, for Christ's sake. Plus Lacey had connects all over the place. I mean between her being a well known actress, and Summer being who she was, that's how I was bumping into all these celebs to blackmail. That rapper Dollar Bill and Nicholas clayman the heavyweight boxing champ I met through Lacey. Plus Lacey and I were friends, so like I said, she still hung out with me, Rodger and the crew.

It was a Saturday night, and we were in China because we were touring with this rock band called Heaven and Hell. The concert was a big hit for Rodger and his band, the Chinese population actually went bananas when Rodger took the stage. Rodger was in good spirits anyway because we had just found out that Patricia was pregnant with his baby. So, after the concert, we had gotten invited to this after-party at this penthouse on the 50th floor that the lead singer from Heaven and Hell owned. The singer and Rodger got along pretty well because he liked the fact that Rodger was a crazy muthafucka, who didn't give a fuck about nothing. It was me, Rodger, Lacey, and Rodger's band at this after-party, getting stoned out of our minds. Everything seemed to be just fine; everybody was having a great time. Rodger and I were in this guy's bathroom sniffing coke off the sink, and just shooting the shit about how far we've come from robbing people's houses whether they were home or not back in Manhattan, to support our drug habit, to touring all over the fuckin' world, and damn near almost being a household name.

"Hey, Casual, who the fuck would have ever thought that we would be in fuckin' China, dude?"

"I sure woulda never thought so," I replied after I sniffed up another line. "I know one thing is for sure, Rodger. I know that the both of us are goin' straight to fuckin' hell to meet the devil when we die, and that's the fuckin' truth. We sure are on the right rock tour."

Rodger began to laugh hysterically as he was suddenly interrupted by a knock on the door. So Rodger and I both turned to look at each other at the same time. And before I could say, 'Hold on, comin' out in a few seconds', this fuckin' asshole Rodger started making sex sounds like two people were in the bathroom fucking.

"Yeah. Yeah. Yeah… Gimme that ass, gimme that ass," And stupid me, I went right along with the shit, making female noises like I was having some sort of an orgasm. So alls you heard was 'Yeah oh Yeah oh Yeah Gimme Gimme Gimme,' and sounds of a female, which was really me screaming out loud. I even took it a step further and tore the shower curtain down to make it really sound like a guy and a girl were really fuckin' in that bathroom. Now I couldn't tell you why we just didn't say hold up, we will be out in just a second, instead of acting like some guy fuckin' some girl. Me and Rodger were just two clowns who were super high on coke and didn't give a fuck, and it must have worked because they knocking stopped.

"Yo Rodger, do you ever think about that little girl that we killed that night?"

"Duude, I couldn't give a shit about that little fuckin' bitch. We are on top of the fuckin' world right now, Casual. Why the hell would I be thinkin' about her for crying out loud? Hell, nobody was worried about me when I was a little boy and my fuckin' father and his friends would burn me with their cigarettes and throw darts at me when they got piss-ass drunk. Why you askin' me this shit anyway?"

"I don't know," I replied. "I just think about it sometimes, ya know. I mean how can I not think of something like that? I'm a fuckin' human bein', Rodger, and not only that, dude, for Christ's fuckin' sake, I have a daughter of my own."

Rodger sniffed up another line and let out a evil, high-pitched giggle, and said, "The only thing that I think about is how many fans I have. Duude, all my life, I've been makin' music, real music at that, and now I have fans all over the world that feel my music."

"Yeah, well, let me tell ya this, Rodger, just enjoy all this shit that's goin' on right now because we are definitely not two of God's favorite children."

"Well, first off, if you ask me, duude, I'm gonna tell ya that my father was the fuckin' devil. Now I know I never met the devil but I tell you what, my dad will do until I meet the real devil. Dude, you answer me this, Casual, do you really think that after all I've been through in my life I actually care what God thinks of me?"

Talking to Rodger was like talking to a damn wall about this touchy situation, so I just shut the fuck up about the whole thing. We both walked out the bathroom and we split up, I went one way and he went the other. I knew if I wanted to talk to someone about it, it definitely had to be Lacey. She was the only one on this trip who had any kind of sense and could understand my situation. Not like I was gonna tell her that the only reason I ended up in California was because I was on the run for the murder of some guy and an innocent, little girl. But at least she was someone I could talk to about where our life was heading. I actually wanted to talk to her anyway because I wanted to know what was going on with our daughter and when her parents were going to give us visitation rights.

As I went all around looking for her, I couldn't find her, I said to myself her crazy ass probably ran off with some random guy to fuck. But then I looked over towards the balcony because a crowd of people was over there. As I got closer, I overheard people talking to each saying, 'Oh my God'. I got out on the balcony and asked one of the girls why everybody was on the balcony, and she said, "Oh my God, you don't know, that girl in the red dress jumped off the balcony and killed herself. There are cops all over the place down there." It didn't hit me until the lead singer from Heaven and Hell, who owned the penthouse came over to me, and said, "Yo dude, Lacey just jumped off my fuckin' balcony, dude. She's fuckin' dead, dude. She's fuckin' dead."

My heart just dropped in my fuckin' stomach. I ran over and peeped over the balcony only to look 50 stories down and see cops and ambulances all over the place. I ran and jumped into the fuckin' elevator down to the first floor. I pushed everybody out of the way including all the cops that were there. And when I saw what I saw, it felt like my world had just ended—there was Lacey's body on top of a car. The impact of her body hitting the top of this fuckin' car had crushed the whole hood, and there she was, dead from a 50-story drop-off of a balcony. I couldn't believe what the fuck I was looking at, I was numb. I just dropped down to my knees as I felt my eyes water with tears. It has to be a dream—it has to be a fuckin' dream—this shit couldn't be for real. I kept telling myself to wake up but the more I tried to tell myself it was a dream, the more real it got. I watched cameras flashing and news reporters live on the scene. It was the most talked about thing on TV and the radio—it made headlines all over. And of course, they added my name in there because she was with me, her child's drug addict father. I was so fucked-up over what had happened that I refused to talk to any media. Even though they were paying a pretty penny to do an interview with me about the last hours of Lacey's life, I totally refused.

# CHAPTER 16

It had been 7 months since Lacey jumped to her death. Mostly every Saturday, if we weren't on some tour, we hung out at this local bar called the Bird's Nest. I don't know what it was about California bars but they were totally different from New York bars. The atmosphere in California was just fun and energetic. People were so much more friendlier in California than in New York. So we were all hanging outside the bar, smoking that good ol' California dust like we normally did.

    Rodger and his crew always had a group of dick-riders around that always wanted to be down. Especially this kid named Paully that we all had met when we first hit the California underground scene. Ever since we had met this kid, he had always hung around with us at the local spots in Cali. Now when I say this kid was a dick-rider for Suicidal, I mean this kid would damn near do any fuckin' thing, just to be down with Rodger and his crew. For some reason, he wanted to go on tour with us the next time we opened up for somebody. He would practically beg Rodger to go. Rodger asked this kid how bad did he want to go, and the kid said that he would do anything that Rodger asked him to do.

## A SUICIDE STORY

We all played a prank on this kid, telling him that if he took a gun and robbed the local Quick Mart store, he could then earn his right to hang with Suicidal. The thing was that I knew the guy that worked in Quick Mart—his name was Nick. I told him that we were gonna have some kid come in and rob him at gunpoint. Now the camera system in this Quick Mart was being repaired and didn't work, so it all worked out. I gave him a whole stack of money to give to this kid so that the he actually thought he was robbing the store. Everything was already staged for this kid. He was gonna think that he was robbing the store but actually he wasn't. The plan was actually pretty cool, if you ask me.

"So Paully, you ready to be a real Suicidal rollin' stone or what?" Rodger asked, as he handed Paully a black 9mm pistol.

"Yeah, I guess I'm ready," Paully responded, as his shaky palm gripped the 9mm pistol. I could tell that this kid was scared out of his mind. He was shaking and his eyes had that look of worry inside them.

"Wait, guys, wait. I don't know if I'm cut out to rob some store. I mean I never even held a gun before, let alone use it to rob someone."

"Oh, quit actin' like a fuckin' pussy, would you? Me and Casual use to burglarize houses for the fun of it, and your cryin' about robbin' a little Quik Mart. Fuck it then, Paully, gimme back my fuckin' gun, and forget about tourin' with me. Because I don't want no pussies with me while I'm on tour."

"No, no, no, no... Wait, I can do this shit. I can do it—I mean, alls I gotta do is put the gun in his face and tell him to gimme the money right?"

"Duh, Paully, it's a fuckin' robbery," Rodger said, as he took a deep pull of dust and inhaled, "What the fuck do you think you're gonna do in there? And don't fuckin' freeze up either, Paully, because you already look scared outta your fuckin' mind." As scared as Paully was, he was still willing to go the mile and rob this store just to get to go on tour with us.

"OK… OK… Let's go do this shit," Paully said, as he tucked the 9mm in his pants. Everything was set-up. I had already called my homeboy that worked in Quick Mart at the register, so we were all on our way. We all packed up in my black truck and headed over to the mart. I told Rodger to drive because I was stoned out of my fuckin' mind, plus I still had a bottle of whiskey in my hand that I was chugging down. We pull up to the store and drove around the side. Rodger looked at Paully through the rearview mirror, and said, "Showtime, you pussy, and you better not fuckin' freeze up in there, Paully." We were all packed up in the truck, me, Rodger, his whole band and this kid, Paully. Skeet handed Paully a Michael Myers mask and

told him to put it on. Paully took two deep breaths and hopped out the truck, and walked into the store. We were all in the car laughing like a bunch of highschool kids. About five minutes had passed by, and I said to myself, 'What the fuck is goin' on in there?'

"Hey, Casual, did you let your fuckin' boy know about this shit because this fuckin' kid is takin' way too long in there." "Now, Rodger, why would you ask me such a stupid fuckin' question? You know damn well I told him—you were standin right there when I did." All of a sudden, my phone rang. I saw that it was Nick, so I picked it up.

"Hello."

"Yo wussup, Casual, where the hell are you guys at? I thought you were gonna send that cornball kid in here—I'm waitin."

"Yo, I'm outside in my truck right now. We sent him in five minutes ago. You don't see him—he has a Michael Myers mask on."

"Casual, I'm standin here right behind the fuckin' register, yo. And there ain't no kid in here with a fuckin' Michael Myers mask. Are you sure this kid ain't tryin' to trick you or some shit?"

"Hell, no, he ain't tryin' to trick us. We watched him go inside with the fuckin' mask on, I'm tellin' you he's inside—look for him."

"Casual, I'm tellin' you I've been behind this register lookin' at the door all fuckin' night, and no one came into this fuckin' store with a goddamn Michael Myers mask on. I'm not fuckin' crazy or blind."

"Well, if he's not in your damn store, tell me where the fuck he is then, Nick, because we saw him walk in."

"You're askin' me where he is? I don't know where the fuck he is—he was with you—why would I know where the fuck he is? Wait, wait, hold up a fuckin' minute, where the fuck are you guys at, Casual . Yo, look across the street, and tell me if you see a damn Burger King."

"A Burger King?" I yelled out, "A fuckin' Burger King, hell no, I don't see no damn Burger King. What the fuck does a Burger King have to do with this shit? Here I am lookin' for this fuckin' kid, and you talkin' about a fuckin' Burger King."

"Ohhhhh shit! Ohhhh shit! Yo, are you across the street from a pizza place, Casual? Look and see if you're across the street from a pizza place."

"Yeah I see a pizza place. Why?"

"Because, Casual, you dumbass, you muthafuckas are at the wrong goddamn Quick Mart. Your at the Quick Mart on the other side of town, you dumbass."

"Nick, you never told me that there were two Quick Marts. What the fuck, holy shit, holy fuckin' shit… I gotta go. We gotta get this kid outta there!"

"Just be careful, Casual, because those muthafuckas got cameras in that bitch."

I didn't know what to fuckin' do at this point. I had the whole conversation on speaker phone, so Rodger heard the whole thing. As soon as I said somebody has to go inside and get this kid, Rodger peeled off outta the parking lot.

"Yo, Rodger, what the fuck, yo, we can't leave that muthafucka back there—that's fucked up!"

"Fuck that! I'm outta here. I ain't waitin around for that clown. He's a fuckin' groupie. Remember, Casual, he ain't one of us by far. If he's smart, and has any balls, he'll shoot his way out when the cops show up." What we thought was gonna be a prank for this kid just to go on tour with us turned into a real fuckin' robbery. Rodger peeled outta there and was going at least 100 miles per hour or better. We were all arguing back and forth about leaving this kid behind. Swerving and dodging cars that were moving too slowly on the road, and arguing with each other, distracted Rodger—he was not looking at the road.

"Yo, Rodger, look out!"

BOOM!!! We had hit an old man that was crossing the street, and we hit this fuckin' guy hard because he flew up in the fuckin' air. Rodger stopped the car and we all got out to see the damage we had done.

"Yo, Rodger, check him and see if he's still breathin'," Skeet hollared from the back seat window, as he let out a evil laugh due to the dust we had just smoked.

"Shut the fuck up, Skeet. I ain't touchin' this old man. Are you stupid? To tell the truth, I couldn't care less if he's dead or not."

Since nobody wanted to check this guy, I rolled him over only to see him coughing up blood. "Ya see, Rodger, I told you to go back for that muthafucka—now we got this old man lyin' here."

"Ohh, quit actin' like a fuckin' pussy, Casual. So what are we gonna do, take him to the hospital and say yeah doc, we are responsible for hittin' this old fuck. We didn't see him because we were drinkin' and we'd been smoking dust, not to mention we fled the scene from a robbery—that's why we were goin' so fast."

"Well, what the fuck are we gonna do—just leave him here?"

"You goddamn right. That's exactly what we are gonna do, so get back in the truck and let's get the hell outta here before the cops come. And you know me, Casual, I ain't trying to go to prison. I will hold court right here in the middle of this fuckin' street, dude." Rodger was absolutely right for once in his dumb life. Plus I knew it would have gotten ugly if we waited for the cops because I knew Rodger was a beer short of a six pack, and he damn sure would have a shootout with the police. The very next day I sat on the couch with Summer watching TV and what came on? The fuckin' news. And who was on it? Paully. The news reporter went on saying how Paully got out of a black truck and walked into the Quick Mart and demanded all the money out of the register. And when the woman didn't give it, he hit her over the head with the pistol. Now here's the crazy part—the guy that was standing behind Paully wanted to play hero, so he grabbed Paully from behind and held him down while almost everybody in the store helped. What a fuckin' way to go out! The only thing was that this kid knew everything about us. He knew about bar brawls that we had gotten into where people had gotten seriously hurt, cut, stabbed, and had even had broken bones. I immediately called Rodger on the phone to tell him that this shit was on TV.

"Yo, Rodger, you know this shit is all over the news. Can you believe this dumbass got held down by the whole entire store until the cops showed up?"

"Duude, are you fuckin' kiddin me? Tell me right now that you're fuckin' kiddin—I have no time for jokes, Casual, this shit isn't funny, you know."

"You think I got time to call your dumbass on the phone and play games with you, Rodger? I hardly have time to call you to talk about serious shit, Rodger! I'm watchin it on TV, dickhead!" Rodger was in the backround cursing and screaming. I could hear Patricia and the rest of the crew in the backround saying what the hell is going on.

"Duude, we gotta bail his ass out, dude. I know you got money, Casual. We gotta bail his ass out."

"We ain't gotta do a damn thing. You got money, Rodger, why don't you bail his ass out? Now all of a sudden you care about this little punk-ass kid?"

"Duude, you don't understand, we gotta bail this kid out. Don't ask any fuckin' questions, Casual, just trust me on this one."

"Rodger, what kind of crack are you smoking over there? I ain't bailin' nobody out. So when you're done smoking your crack that has your mind all fried up, you call me back, you stupid ass!"

"I'm tellin' you we gotta bail this kid out, Casual. He used the same gun to rob the store that we used when we killed that little girl."

A moment of silence came between us for a long period of time to the point where Rodger was saying 'hello, hello', as if I had hung up the phone. "Rodger, you should just take a gun and shoot yourself right in the face. You should kill yourself you, stupid ass. You're tellin' me that the gun you gave him was the gun that accidentally killed that girl? Now what the fuck are we gonna do you, fuckin' genius?"

"I just told you what we have to do. We gotta bail this kid out before he spills all the fuckin' dimes. They're gonna try and pin those murders on him, and that's when he's gonna crack and say who he got the gun from, Casual. We gotta bail him out." I dropped the phone and just laid back on the couch. I thought to myself why in the hell would Rodger give this kid the same damn gun to rob the store that we used in New York. I felt like a black cloud was hovering over my head at this point in my life. Everytime we took 3 steps forward, we fell 12 steps back.

## CHAPTER 17

"Hello"

"Well, hi there, Mr Heavyweight Champion of the world. I hear you gotta big fight comin' up. I hope you're training hard there, tough guy."

"Aww man… what the hell do you want—not you again—can't you leave me the fuck alone? You already blackmailed millions of dollars outta me. What the hell do you want now?"

"Now, now… Mr Clayman, is that any way to talk to the man that has you on tape raping some innocent white girl? Quite frankly, I think that you should be happy to hear from me. You should be saying 'Hey Mr. You Got Me On Tape Raping Some Strange Woman, what can I do for you? Or better yet, how much money can I offer you today? You know I really don't like your tone of voice, Mr. Clayman."

"Well, what the hell do you expect from me? I gave you millions already. What the hell else do you want from me dammit!"

"What do I want from you—are you asking me what I want from you? I want everything you fuckin' have, you muthafucka! I own you, do you fuckin' understand me—I own you! You are my financial slave, so I'm gonna call you whenever I get good and goddamn ready to call you, and you will answer, and you will give me what I want, because the minute I get bored with what's on TV nowadays, I'm gonna send this video of you raping this girl to every fuckin' news channel that exists. And that sure will change what's on TV these days, don't you agree, Mr. Fuckin' Clayman? So what I would like from you is another 2 million and you can go on about your business until I decide to call you again. Now you already have my banking info, so make that happen by tomorrow. Good bye."

I made that phonecal while me and Summer were sniffing up some coke off of her coffee table early in the morning. She absolutely loved it when I called these muthafuckas on their phone and demanded money. I mean we would literally sit around and sniff up some coke and call these fuckers on the phone and fuck with them. There was really no sense in me having Summer get raped by anyone else. I mean alls I needed to do was call these fucks on the phone every now and then, and have them send me money. What were they gonna do about it—I had them by the balls and they knew it. And they already knew that if they changed their phone number without me knowing and they tried to dodge and hide from me, I was automatically gonna have them all over the news. Summer especially loved it when I called Kevin Roberson on the phone—I really put on a show when I called his ass.

At this time Patricia was as big as a house—she was 7 months pregnant, and she actually looked normal for once in her life. She gained weight and stopped using drugs for the sake of the baby. Rodger was happy as hell, but they kept on coming up with these dumbass names like 'Brock' and 'Lester' and 'Fabian'. Summer and I couldn't help but intervene, and tell them that those fuckin' names were horrible. Now the new drama that was going on was within Rodger's band. One night, Skeet walked in on his girl sucking Frenchy's cock—and now we were out of a guitar man because Skeet said if Frenchy stays around, he was not gonna play. Now if you ask me, the band could have made it without Frenchy—he was nothing but a hypeman, a backup singer . Alls he did was hype up the words that Rodger was saying. Now Skeet was somebody that Rodger needed in the band—he was a hell of a guitar player, and that fuckin' Frenchy was dead wrong anyway. So one night Rodger decided to let Frenchy go from the band. Skeet was crushed—this guy's heart was fuckin' broke. And the girl was actually a pretty fuckin' girl too. I knew she was a whore though because she just had that sneaky whore look about her. I actually had sensed that Frenchy and her were fuckin' around because they were always flirting around with each other. But it wasn't my business to say something and nor did I give a fuck to even say anything. But Frenchy took it like a man and left the group. Not only did he leave with just himself, but this fuckin' guy also took Skeet's girl right along with him. I thought it was the funniest thing since a joke from Richard Pryor.

Now on the flip side of things, we had the money to bail out Paully from county jail but when we went to bail him out, they told us that he was being held without bail. Now that was not good news at all, because that information right there meant that they had traced that gun back to the murder of Fritz and that little girl in New York. There was no way in hell they were denying bail just based on Paully robbing this store. I knew for a fact that they had denied his bail based on the fact that they were investigating him more because they had tracked that gun. I had that gut feeling in my stomach. After a couple days had passed, we got a call from Paully's sister, and she told us they were keeping him because they had traced the gun back to the murders of some little girl and a man in New York. The fucked-up thing about it all was that she told Rodger that her dad was a detective working for the police department. And can you believe this bitch actually told Rodger that we better fix this situation or she was going to tell the cops everything that we were involved in. And let me tell ya, she knew a lot. Like one night, at this local underground spot where a bar brawl broke out that, of course, we were involved in, and a guy ended up getting paralyzed due to the severe beating we gave him. And she knew about a lot more shit that could lead to us being investigated and locked up for a long time.

I couldn't believe this shit—I felt like I was being blackmailed. Yeah, me of all fuckin' people, was being fuckin' blackmailed by this bitch. But I wasn't being blackmailed for money—I was being blackmailed for my damn freedom. It was either all or nothing at this point, so I grabbed the phone from Rodger, and told that dumb bitch to do whatever it is that she felt like doing and hung up the phone. I wasn't admitting to shit—if I was gonna go do any time in jail, they were gonna have to catch my ass. And damn sure the newspaper came out a couple weeks later, and said that Paully was being held for the possible murder of a little girl and a man back in New York. It seemed like everything was going downhill from here. Out of everything that could possibly happen, Rodger had to to give this fuckin' kid the same gun that we had used in New York to rob Fritz. But I wasn't gonna let this shit bother me now, hell, I was damn near almost on my way to the top of the fuckin' world. And I wasn't gonna let this situation slow me down—no fuckin' way.

Two more months passed. It was a rainy Saturday night. Rodger and I were on our way to the hospital because Patricia was in labor and she was about to have the baby. Rodger was so fuckin' happy that it actually made me feel good to see him this way. Rodger always wanted the opportunity to raise a son and be the father to him that Rodger's father never was to him. Throughout Patricia's entire pregnancy, he would bend my fuckin' ear about how much of a super dad he was going to be. He actually told me that he was gonna give me some lessons on how to be a father because he always said I sucked at being one. They knew the baby was going to be a boy, so they prepared everything in boy colors for him to come home in. They were gonna name him 'Brock'—now to me that was a really fucked-up name, but hey, it wasn't my kid so what the hell! Rodger was speeding to get to the hospital. He couldn't wait to see his firstborn son come out. He actually didn't do any hardcore drugs or any hard liquor this time. I mean he was really excited about this whole thing. The only thing that fucked everything up was the fact that it was raining really hard out. You would think that a day like this would be a nice sunny day with a light breeze but it sure as hell wasn't. When we got to the hospital, we took the elevator up to the 3rd floor, which was the baby ward. We rushed into the room to see Patricia's mom and Summer.

We got there just in time—Patricia was trying to push this baby out with all her might. Rodger was pacing back and forth—he didn't know what to do with himself. So I told him to go over and hold her hand and help her push. And that's exactly what he did. The doctor was between her legs telling her to push, and everyone in the room was giving their full support waiting for little Brock to come out. I looked up to see Rodger give Patricia a kiss, and they both smiled at each other. They were both ready to be parents at any moment now. I have to say, I was happy for the both them, and the baby hadn't even come out yet. I couldn't wait to see Rodger's face when his firstborn son came out. I just knew that he was gonna hold him and embrace him real close to him. If anybody knew that Rodger had a fucked-up childhood, it was me. Rodger never knew what a father was, and I just knew he was gonna be a different father than his father was to him. But this sound went off on the monitor for the babies heart beat. The heartbeat had stopped. It all happened way to fast for my mind to fathom, Patricia delivered a stillborn. And the fucked up thing about it all, is that she still had to push out the baby even though it was already dead.

When the baby came out, he was limp and not moving. The doctor and the nurses then rushed to the baby's aid. Something wasn't right—a sense of coldness came into the room and hit me. I felt cold and eerie, my stomach dropped and my heart began to pump. I looked over at Rodger, and he just looked confused about what was going on.

Here I stood, staring at this little, tiny infant, helpless, lifeless, and not moving. Rodger was beginning to push the nurses out of the way. I went over to grab him but he went absolutely crazy after that.

"Casual, what the fuck is goin' on? What the fuck is goin' on with my baby? What the fuck!"

"Rodger, calm down, man, just calm down. Let them do their job, please."

"No… No… No… No!! Something is wrong, Casual. Something is wrong! What the fuck is wrong with my baby?"

Rodger was going crazy at this point. He knocked me over and then ran over toward the doctors and the nurses. I got right back up and pushed him over to the wall—it took everything I had to try and hold him back. And Rodger was a big mothafucka, I can't even explain the feeling that I had in my gut—it was like the fuckin' world got put on pause for a New York-minute.

The very next day, Rodger was slumped in the chair with a finished bottle of tequila, and lying right next to him was a double shot glass with the hot sauce next to it. That's the way we all drank when we wanted to get so drunk that you start talking to God, or the devil, for that matter. You fill a double shot glass with 100% agave tequila and put some hot sauce in the shot with a jalapeno. We had been kicking it with some hardcore dudes from Guatamala one night, and they called it 'Devil's blood'. When it went down, it went down hot, and it burned. Then you gotta chew the jalapeno, steamin' hot devil's blood in your veins and it makes you sweat like crazy.

Rodger was completely drunk and he hadn't showered, so I knew he was all fucked-up in the head. We didn't even have a funeral because we knew we were on the run. So Rodger had the little baby boy that they were going to call Brock, cremated, and they kept the ashes in a jar. Man, let me tell ya, Rodger and Patricia were real fucked-up behind losing their first child. I tried to at least give him some words of encouragement from time to time, but it really didn't help.

It took at least another two months for Rodger and Patricia to get back to reality. And when I say 'get back to reality', I mean they were hitting up some hardcore drugs every fuckin' night just to ease the pain—smoking red devil dust, sniffing coke, tripping on LSD, shooting heroin and every damn thing else. Rodger and I got so fucked-up one night off of some crystal meth and moonshine, he made up a song about his fucked-up childhood and how he was going to change it all, and give his new son the world but never got a chance to. The song was deep, emotional, heart-wrenching, and needed to be heard by the American people. I interpreted the song as a masterpiece to all fathers who would die to have the chance to erase a fucked-up childhood by fathering their firstborn child, and any other child the way a father is suppose to father a child. The song actually made me think of how much a fucked-up father I was to my kids.

I let the song leak to a couple of big-time rock managers who worked for big-time labels, and they loved it. I mean they already knew who we were, not to mention they were ready to skin somebody alive just to get Rodger and his band to sign to their label. I figured that these record labels could do twice as much as I could do. Plus they could get Rodger exposure at a rapid rate. So I created a bidding war with these labels. I knew they were willing to invest in Rodger because they knew it would come back. I mean he damn near had a better fan base than most bands that were signed. So it would be a great investment to these rock labels to have Rodger as a part of their entourage. And it was a strategic chess move for me, because I knew we were going to the biggest bidder, no doubt about that. Once the tabloids found out that the labels were having a bidding war over Suicidal, it was all over every major rock radio station. It was the talk soup of every state—who was Suicidal going to sign with.

Two more months had gone by, and Rodger was pretty much over the fact that Patricia had delivered a stillborn. We were all now focused on who we were going to sign with. It was between two record labels that were bidding for us, the rest of the labels fell to the side due to the fact that they knew they couldn't compete with any of the top dog rock labels, especially the two labels that were having a bidding war over us. It was between Lime Light Records and 6 Feet Deep Records. After thinking about it all, we figured we would sign with 6 Feet Deep because it just went with our style and our name. I mean the band was called Suicidal, now suicide indicates death, and when you die, they bury you 6 feet deep—so it all made sense. Everything was looking cool, exept that Rodger was always up Patricia's ass because she was a little depressed still about the baby dying during birth. Which is totally understandable—I mean that was hard to swallow even for me, and I didn't even have the baby.

There were meetings on top of meetings, paper signings, sessions with lawyers, sessions with producers, managers, makeup artists, promoters—we were finally in the door. When I tell you we were on the front page of every fuckin' rock magazine, I mean we were taking pictures for everybody. We were the new hot commodity on the rock scene. And people knew we were the real deal because the underground scene in New York was behind us like an army. Every skinhead, Megadeath freak, skateboarder, hardcore biker, and die-hard brawl out Anthrax fans from New York city were Suicidal fans. Plus we had the whole underground night club scene out in California. They knew we were a bunch of bad-to-the-bone hardcore heavy metal muthafuckas, who didn't give a fuck about shit. Money or no money, in the blink of an eye, you would have a gun in your mouth for being disrespectful to any Suicidal member. And the fans knew that, and that's where we got our respect from. Not to mention, Rodger's music was great to these people. They really related to him in a soulful way. I have to say, I was actually shocked by how many black people worked in this industry of rock music. Just because Rodger was my best friend doesn't mean I liked fuckin' rock music—because a lot of that shit to me was just straight fuckin' noise. I was more of an R&B and hip hop type of guy. I actually wanted Rodger and his band to maybe do a song with a hip hop artist, just to get that crossover exposure.

# CHAPTER 18

Now even with all our exposure with this music thing blasting off, I still felt that I needed to put more and more money in my bank account. Ya see, an opportunity came across the table that I just could not pass up. I was up late one night, sniffing up a couple of lines and shooting the shit with Summer about politics and how fucked-up the government was. It just so happened that we started talking about the mayor of California, who was also a big-time actor who played in a lot of major movies. Now how his ass got from the big screen to the mayor of California was the topic of our conversation.

As I sniffed up the last line of the glass table and laid back on the couch, I heard Summer say, "You know I know that fat motherfucker right." I damn near choked on the coke that I had just sniffed up my nostril. I began to cough real heavy, trying to catch my breath. As I got my breath back, I looked over at Summer, and said, "What the fuck did you just say?"

"I said I know him. You heard what I said, Casual. That's why you choked," Summer responded sarcastically.

"Yeah, you're right, Summer, I did hear you loud and fuckin' clear. I was just checkin' to see if what I heard was what I really heard. What the fuck do you mean you know him—you actually know Mayor Luckerman?"

Summer actually got kind of offended because it was like she felt that I didn't believe that she knew the mayor of California. She started to explain how he was a big fan of basketball, and she would see him at some of the games. But that didn't mean a damn thing to me, so that's exactly what I said to her.

"Ummm… what the fuck does that mean, Summer? Ooooooh big deal, you've seen the mayor of Cali at a couple games. Big fuckin' deal. That don't mean you know his ass. Dammit Summer, you made me choke on this coke for fuckin' nothing!"

"Well, if you let me finish, asshole, I'm gonna explain to you the rest of the story of how I know him. Don't worry, baby, you choked on that coke for a good reason," she said, as she laughed. "There was a girl on my cheer squad that was his niece. I always would wonder why she was givin' this guy all these big hugs at the games. I mean at the time he was still playing in big movies, so we were all like 'Damn girl, you know Joseph Luckerman'—we were all shocked. Then she told us that he was her uncle."

I cut Summer off again because I still was not impressed by her story of how she claimed she knew this guy. "Summer… Summer… You sittin' up here tellin' me about how you was on the same team with a girl who was his niece? That don't mean a fuckin' goddamn thing ok! I'm sittin' here thinkin' you had dinner with this cocksucker or had a couple drinks with him, and you tellin' me about how his niece was on your cheer team. I couldn't give a fuck less if that bitch was his niece. Fuck her, Summer! Just because you know her, that don't mean you know him ok!"

"Casual, will you just shut the fuck up and let me finish the damn story please?"

"Yeah...Yeah... yeah...Whatever, girl, hurry up and get to the point OK?"

Summer had this real big smirk on her face—as if she had some shit on her mind. As she was she finishing her little story, what she was saying was just fading away, going in my one ear and right out of the other. At this point, I really didn't even give a fuck what she had to say about this faggot-ass mayor, so I just tuned her out. Until I heard her say the words, 'I would love to be your secretary.' Then my attention jumped right back at her. "Huh, what the fuck did you just say? Did you just say something about you being his secretary?"

"Uhhhh... yeah," Summer replied, "If you had been listening to my whole story, you would have heard me."

"So this guy wanted you to be his secretary? Why in the fuck would he want you, Summer? You don't even have half the credentials that it takes to be a secretary for the mayor of California. I mean you were a professional cheerleader, for Christ's sake, why would he just choose you out of all the college grads that went to school for something like that?"

"First of all, Casual, if you had been listening to what I was saying, you would have heard me say that he was offering an internship to work with him, and I was interested."

I laughed when she said that, and responded by saying, "Ya see, what I'm saying, Summer, is your ass is too damn dumb to even accept an offer like that. Who in their right mind would say 'no' to some shit like that especially when they ain't got shit else goin' on for themselves, and I know you didn't have a damn thing going on for yourself, so don't make it seem like you did."

"Ya know, Casual, you can be such an arrogant, ignorant, son of a bitch—like I said, if you had been listening, you would have heard me say I had way too much going on in my life at the time, and I couldn't fit that into my schedule. But I have all the time in the world now to do something like that," she whispered in my ear real soft and slow, sticking her tongue gently in my ear, and biting my earlobe at the same time.

Even though it did make my cock get hard, I said to her, "Summer, why in the hell would you wanna do that now? Its called an 'internship', which means you ain't getting no damn money. You are a grownass woman, Summer—grown muthafuckas do not participate in internships OK. Young kids do internships, not adults. And you wonder why I ignore all the shit that comes outta your damn mouth. I feel like I'm talking to Rodger, for Christ's fuckin' sake."

Summer put her tongue on her top lip, and began to carress my leg. She leaned forward and kissed me on my lips, and began kissing me on my neck. We went from talking about an internship with the mayor to tongue-kissing on the couch. She then unzipped my pants, took out my cock, and put her hot mouth around it as she caressed my balls. My cock was so damn hard—at this point, I had forgotten about the whole conversation and focused on her as she put her tongue around the head of my cock in a circular motion. As I slumped down in the couch, she looked up into my eyes, and said in a real sexy voice, "Do you think the mayor would like it if put his cock in my mouth while I play with his little balls?"

We just looked at each other, eyes wide open, and I said to her "Are you thinking what I'm thinking—because if you are thinking what I'm thinking, I want you to know that I think you're a fuckin' genius, Summer."

"I know I'm a genius, Casual, I'm always two steps ahead of your ass. Don't worry about a thing. I know how to get in contact with him and everything. What I want you to do is just sit back and let me work."

A month had passed by, and Rodger and his crew were in the studio making their first single for their album. Day in and day out, they were in that studio. I was spending a lot of time with Rodger and his band—I was excited about this whole record deal thing. I truly believed that we were going to takeoff from here. The producers and promoters wanted Rodger to come up with a party song to introduce them to the public, so that's exactly what they did. The studio became like our apartment. We had every fuckin' drug in that studio—from coke to dust to heroin to weed to acid, shrooms and hash. There wasn't one sober day as we cut Rodger's first single. Hell, I got so fuckin' high one night, even I started screaming into that microphone—it was so damn funny that Rodger actually put me in one of his songs. It almost became a party in there. One week, four people from the label showed up. The next week, there were at least ten people from the lable in that studio. From there it turned into all types of groupie girls showing up half-dressed and ready to party. And from there, it turned into people having sex in there. Girls were making out with girls, and all types of orgies were going on while Rodger was cutting his album. I remember, one night, I was so high on coke that I was fuckin' this girl, and she was eating this other girl's pussy at the same time, inside the studio, while Rodger was recording one of his songs.

It was absolutely fuckin' crazy in that studio—we had groupies of all kinds ready to do anything we wanted them to do. Two girls actually had gotten into a fight one night over who was gonna be inside the studio room while Rodger was doing a skit. This girl had gotten so drunk that she took it as an insult that Rodger didn't want her in the room. Now the reason he didn't want her in there was because it was way too crowded in the studio in the first place. So he told her that she had to go. The funny thing was that this girl who couldn't stay and the girl that could stay were best fuckin' friends. The one girl was telling her friend, "Hey, if we both can't go in, then we should both leave." But the other girl said, "Hell! No, I ain't leaving." She wasn't willing to give up the opportunity to be inside the studio with the next up-and-coming rock star while he was making his first album. So they started to fight inside the studio and we all sat there and let them fuckin' fight. As a matter of fact, while they were rolling around on the floor pulling each other's hair and punching each other in the fuckin' face, I stood up and shouted, "Yo, I got two thousand dollars on the Spanish girl." Everybody in the studio jumped up and started placing bets while these two fuckin' girls were trying to kill each other in there. They both were bleeding badly and screaming at the top of their lungs. Now on this specific night, we had all been chewing on shrooms and popping acid, and so were these two girls. So they were bound to kill each other in that studio—but we didn't give a fuck about who got killed. At this point, I was beginning to tweek on the acid and the shrooms that I chewed. As I was looking at these two girls pulling out each other's hair, scratching and biting each other, the acid really started to kick in. First of all, they had torn each other's shirts off, so both of their tits were out. We were all shouting like we were at a damn MMA cage match—these girls were not gonna stop fighting until one of them was dead. And they picked the right night to fight because none of us was gonna break it up. So one of them was just gonna fuckin' die in that studio. Plus I had two thousand dollars on the fuckin' line, so I certainly wasn't breaking it up. It went on, till Summer walked in and started breaking it up. I was so fuckin' pissed that she walked in there and did that. I mean I had money on the fuckin' line and this idiot just walked in out of nowhere and broke up these two girls.

"Yo, yo, yo, Summer, what the fuck are you doin'!"

"What does it look like I'm doin', you asshole. You're just standing there and you see I need help breaking these two bitches up, Casual!"

"Ummmmmm... that would be because I want them to fight. Why don't you mind your fuckin' business. We were doing just fine in here until you came in here with your shit!"

But even though I was mad that Summer had broken up the fight, I had to help her separate these two girls because she was struggling with them. I was so pissed off that I pulled both of them apart and kicked both of them out. These were the kinds of things that were happening in the studio—it was out of control. Now the video shoot was even more fun. Rodger had come up with the idea of having a bunch of convicts being transported on a bus to another prison. While the bus was traveling, it was going to flip over in an accident causing the guards to be unconscious. Of course, the inmates were played by Rodger and his crew, so they'd get the guards' keys, uncuff themselves and escape from the flipped-over bus. As they are on foot, running from the scene of the accident, they come upon a mansion with a gate in the front. Their intentions were to hold whoever was in the house hostage, and steal a car or two. When they get to the back of the house, they notice a huge house party going down, so they jump right in. And that's the whole video, until the cops surround the mansion and rearrest Rodger and his band. We had groupies on top of groupies running around with two-piece bathing suits, looking as if they had just fallen from heaven into a pool full of party animals. There were girls kissing girls, dudes ripping the bras off girls' chests, exposing their tits, and people just havin a good fuckin' time. The song was actually called *Party Animal*, and when it hit the big screen, it became the number one video. It also became the number one song on the pop charts. Suicidal was finally in everybody's home, taking control of the young minds of America's future. I couldn't believe this was actually coming true—we had come a long way from burglarizing houses just to get high— and now we were living the dream. We were travelling from one airport to the next, on a plane, off a plane, city to city, from one coast to the next coast, flying overseas, rockin sold-out arenas in other countries, signing autographs, waking up in a luxury hotel with strange women in the bed, and unfinished lines of coke across the dresser. We were giving interview after interview, tabloids followed us all around snapping pcitures, and of course, you know Rodger made that exciting. Sticking his middle finger up at the camera, screaming things like,

# A SUICIDE STORY

'One life to live, so live it hardcore, sniff coke, drink heavy and spend money, fuck the whole world'. The magazine labled him a maniac on wheels, a ticking time bomb ready to go off any minute.

One time on the red carpet at the VMA Awards, he was asked a simple question about how he feels about this year's VMA awards. This fuckin' guy turned around, pulled his pants down, spread his ass cheeks, and farted right into the camera. That shit was the talk of every radio station, television show, and on the cover of every magazine; it was absolutely insane. Rodger and his band were raunchy, raw, hardcore, and just didn't give a fuck. They said anything they wanted, and did anything they wanted, and there wasn't anybody that was gonna say a damn thing. After his album was finished and put out into the stores, there was even more pandemonium. His album was titled, *A Suicide Story.* There was a picture of a evil clown on the front with rotten teeth, pointing a .38 caliber pistol to his head, pulling the trigger, and blowing his brains out of the side of his head.

# CHAPTER 19

Patricia was not doing well at all. We had just gotten back from doing a show in Paris, and Summer had called Rodger and told him that Patricia was not doing so well. She had fallen into a deep depression, and wasn't speaking to anyone. She began using heroin real heavily and drinking like she was trying to kill herself. The sick thing about it all was that Rodger would actually insert the needle for this girl, even after knowing what kind of mental state she was in. In Rodger's sick mind, he actually thought that by getting her high and keeping her high, she would forget about the death of her child. She had absolutely no good veins left on her whole damn body, from being a heroin addict for most of her life. This fuckin' girl was now getting heroin injections under her tongue. I couldn't believe that she would stoop all the way down to that level just to get a dope high. And what was sicker was the fact that Rodger was the one giving it to her. It was none of my business, so I didn't say a damn word. But what was I even thinking—it wasn't like Rodger was a normal dude anyway. He would inject that needle under her tongue, and then stick that same needle in his arm, and they would both pass out on top of each other—now that's some real drug love for you if you have never seen or heard of it before.

One night I actually told off Rodger. I asked him, "How the fuck can you be so stupid that you can actually get her high on that nasty shit, knowing the condition that she's in?"

This fuckin' idiot just looked at me, and said, "Damn, you're right, Casual. You think I should tell her to stop?"

"Huh, what, are you serious Rodger? Are you serious, I mean I know your half-retarded, but damn, Rodger, you can't be serious."

"Well, I don't know what else to do about her. She's always crying and tellin' me that she isn't worth shit because she can't even carry a baby and give life. She told me one night that she thinks her womb is corroded with death. She said life can't come out of her womb."

"Uhhhhhhhhhhh… Rodger, it's obvious that she is depressed beyond any help you can give her. The answer is not injecting her with dope, my man."

Talking to Rodger about anything that made sense didn't make any sense, simply because it was a waste of time. He wasn't going to listen any damn way.

Now on the good side of things, one morning, I woke up to Summer playing music extra loud in the house. As I opened my eyes, I saw her in the mirror modeling a tight-ass dress that I supposed she had bought, and wanted to see how it fit. But to be doing that so early in the damn morning with the music on full blast pissed me off.

"Yo, it's fuckin' 9 in the morning, Summer. Do you really have to have that fuckin' music up that loud, I mean really?" She didn't say a word—she turned and began catwalking toward me in these red high heels.

"So how do I look? Do you think this dress is too much or what?"

I was so mad that she woke me up with that loud music that I just put the covers over my head and turned away.

"Aww… Come on, Casual, tell me how this dress looks on me!"

"It looks fuckin' horrible, OK! You look like a hooker, a slut, a whore—as a matter of fact, you know what, my dick is hard now. Since you woke me up to this techno music at 9 in the morning modeling a hooker skirt in the mirror, I'm wide awake now. I can't go back to sleep and now I wanna fuck."

"Wrong answer, you arrogant asshole. If you really wanted some of this pussy, you would have told me the truth about my new skirt. Like 'Wow, Summer, you look gorgous in that skirt'. But since you wanna be a dick, I think I'll pass on that."

"Bitch, I am telling you the truth. What the fuck! You look like a slut who wants to get fucked, so now there you have it. That's the truth. That's what you wanted, right. Now get the fuck over here and sit on this black dick."

"Damn, you know that's too bad. Because ya see, I thought this dress was gonna make Mayor Luckerman go crazy. I guess I should just take it back to the store and cancel my appointment with him today."

I jumped up in the bed, butt naked, with a smile on my face.

"You hooked this up already? How come you didn't tell me?"

"Come on, Casual. I'm always telling you that I'm always two steps ahead of you—you move too slow, Casual."

"Wait… wait… wait… Hold the hell up, Summer. So you're tellin' me that you got that internship with this fuckin' guy? That was fast! I mean we were just talkin' about it not too long ago, and now you already got an in with this dude. I gotta tell you, girl, you're slicker than I thought. I like your style. You deserve to suck on my cock before you leave. You worked hard, baby, now come over here and get what you deserve."

"Nah... I think I'll pass on that, darling. I'd rather suck Mayor Luckerman's cock. I think I need a little political dick in my life. There's something about a man in power that just makes my pussy wet."

"So then get the fuck out, and get to work. Why you still here in my face, waking me up outta my beauty sleep. You should have been left outta here, girl. You need to hurry up before he gets another little freak to do that internship for him"

As rude as it sounds, that was the relationship that Summer and I had. We were so cool with each other that we spoke to each other that way. I couldn't believe that she really hooked up with this fuckin' mayor fag. I watched her walk out the door and I thought to myself I am gonna rape this mothafucker for everything he has in his bank. Being the fact that I was a big-time anarchist, and I hated government officials anyway, I couldn't wait to have that faggot in the palm of my hands. I lay down in the bed and closed my eyes, and just pictured myself swimming in a pool full of this dude's money and laughing hysterically.

Then, I heard a hard knock at the front door, as if someone was trying to knock the damn door down. Now I figured whoever was knocking at this door this hard deserves to see me butt naked, and that's just what they are gonna see, just for knocking at my door like that. I didn't give a fuck who it was. So I got up and walked towards the door with absolutely no damn clothes on. I didn't even look through the peephole to see who it was. I just swung the door open and gave who ever it was a real surprise. A butt naked black dude with a big dick.

Now what I saw when I opened the door was two white men dressed in suits, both flashing police badges in my face. I couldn't figure out for the life of me why they would be at my door. But I'd been involved in a lot of shit—from burglarizing homes back in Manhattan, to murder, to bar brawls in California, burning down houses and all types of devilish shit. So I knew I had to play it cool in front of these pigs—and that's exactly what I did.

"Can I help you gentleman? Are you lost?"

"Yes, as a matter of fact, you can help us. I'm Detective Jonson, and this is my partner, Detective Graham. We are looking for a Damion De Voh better known as Casual. By the way, my daughter is a big fan of your music, well, not your music, but the band that you roll with… ummmmmm…Suicidal, yeah, that's it."

"Yeah, I'm Casual. How may I help you pigs today, ooops, I mean gentlemen. You guys can come in. I was just about to make some bacon—I know you guys looove bacon, don't you?"

"Yes, as a matter of fact, we would love to come in. Such a beautiful home you have here, Casual. Don't mind us—we have seen plenty of naked criminals before, ooops, I mean people. So putting on clothes won't be necessary, we don't mind."

This cop was a real sarcastic bastard, and I could tell he knew his shit, he was belligerent, quick with his speech, arrogant, and cunning. So I was going to play his game right along with him.

"Now why would you call me a criminal? Is it because I'm a black man with a better home than you?"

"No… no… no… Not at all, Casual. Let me ask you, do you prefer me to call you Casual or Damion?"

"Sir, you can call me whatever the fuck you wanna call me—I couldn't care less. Now let's cut to the chase and let me know why you're even here, interrupting my beauty sleep."

"Well, Casual, since you have interrupted time with my family with this case I now have to investigate, I figured, let's return the favor by interrupting your sleep."

I just laughed when he said that and started scratching my balls, and I was really scratching my balls real good too. After I finished scratching them, I extended the same hand that I scratched them with, and said, "Listen, gentlemen, we got off to a wrong start. Let's shake hands and start over. I'm Damion De Voh, nice to meet you."

As I held my hand out, waiting to see the reaction of both detectives, the one who was doing most of the talking, Detective Johnson, just looked down and spit right on my hand as I held it out. Right then and there I knew I was dealing with some crooked asshole cops that would do any fuckin' thing to solve a case. But I wasn't gonna crack by any means necessary—I wiped that spit right on his partner's trench coat.

"Now don't you cops just wanna fuck me up in here? You should just kick my black ass in this house—like you guys did Rodney King, beat me down in my own house, please—I deserve it. I just wiped spit on your jacket—doesn't that amount to a fuckin' ass-kickin'? You fuckin' cops are soft because if I were you, I woulda kicked my black fuckin' ass right in this house."

"Now why would we do a thing like that—so you could get a fat law suit? I can see it now—two white cops fuckin' up a nigger in his house for no reason at all. Now that would make the fuckin' papers wouldn't it, Detective Graham."

I couldn't believe this asshole just refered to me as a nigger. I mean I wasn't surprised by it, but it was a little insulting, and I gotta tell you, I wanted to bust his fuckin' lip wide open. But I wasn't about to let them win. My mind was going back and forth, wondering why they were even in my house in the first place. I had done so much that it could have been anything that coulda put me away. But the only thing on my mind was, the next place they would probably go to would be to Rodger's. Now that was dangerous, because Rodger was a time bomb—ready to blow the fuck up. He had no respect for the law at all, so in my mind, I'm just thinking that this dummy would either sink us because he is not too bright or he would just shoot it out with them right on the spot.

"Well, Casual, or Damion De Voh or whatever they fuckin' call you, the reason for our little visit here is a pistol that we have in our possession, which is a .9mm we caught on a kid named Paully. Furthemore, this kid Paully was snatched up for a robbery that he committed and this kid is doin' a lot of talking, aka cooperating aka snitching. So I can imagine what you're saying to yourself right now, Casual. I have been doing police work long before your parents even thought about fuckin' each other to conceive you. So I'm gonna leave you with my card here. Call me if you think you know anything about this gun. Now I know I know you're saying to yourself, 'Why doesn't this guy just arrest me right now, if he thinks this is my gun?' But to tell you the truth, the gun is being checked out for all types of prints and you know murders. This here is just to let you know that I can find you whenever I want. You can't run anywhere. So if you have any info on this gun, please call me—don't hesitate. I mean it's only your freedom we're talking about here. And I know you niggers know a lot about wanting to be free, especially after 400 years of oppression." He pulled out the card and just dropped it on the floor, and just walked out with his partner.

My heart was pumping like a muthafucka. I was stiff and my blood was running through my veins, as if a marathon was going on in there. This fuckin' kid folded under police pressure, and I know in my heart, he told those faggots that we made him do it, as well as gave him the gun. But the fucked-up thing about the whole situation was that I couldn't remember if Rodger and I had on gloves when we robbed Fritz. That poor innocent girl lost her life because of us. I knew that eventually, I was gonna have to pay for her losing her precious little life. The gun that Rodger used in the robbery that had turned so deadly was the same gun that these cops had in possession. It was the same .9mm pistol that stole the life of a little girl, not to mention, a woman was raped violently at gunpoint, and a man had been killed. Alls they needed to do was run the prints on the gun, track it back to

Manhattan, and they would be at the scene of a grizzly murder. Not to mention the fact that the woman who was raped was still living—so she could easily be a witness because we didn't have a mask on at all.

I immediately called Rodger on the phone and told him I was heading over to his place to talk to him. He knew it was important by the sound of my voice. When I got over to Rodger's, of course, it looked like a fuckin' mess. Liquor bottles all over the place and a cloud of cigarrete smoke that you couldn't get rid of with an industrial fan. Patricia was on the couch, looking like death. She was pale and her lips were chapped and had a dark blue color to them.

"Hey, Patricia, I see you're looking alive and well. I don't ever remember seeing you happier!" There was no response after I made that little comment. She just stared at me with a blank look, as if I wasn't even standing in front of her. Finally, she leaned forward slowly towards me.

"It was you. It was you. I knew it all along—you stole my baby, you motherfucker. It was you—it was you." I didn't know whether to walk away, or stand there and try to figure out why this bitch was looking the way she was looking and talking crazy at the same time. She began to start screaming at the top of her lungs that it was me that stole her baby, and that I was the fuckin' devil. Her teeth were yellow and filled with plaque, and her lips had been so dry that they began to crack and bleed when she started yelling. Then to make matters worse, this fuckin' bitch spat on me, and began attacking me, yelling at the top of her lungs that it was me that stole her baby. I was pissed off that she spat on me, and I began to back up towards the wall until Rodger came in and grabbed her. He picked her up over his shoulder and carried her back into her room and locked her in there, as if she were a wild animal. I could still hear her banging on the wall and shouting, "It was you. It was you. You stole my baby."

I immediately turned to Rodger, and said, "Yo, what the fuck is wrong with her crazy ass now? Yo, Rodger, you need to take that bitch to the goddamn doctor, yo. That shit is crazy. First of all, she looks possessed. She hasn't brushed her teeth in I don't know how long. What the fuck is going on, Rodger?"

"Dude, I gave her two tabs of acid so she would leave me alone. She kept buggin' out about losing the baby and blaming herself, so I said 'fuck it'. I gave two tabs to get it off her mind."

"Yo, alls I'm saying, Rodger, is that you need to get that fuckin' girl some help. Anyway, I didn't come over here to talk about that. Yo, can you believe I had two detectives at my damn door this morning?"

Rodger didn't look surprised at all. As a matter of fact, he began to chuckle and laugh like what I said was funny.

"Ummm… Rodger. last I checked, I wasn't a comedian. So I don't know why the fuck you are sittin' there laughing at what I just said."

"No… no… no… It's not funny. It's just that those same fuckers showed up at the studio when I was doing one of my tracks." There was a moment of silence between me and Rodger at that point. I was waiting for him to elaborate on what was said between him and those two detectives, but I guess Rodger didn't get the fact that I wanted to know what was said. I felt like smacking him right in the face.

"Uhh… Sooo… yeah… like what the fuck did they say, Rodger? I'm sure they didn't show up at the studio to hear you scream on the microphone live in person. They came there for a specific purpose, Rodger."

"Dude, they didn't say shit, alright, and most importantly, I didn't say shit. So they didn't get shit. Why the hell are you so damn paranoid anyway?"

"Rodger, you and I both know that you ain't the brightest person ya know. For all I know, you probably slipped up and told them some shit—some shit like where the hell I live. How did they know where I live?"

"Well, one night they pulled me and Patricia over. Thank God, she was driving, and they asked me where I was coming from, so I told them."

"Wait a minute, hold up. They pulled you over? When the hell was this Rodger?"

"I'd say this was about two months ago or so, give or take. Those fuckers have been harassing me forever. I wish they would just quit it."

"TWO FUCKIN' MONTHS! TWO FUCKIN' MONTHS, RODGER!" I was pissed now—I mean, you could see the smoke coming outta my ears. I started to raise my voice higher and higher. I couldn't believe this damn dumbass didn't tell me about these two detectives.

"Rodger, could you please tell me why you wouldn't tell me about this, you can't be that dumb, my man. These two assholes have been talking to you and asking you questions for two damn months, and you didn't think it was the least bit important to tell your best fuckin' friend that 'hey, yo, Casual, the cops have been on my ass. They might be on to something. Lay low.' I mean, you just don't say shit! What kind of dumbass are you?"

## CHAPTER 20

Summer had been interning for Mayor Luckerman for sometime now, and she was making progress at a rapid rate, let me tell ya. I was busy going from city to city with Rodger and the band, doing shows and interviews for radio stations. But everytime I spoke to her, she was preparing to go somewhere with this lame.

    One night, she had asked me to attend a dinner with her that he had invited her to. It was gonna be filled with a bunch of politician lame-asses, just like the mayor, but she wanted me to go as her date so that it would make him jealous. It was actually a great fuckin' idea, but of course, I had to add my magic to it. My plan was to act like a complete dickhead towards Summer.... Kind of like a deadbeat boyfriend who doesn't appreciate her beauty at all. And man, was I the perfect character for the part. Ya see, what that was gonna do was draw him closer to Summer—kind of like a captain save a hoe type. He would see how I was treating Summer, and in his lame, little mind, it would upset him and he would feel that he would be the one to save Summer from a deadbeat arrogant asshole such as myself. And starring in the role of this deadbeat, arrogant asshole was a deadbeat, arrogant asshole—me—acting as myself. I was high as a fuckin' kite—loud, obnoxious, rude, raunchy, and real niggerish.

When I shook the mayor's hand, I taught that muthafucka how to give a pound. You know, like one of those pounds you give one of your homeboys from your hood that you haven't seen in a while—like he just came home from doing prisontime. It was a pound and a hug. I told him to bring it in for the real thing, because this was the first time he was ever gonna shake someone's hand that was more influential than him. And when I did that, I wasn't acting at all, that was sincere, 100% genuine. I mean who the fuck was he to me—who the fuck wants to grow up and be a mayor, I mean really? What a boring life—he's all tight and uppity and proper. And I was a real star—'The man' behind the success of the most popular rock band in America. Or better yet in the whole world. And the plan worked out. We baited that bastard right into the palm of our hands. He told Summer that I was a complete asshole, and that she has no business with a low-life such as me. And that's exactly what I wanted him to think.

What I wasn't expecting was Summer to show up at the studio where Rodger was recording his next album, all happy like she just hit the lotto. She reached into her pocket and pulled out a box that was all wrapped in wrapping paper with a bow on the top. She danced her way over to me to the beat of Rodger's song, and dropped it on my lap. So, of course, I opened it, and it was a little mini camcorder. And it said, 'Open me and play me.' I was confused as hell about what this was all about, so I did as the note said, and what I saw absolutely blew my mind.

It was Summer fuckin' the shit outta this dude—and when I say 'this dude' I mean Mayor Luckerman. I jumped up and gave Summer the biggest fuckin' hug. I couldn't believe she had pulled it off by herself—this was a slick bitch let me tell ya. Because of her, I just pulled off the heist of the century—out of every heist that was ever committed in the history of committing them, this was the one in my opinion that should go down in history. Hell, with a heist like this, I shoulda been a motivational speaker for those who are to scared commit them because they don't believe it will work. It was the most orgasmic feeling I've ever had—yeah, better than fuckin' sex. Just to know that I had the mayor in the palm of my hands—he was mine. Fuck how many speeches he had given, fuck how many hands he had shook, fuck the fact that he was in charge of California! Here you had a man that graduated from Ivy League schools all his life, and probably had it locked in his mind that he was the most successful man in terms of what he had accomplished. And look at me—I barely got outta high school, then had the audacity to go to college. But the difference was I was the most influential mufucka on the planet. And after my death, I was gonna be a fuckin' legend, and nobody could deny that or take that from me.

A couple days had passed. Summer and I were literally making like hundreds of copies of this shit. I just couldn't wait to give this asshole the phone call that was gonna change his life for worse. There was actually a commercial that came on one night that featured him, his wife and his kids. They looked like such a happy family—the smiles, the laughter, the innocence that they betrayed. It was almost iconic to watch this so-called successful mayor on TV with his wife and kids. And I was about to fuck all that up—it made my dick hard to know I possessed that kind of power. And this is what I mean when I say power—ya see, I didn't want any fuckin' money from him. I wanted to strip him of his so-called success, his so-called family innocence. Here this guy was on TV promoting how important family was to all these Americans. Americans don't deserve to be lied to by a muthafucka who sits on this throne of California, and acts like he is the American dream. My plan wasn't to blackmail him and take his money. I wanted more. I wasn't giving that son of a bitch the satisfaction of saving himself from his fuckup of tearing apart his family. I want his daughter to feel pain; I want his son to feel anger; I want his wife to feel embarrassment; and I

## A SUICIDE STORY

want him to feel suicidal. I want to be the reason that he killed himself. I was his God—I was gonna sit there on my couch when I called him while I was sniffing up a couple lines, and decide his fuckin' fate. The plan was to call him and let him know I had one of his most darkest secrets on camera, and to let him know what I had on him. Then send that shit to every news media in the world—even the newspapers were gonna get a copy. Even the NY Times was getting a copy, courtesy of me because that's where I was from. TMZ was getting a copy. It was a Tuesday night and we all sat around drinking and getting fucked-up. It was showtime. I was making the phone call that was gonna tear the mayor's life apart. Not to mention this was gonna make Summer as famous as your everyday actor. She was gonna become a regular household name after I was finished with this fucker. I invited everybody to the show that was going down at the house. I even charged Rogder and his band to come in and have a front row seat on the couch. I even put on my best suit, fuck it, I even went out and brought a disco ball. I wanted the lights out and the disco ball spinning for this shit. Summer had told me that I was losing my mind but it was a show to me, fuck that. How many people are you actually gonna meet in the world that have the fuckin' balls to do what I did. I told Summer that this was her coming out party—she was gonna be famous, so please… please… thank me later, just let me work.

Summer passed me the phone and the number to call, which we both knew he was gonna answer because he thought it would be Summer calling. The lights went off, and I told Rodger to hit the switch for the disco ball. I dialed the number and put it on speaker—it was fuckin' showtime. The phone rang about 7 times, and when Mayor Luckerman picked up, he got straight to the point as he thought it was Summer.

"Well, hello there, doll, I was wondering when you were going to call."

"Mayor Luckerman, how the hell are you, Sir? Hey, let me just tell you, I am delighted to hear your voice. I mean its not every day that someone gets to talk to the mayor, ya know."

"Yes this is Mayor Luckerman. Who am I speaking with, may I ask?"

"This is the devil, Mayor Luckerman. I bet you never thought you would be talking to the devil huh? Please, whatever you do, don't call on the Lord now because it ain't gonna do no fuckin' good." At this point, Mayor Luckerman started to get a little frustrated.

"OK OK enough of the silly games. Do you know who you are speaking to—this is Mayor Luckerman. You can be in a lot of trouble for this little prank, you know buddy."

"Ain't nobody in trouble here but you, Sir, and trust me, this ain't no fuckin' game. Let me get straight to the point here, Mayor Luckerman. I am here to tell you that I am the last voice that you are gonna hear before your life goes down the fuckin' toilet, like the piece of shit you are. You haven't been a good little boy now, have you Mayor Luckerman? As a matter of fact, I saw your commercial on TV the other day, you know, the one where you are smiling and laughing with your wife and your kids, potraying like you are a loyal husband and a honest father. Let me just add that I throw up in my mouth everytime I see that shit. Nothing's gonna make my stomach feel better than to see you suffer when your wife and kids look at you as a man that they can no longer trust."

"Is this some ridiculous prank? Look, whoever this is, I don't have the time to entertain you and your silly games. I'm going to hang up now."

"Well, Mayor, you can hang up if you choose but at least let me explain to you why I'm even calling you in the first place. I mean why wouldn't you wanna know that I have you on camera having sexual relations with a woman, who is not your wife…"

"This is insane. Who is this?"

"I told you that I'm the devil, oh what, you don't believe me"

"You don't have me on tape doing anything because I haven't done anything. So you have a nice day."

I couldn't believe that this bastard actually hung up the phone on me—he actually hung up the fuckin' phone. I wanted to ruin his fuckin' life, and that was just what I was gonna do. And at the same time, I was gonna make a star outta Summer. I figured, if I tell Summer to go straight to the press with a story of betrayal, adultery, and lies, from a mistress who was having sexual relations with the mayor of California, I could make Summer a star overnight. I masterplanned it all out in the next three weeks. I got Summer to get the information for all news media stations that were thirsty for a story and she let him all have it. CNN was the first to contact us, and after that, we were getting phone calls from all over. Now I played the role of an innocent boyfriend, who didn't want this out for people to know. What that did was make all these paparazzi news fuckers to offer a pretty penny for Summer to spill the beans. Instantly, Summer became a fuckin' celeb. We were getting calls to do interviews from everywhere—even daytime talk show hosts started ringing our phone to get the story. It was on every fuckin' news channel in America—as a matter of fact, it made every fuckin' channel on TV.

Everyone wanted to know who this pretty, young brunette was, who was having an affair with the mayor of California. And she played the role of a young woman who was lied to and betrayed and kept a secret, like a Grammy award-winning actor. She told reporters how Mayor Luckerman had lied to her about leaving his wife for her and starting a life with her. Summer was portrayed on television as a young mistress, who was used as a piece of meat for just wild sex. She even told the press of all the freaky, nasty fantasies that Mayor Luckerman wanted her to fulfill. She had no shame in telling the press all the details of her and Mayor Luckerman's sexcapades. I kinda felt sorry for his wife, as she looked so pitiful on TV standing next to her husband. Then I got over it 3 seconds later, after seeing how good Summer looked on TV.

While Summer was on her tour, doing interviews all over America about the sleaze of California Mayor Luckerman, I was touring with Rodger doing concerts. At this point, Suicidal was the hottest band out, and the limelight was nothing if it wasn't shining on us. I remember one night, Rodger incited a mosh pit so big, it actually looked like a damn rumble was going on in the arena. We were performing at the Staple Center in California. The next thing I know, this crazy bastard jumps into the crowd, and starts swinging his fists and kicking like he was beating up his own fans. Then it dawned on me—he was actually performing one of his songs called *Penalty Pit*. This is where he calls everyone from New York to Florida to Texas to California and all major cities in America, to come together in a circle and mosh. It was actually a dance that he called the 'penalty pit'. If you are soft, don't enter; the penalty pit was for warriors only. So I kind of understood why this maniac jumped into the crowd and did this, I mean, hell, it was his fuckin' dance. I didn't even like to call it a dance because it wasn't dancing to me at all. These mufuckaz were beating the shit outta each other. After the concert was over, we were taking pictures with a bunch of groupies, of course. And Rodger's eye was swollen, he had a fat lip, his nose and his mouth were bleeding. And this fuckin' dude was still takin pictures with girls. The thing that shocked me the most was this one girl actually took off her shirt and cleaned all the blood from Rodger's face, and then asked him to autograph it. So not only did she have a pic with him, she had his blood on her shirt straight from one of his hit songs the *Penalty Pit,* with his autograph on it. The thing was if you went into the penalty pit and didn't come out bloody with a black eye or a fat lip, you weren't doing the dance properly. Now tell me if that ain't the sickest shit you ever heard of in your life. After all the groupie love, we finally broke out and headed home—we were all gonna crash at Rodger's house. We didn't have to be at the airport until next week—we were headed out to Phoenix, Arizona, for another concert. Now I was sitting there looking at Rodger, and I said to him, "Yo, Rodger, please tell me how is that sexy—the fact that you are going to lie next to Patricia lookin all beat the fuck up."

"Duuude, you wouldn't understand, she fuckin' loves it when her man comes home lookin' like a warrior."

"Uhhhhhh... I guess, I mean I don't understand how any woman would find that attractive, but then again, we are talkin about you and Patricia here, so I don't even know why I brought it up. My apologies, Rodger."

As we walked into the house, we were all just a little too loud for Patricia's taste—she hated it when we came in and we were loud. For some strange reason, she didn't like a loud atmosphere. The house was absolutely empty when we walked in. Rodger called Patricia's name a couple times, waiting to hear her normal response, which was for him to stop fuckin' yelling. But we didn't hear an answer. I told Rodger, she was probably out with Summer looking for black guys. I loved fuckin' with Rodger about his girl wanting to fuck a black dude. Everyone took a seat on the couch but I had to go to the bathroom. I had been holding my piss for too damn long. I barged open the bathroom door, opened the toilet and let it go. As I was pissing, I heard water dripping in the bathtub. Since the toilet was right next to the bathtub, I just reached over and pulled the curtain back. And what I saw spooked me out of my shoes. I thought I was having an out-of-body experience. There was Patricia, lying in a tub full of red water, which looked like blood. I got so scared that I froze and began to shake. I said to myself, why is the tub water red. As I bent down to pick her up, I noticed both her wrists were cut deep. Her body was cold, and she was indeed dead.

"RODGER!!! RODGER!!!" I screamed at the top of my lungs. "RODGER!!! Get the fuck in here." Rodger came busting through the bathroom door and when he saw Patricia in the tub full of bloody water, he threw me to the side so hard, I hit my head on the wall.

"PATRICIA! PATRICIA! Get up, baby, get up, baby. What the fuck did you do to yourself?" he screamed. His voice trembled, and tears began to run down his face. I sat back and watched the whole thing play out in slow-motion. It was as if I was having another out-of-body experience—as if my soul had separated from my body, and was looking down on what was happening. Rodger pulled Patricia's body out of the bloody water in the tub, and just held her in his arms. He held her and rocked her back and forth, just asking why she did this. He was talking to her as if she was going to respond. But by the looks of it she was long dead, before I even went into the bathroom. This was not a good thing at all for Rodger. Patricia was what kept his heart beating in the first place. And to be honest, I always thought it was gonna be the other way around. I always thought it was gonna be Patricia hovering over Rodger, trying to bring him back to life.

My cell phone started to ring in my pocket. I picked it up to see who it was, and it was Summer. I ignored it at first, because I was speechless at this point. I didn't know what to say or even how to say it. I was hoping that she wouldn't call back, and for a minute, she did just as I was hoping. Until my phone rang again, and damn sure, it was Summer. I said to myself, 'Just pick up phone, Casual, just do it. Just do it.' And I did.

"Hello"

"Hey, pumpkin. You'll never guess who I just got off the phone with."

Summer sounded so fuckin' cheerful and happy that I started to get queasy, and then I got sick. Just thinking of having to tell her what I was looking at, and what had happenend was making me sick to the core of my stomach. I didn't wanna tell her but I knew that I had to. I knew I had to say something. For Christ's sake, her own blood cousin was dead, and the worst thing about it all was the fact that she had taken her own life. Rodger was still screaming at the top of his lungs and crying, at this point. I knew Summer had heard all the noise, so I was just waiting for her to say what the fuck is going on over there. I paused for about a second. The words were at the tip of my tongue but they wouldn't come out. I sat down on the bathroom floor and and began to look up at the ceiling. I could hear Summer on the other end of the phone, saying, 'hello.' But it took me a couple seconds before I could even acknowledge her.

"Summer, we found Patricia in the bathroom dead."

"What!!! Stop playing around. That's not even fuckin' funny. You're such an ass!"

"Summer, I'm not kidding. We found her in the tub. She's dead, Summer. She's gone… She's gone."

## CHAPTER 21

It was the most influential time ever. Rodger and his band were invited to come to the staple center to escort the famous WWE world champion wrestler Mr. America to the ring. Mr. America was one of Rodger's biggest fans—the theme music that he was introduced to was Rodger's song, *American Nightmare*. So Rodger actually got to walk this musclehead to the center of the ring. Of course, the rest of the band and I were in the front row. I almost couldn't believe it. These fuckin' wrestler dudes were huuuuuge—I mean they looked like super heroes on steroids. Like they had steroids for breakfast, lunch, dinner, and cocaine for dessert. Now you know you're a superstar when you get invited to the WWE to escort the world champion to center ring. Now here's where the shit gets influential, and just plain outright the' craziest shit ever done in the history of sports and entertainment. It goes back to when we all would get fucked up and go to either a basketball game or a football game. We would get season tickets to damn near any game that was being played anywhere. We even got hockey tickets, even though we didn't go.

Now what we would do was get real fucked-up and shoot rock, paper, scissors. Whoever lost would have to run out on the court or the field, and try to steal the ball. Fortunately, I always won, for some strange reason, so it wouldn't be me making a fool out of myself. One time, we were at a Lakers game, and Skeet lost, he threw out a paper sign, and I threw out scissors. So he had to run out on the court and try to steal the ball from the point guard on either team. We always had courtside seats, so it was nothing for one of us to just run out on the court and do something stupid. So this fuckin' idiot takes about three deep breaths, and runs out on to the court, somehow he snuck up behind whoever the point guard was who was bringing the ball up the court from the LA Clippers, and this little muthafucka stole the fuckin' ball. Now instead of running around the court with the ball, he runs back over to where we were sitting, and throws the ball at me. Why he did that, I had no fuckin' clue—he should have been looking behind him for those security guards who tackled his ass like a bunch of linebackers. I actually thought I was gonna be able to keep the damn ball, but of course, they asked for it back.

So now here we were, at the the main event—the final match of the night for the championship belt. Mr. America VS Guerrilaman Guterrez. So here these two were going at it in the ring, body slam after body slam, leg drops, flying elbows, and top rope body collisions. Rodger came over to us, as we were yelling and screaming for Mr. America to kick this guy's ass. He had this crazy look in his eyes—like he was getting ready to do some real dumb shit. I knew Rodger long enough to know what that 'look' actually looked like, and it looked familiar. He grabbed me by my shirt, and said, "Duude, I'm about to jump in the ring and start kickin' Guerilla Man's ass." The fucked-up thing about what he had just told me was as I looked in his eyes, I could tell that Rodger was on acid because his pupils were so dialated that they were completely black. There was no talking Rodger out of what he was getting ready to do. So I told him go right ahead and get his ass fucked up in that ring by that big muthafucka. Rodger was so pumped up that the grip he had on my collar was starting to hurt.

Before I could say 'Get your damn hands off me,' this cocksucker let me loose, and ran full-speed into the fuckin' ring. I couldn't believe it—I could not believe that asshole had just run into the ring. I didn't think Rodger had it in him but after he jumped on Guerilla Man Guterrez, he actually picked this fuckin' guy up and slammed him on the mat. The crowd went absolutely bananas—it was pandemonium in that arena.

I thought to myself maybe this might boost how Rodger has been feeling ever since Patricia's death. As crazy as the situation was, he actually looked alive in that ring. He began to look like himself all over again, because let me tell ya, Rodger was beginning to really slip into a deep, deep depression. I mean that was a lot for anyone to handle. First his baby was a stillborn, then his girl takes her own life—now that is some back-to-back fucked-up shit. But as I looked at this maniac in the middle of that ring, running around, getting the crowd pumped up, he looked just fine to me. The promoters and managers of the WWE must have been stunned themselves because it wasn't like security was coming into the ring to drag Rodger out.

It actually turned out to be a good publicity stunt for the WWE and Rodger. Kids were absolutely in love with Rodger after this. He was the new idol in children's eyes all across America. Amazing how a simple joke betwwen us all could turn into Rodger becoming a fuckin' hero in kids' eyes. The only problem was little that these kids knew Rodger was a drug addict beyond all belief, and a dude that was responsible for the murders of a little innocent girl and a big-time drug kingpin named Fritz. The bell had rung at this point, and the ref came in and started to break everything up. I thought it was all over until Rodger picked up the fuckin' ref and threw him out the ring—this guy was really acting like he was a real wrestler. Now Rodger didn't get into any kind of trouble for it, but he sure wasn't allowed back to any WWE event for a long fuckin' time.

The whole thing about it was that Rodger was like Dr Jekyll and MR Hyde. He started to develop two personalities, one week, he would be happy as a muthafucka; the next week, he would fall into a deep depression. I mean it was a depression so deep that he wouldn't even talk—he would just stare into space and rock back and forth. One night, I caught him whispering to himself in the dark with a loaded .38 in his hand. I called his name a couple times but he wouldn't answer. Then all of a sudden, two hours would pass, and he would be as happy as ever, laughing and joking like he wasn't just sitting in the dark whispering to himself with a loaded gun in his hand.

One day, Rodger and I were both out at a local coffee shop, just shooting the shit and who decides to pull up a chair and join us—Detective Graham and Detective Jonson. Rodger was already in a bad mood, so I knew this was gonna be a very interesting conversation. I told Rodger to just shut the fuck up, and let me do all the talking. They both came to our table, rudely pulled out some chairs, and just sat down. Just as they sat down, the waiter came over to the table as if we were all cool and wanted to make a big order.

"Hi, how are you guys today? What can I get you gentlemen? We have a special on our Cappuccino Express with a sugar roll." So, of course, this fuckin' pig Detective Jonson comes right out and has the nerve to place an order.

"Yes, I would like to have that Cappuccino Express, as a matter of fact, make that two orders—one for me, and one for my partner. So how are you, Casual? Hey Rodge, how's the album going? Hey, before I leave, please you gotta give me your autograph. My son loves your music. And that stunt you pulled on WWE last week—holy shit, let me tell ya, that was something."

"Alright... alright... alright... Dickdective Jonson, ooh... I'm sorry, I meant Detective Jonson, what do you want now? Don't you have a wife to go home to—ya know how you cops are... you don't spend enough time with the family because you're always out chasin' guys like me, and then your wife ends up fuckin' guys like Rodger here. It's bad enough your son is a fan, he might start actin' 'suicidal'. Rodger's album isn't exactly what you want your kid listening to. Ya know, your son could be out playin' basketball or some shit. Ooops, I forgot his daddy is never home to teach him how to play." A sarcastic chuckle came from both Detective Jonson and Graham.

"Now that was funny," said Dectective Jonson, as he folded his hands on the table stirring up to start mindfuckin' me and Rodger. "Well, now, let's get right to the point here gentlemen. There's no sense sitting here, trying to make a joke out of why we are here because quite frankly, I've got something to share with you two fellas that ain't so fuckin' funny. Hey, you guys remember that kid that we picked up... Paully was his name, you guys remember Paully, don't you... Of course, you do. Well, it seems that the gun that Paully had was linked to two murders in New York. Now what's so strange here, gentlemen, is that we checked out Paully's alibi on the night of those two murders, and it seems that his alibi matches where he said he was. How could he be in New York at that time when he was in county jail for breaking his probation? But wait... wait... wait... It gets even better. Ya see, he told us that he got the pistol from you guys. But what's so strange about the whole thing is that the murder was committed not too far from where you guys used to live in New York. I bet you didn't think we would ever find that out, huh. Ya see, all those hours I spend away from my wife do pay off, huh. So if it means my wife is sucking some guy's cock behind my back while I'm investigating pieces of shit like you, it's well fuckin' worth it. But I forgot to mention one detail to you, Casual. My wife has been dead for over 5 years now. So I spend every last waking moment putting scum like you away for good."

This cop was on ontop of his shit—I mean he was right on. But I wasn't gonna sit there and let him know that he had me trapped in a fuckin' corner. And just when I thought they weren't gonna ask Rodger a fuckin' question, Detective Jonson turned his attention towards Rodger.

"So what do you have to say about any of this, now you gotta excuse me if I seem a little nervous. I have never sat in front of a rock star before. So please excuse my nervousness. But it looks like you guys are in a little bit of a jam here. Now I can't really prove it now, but I sure the fuck am working around the clock trying to figure this out. You don't talk much, Rodger, damn, you must be saving your voice for all that screamin' you do on the microphone."

As Rodger fixed himself to say something, I pinched his leg under the table as hard as I could. And what the fuck does this dickhead do—he jumps up out of his seat, and yells out, "Dude, what the fuck are you pinchin' me for? That shit fuckin' hurt, dude."

I couldn't fuckin' believe it. I just couldn't fuckin' believe how dumb this dude could be. I felt like the dumbest muthafucka in the world. You shoulda seen the look on these cops' faces. I quickly just jumped right in.

"Look! I'm getting quite sick of you two cops harassing us over this kid, Paully's fuck-ups. If you ain't got no warrant to lock us up, I would appreciate it if you two would leave us alone. I got up from the table, pulled out some money, threw it on the table, and told Rodger, "Let's go." As we were walkin away from the table, Detective Johnson made a smart comment that made me wanna turn around and punch him right in his mouth. This muthafucka had the balls to say that I would be the first nigger superstar that he put behind bars in his career. But I knew he only made that comment to make me mad, and possibly make me start an argument with him. That's exactly what he wanted, and I wasn't gonna give him the satisfaction. But the bottomline was that they were trailing right behind all of our fuck-ups. And it was only a matter of time before they figured out that it was us that had committed those murders. What the hell was even on my mind that night listenin' to Rodger's ass! But what really pissed me off was Rodger's stupid ass making it obvious that I wanted him to shut the fuck up.

Time had flown by, and the weather was absolutely beautiful. I mean you couldn't ask for better weather. Not too hot, not too cold, but just right. Summer had planned a big-time birthday party for one of her friends but what was fucked-up about it was that this dude was a flaming faggot. I mean he had to be the gayest muthafucka I had ever met in my life. The second fucked-up thing was that it was in my house. Summer had begged me to have it at my house. I mean my house was a masterpiece, designed by a master architect. So I let her, of course, I mean what the hell, I figured that there would be at least some girls in there. I mean gay dudes do hang with girls—at least that's what I thought. Now when I tell you I could count on two hands how many girls showed up, I mean you could literally count on two hands how many girls were there. I had a packed house full of gay dudes, and not just your average gay dudes, I mean like some super faggots were in there. She actually had guy strippers there that were dancing for these dudes.

So here we had in my living room, a bunch of muscle bodied men with a bow-tie and bakini underwear, oiled up and shiny like somebody had just polished them all. I had a bunch of men in my living room going crazy and screaming like bitches over a bunch of men. Men getting turned on by men—what the fuck is this world coming to, I thought to myself. These dudes were picking up these other dudes and twirling them around like they were women. So I had to ask—I had to ask one of the strippers how much he got paid for doing this. I had never seen such madness in my life.

I walked over to this black guy who absolutely looked like he was having the time of his life and I tapped him on his shoulder.

"Excuse me, Sir, but can I ask you a question?"

"Yeah sure," he responded.

"Please don't take offense to this please, but are you like… Ya know… like… ya know… like… are you a fag, brotha? Because you don't seem like you're gay but then again you never know…"

As this dude danced his way closer to me, he came close to my ear, and said, "If you wanna hook up, I charge 200 an hour but you have to talk to me after I m done working, OK."

"What! What! Look muthafucka, I ain't no faggot OK! I just wanted to know if you were like the rest of these gays in here or are you just getting paid."

"No, no. I'm not gay. This is my side job. I do it because its good money and its easy money."

Now I'm sayin to myself, "side job". Did this muthafucka just say "side job"? If this is his side job, I could only imagine what the fuck his full-time job is.

"If you don't mind me asking you, what is your full-time job?"

"Well, Imma pediatrician. I've been doing that for about 7 years now."

I almost choked on my own air going into my nostrils. This fuckin' guy just said he was a fuckin' pediatrician. I had a pediatrician with mucsles in my living room with a bow-tie and bikini on, stripping for a bunch of fuckin' faggots. Now what mother would ever think that her child's pediatrician was a goddamn male stripper for faggots? I mean you have got to be kidding me! I knew right then and there, this world was coming to an end real fuckin' quick.

"So you're not gay, and you're a pediatrician. Are pediatricians not getting paid the way they are supposed to these days or what?"

"Well, my wife is not working right now. We have decided that she's just gonna stay home and raise the kids."

"Wait… wait… wait… What the fuck did you just say! Yo bro, you're fuckin' married? Like you have a wife at home—a woman with tits and a pussy? And you have kids? Are you shittin' me right now? This conversation is getting worse by the fuckin' minute."

This dude stopped dancing and had the audacity to get offended by what I had just said to him. How in the the fuck could a full-time pediatrician, who has a wife and kids, be a part-time gay stripper?

"Excuse me," he said, with a look on his face as if he wanted to start throwing blows at me. "As a matter of fact, yes, I do have a wife with tits—very nice ones, and yes, I do have kids, two beautiful ones. So what the fuck is your problem? Because if you have a problem with that, this full-time pediatrician slash part-time male stripper ain't got no problem whoopin' your ass up in this mufucka."

I guess this dude actually thought he was gonna intimidate me with all his muscles. He was fooled by my bright pink suit and my big gazelle glasses. He actually pissed me off because he actually thought that what he was doing was OK

"Yo, first of all, brotha, I do have a big problem with you. Three minutes ago, you were willin' to take 200 dollars from me because for some fuckin' reason, you thought I wanted to fuck you. Then you turn around in the same breath and say you ain't gay. Well, I'm here to tell you that you are indeed a fuckin' pillow biter. Then you tell me that you are a pediatrician full-time—what fuckin' pediatrician dances for faggots part-time. Then you tell me you have a beautiful wife at home with kids. That means you dance with other men, and possibly for an extra fee, you stick 'em in the fuckin' asshole. Then you go home and kiss your wife and kids. Fuck you, I was just asking you why you do what you do, and how much you do it for. I wasn't gonna pour out how I feel about it. But since you brought it out, I think you're a piece of shit."

"Hey, fuck you too, asshole. Who the fuck do you think you are?"

Summer must have found out that this dude and I were arguing, so she ran over, put a drink in my hand, and pulled me away.

"Casual, what the hell are you doing?"

"I ain't doin shit. I was just askin' the dude a question, and he got mad."

"Yeah, right, Casual. I know you—I know you said something slick to him."

"Well, what the hell do you expect Summer? You got about 350 to 400 people in my house, and more than half of these people are faggots."

"Casual, don't do this to me. You knew I was throwing a party for my friend Vinny. I told you he was gay. You should have known there were gonna be gay people here."

"Yeah, but what you didn't tell me was that you were gonna have male strippers that dance for faggots part-time. And have a career in caring for young children. What the fuck is that about!"

"It's none of your business, Casual, that's exactly what it is. So can you please just try and enjoy yourself?" So out of respect for Summer, I walked away and just began to drink like a fuckin' fish. I can't even believe I agreed to do this dumb shit. The music was loud and the alcohol I was taking down was now starting to get to me. I couldn't take it anymore—it wasn't like I had a phobia of gay people but it was real fuckin' overwhelming to have over 300 gays in your house doin' shit to each other that God only intended for men and women to do.

So I just went right to my room and crashed. I slept like I was going under for surgery. Now everyone knows when you take in a lot of alcohol, you're eventually gonna have to piss it all out. I felt my bladder filling up as I was slept. I knew it couldn't have been a dream because it was hurtin' like hell. I really had to pee, so I opened my eyes and began to stretch. As I was stretching, I heard what sounded like two people moaning. And when I tuned my ears in a little more, it began to sound like two people fuckin'. You know that slapping skin sound when you're really giving it to a female—that sound when you're trying to really prove a point to that female by fuckin' the shit outta her. Alls I heard as I tuned in more and more was the sound of slapping skins when someone is fuckin'. But who the hell could it be in my fuckin' room having fuckin' sex. Now my room was kinda big, so I lifted myself up from my bed, and what did I see in the corner of my fuckin' room. Two fuckin' dudes had the fuckin' balls to screw in my fuckin' bedroom while I was in my bed. It was the ugliest thing I had ever seen in my life. Alls I saw was a hairy chested white dude fuckin' the hell out of this dude from the back in my goddamn bedroom.

"GET THE FUCK OUT! GET THE FUCK OUT! I swear to God, I'll fuckin' shoot both of you muthafuckas in the face. Where's my goddamn gun!" As I'm searchin for my gun, I get tackled from the back by both of these muthafuckas. I couldn't believe it—I was getting jumped by two fuckin' gay dudes in my own damn house. Now here's the real bullshit. When I go to sleep, I sleep naked. It's been something that I just did for a long time. And when you have silk fuckin' sheets, its like heaven under them covers. So here I was, butt fuckin' naked, trying to get out of a bear-hug from one naked gay dude, while the other one tries to hold my legs. I had forgotton where I put my gun and when I saw those two dudes fuckin' in the corner of my room, I just lost my mind. I wasn't thinking about finding my clothes. The only thing on my mind was shooting both of these muthafuckas in the face.

Now somebody must have heard all the crashing and banging in my room because my door opened, and two other dudes walked in. There must have been a gay gang in my house because I had thought these two dudes were actually coming to either help me out or break up the fight. I was dead wrong—they actually joined in and started beating on me. I couldn't fuckin' believe it. I was getting jumped by a bunch of gay dudes. It was four on one, so there were 3 naked dudes and one of them was me, and two other dudes. This was not a good look for me at all. Even if I had been kicking their ass, you don't get any brownie points for kicking a fag's ass. Now I don't know what kinda fags these guys were but they really knew how to fight. What are the chances of two dudes fuckin' in your bedroom and when you try to kill 'em, they end up jumping you? And not only do they end up jumping you, they end up kicking your ass because they know how to fight. And then on top of that, two more fags join in on the straight man's ass-kicking.

By this time, I guess Summer had heard what was going on in my room, so here she came to the rescue. But it was too late. I was already fuming. I tell ya, if I woulda had my gun, there woulda been some shot-up gay dudes in my house. I probably would have gone on a gay dude-killing spree in my house. Running from room to room, just killing every gay in my house.

I fuckin' hated Summer for a long time for what happened. She thought it was the funniest thing ever. I couldn't go anywhere without her or Rodger bringing that up and laughing about it. I told Summer, she was lucky I didn't find my gun because I probably woulda shot her fuckin' ass along with all her gay friends. It took every gay muthafucka in my house to hold me down that night. And let me tell ya, she had some big strong tough gay friends that got the job done. I wondered if what they did was considered a hate crime. Hell, if me and my fuckin' friends jumped and beat up a gay dude, it would have been a hate crime. But since a couple of gay dudes jumped a straight dude, I wondered if it would still be a hate crime.

## CHAPTER 22

I was thousands and thousands of feet in the air, looking down at the ground from a small plane with a bunch of coke-sniffing, adrenaline junkies who skydive because they say, living life on two feet has gotten boring. You can almost guess who I was with—of course, Rodger and his fuckin' idiot friends. I actually let this fuckin' guy talk me into jumping out out of a fuckin' plane! These were actually Bulldog's friends—everywhere Bulldog went, he made friends. Out of everyone in Rodger's band, he was the one that had the most sense. So here I was, thousands of feet in the air with a bunch of fuckin' maniacs, preparing myself to jump out of this plane. Of course, I didn't have the experience to jump on my own. So I had to do a tandem jump. That's when an experienced jumper is on your back when you jump, and he is the one that pulls the parachute for the both of us. What I couldn't understand was that these mufuckas were actually sniffing coke before they jumped. Not me—fuck that! I was already scared out of my mind and everybody knew it. They were actually laughing and cracking jokes that I was gonna die on my first jump. I was cursin myself out in my head, calling myself all kinds of dumb asses for being this high in the air and jumping out. As I turned to look at the guy behind me that was jumping with me, I noticed that he had coke on the tip of his nose.

"Yo, my man, my man. Don't tell me you over here gettin coked up, and think imma jump out this fuckin' plane with you!"

"Don't worry, my friend. You're in good hands. As a matter of fact, you should take a bump—it will calm you down."

"Take a bump!" I yelled out, as if my life was on the line. Well, then again, my life was on the line. I was jumping out of a plane with this cokehead attached to my back. "Take a bump—I ain't takin' shit, and you don't need to be takin' nothing your damn self." At this point everyone had jumped out of the plane. They flew away like they were birds in the fuckin' sky. My heart was poundin' like a muthafucka. I couldn't remember a time that I was so scared.

"Are you ready? We are jumpin' on the count of three. Are you ready?"

I thought I was ready, but I really wasn't. So I couldn't answer him. My jaw was completely locked. That's how fuckin' scared I was of jumping out of this plane. The only thing that kept going through my head was why in the fuck did I let Rodger and Bulldog talk me into this shit. They had jumped out of the plane a long time ago, and here my ass was, still in the plane.

"So listen up, my friend, I'm going to count to 3 real slow, and then we're gonna jump outta this mutherfucker OK? Real slow. 1… 2…"

This muthafucka didn't even get to 3! He just lunged real hard and both of us fell out of the plane. I was screaming like a bitch literally—my stomach ended up in my brain from the butterflies. I was completely terrified. I mean I was flat-out fuckin' scared. A couple of seconds passed by and I was starting to get a little used to the feeling. I mean I was still terrified but the feeling, I have to say, was a little fun. It was a mixture of being absolutely terrified combined with severe butterflies and a little bit of laughter. I was actually starting to crack a smile.

"Hey listen, my friend. I don't want you to panic OK. Try and stay calm."

"I'm as calm as I'm gonna get mufucka. This shit is crazy."

"Well, I'm saying that to you because I'm trying to pull the cord, and it's not pulling. I've been trying, but something is seriously wrong."

"What the fuck do you mean something is wrong—what fuckin' cord are you talkin' about?"

"I'm talkin' about the cord to pull for the parachute—it's not working. I don't know what the hell is going on!"

"WHAT! WHAT! What the fuck do you mean, you don't know what's goin on. You better figure it out, muthafucka. Don't fuck with me. Do not fuck with me!"

"Dude, I'm not fuckin' around. I can't pull the cord. We are supposed to be parachuting right now. You might have to brace yourself for a real fucked-up landing, dude. I can't get this fuckin' thing to pull."

In a quick second, my mind went from trying to enjoy falling from the sky at rapid speed, to sheer terror—I can't explain the feeling of sheer terror just knowing that you're gonna hit the ground because your chute wouldn't open.

"PLEASE, PLEASE! Do something! Oh my God! I'm gonna fuckin' die. I'm gonna fuckin' die. Please God, please God!" As I was pleading to God, and begging for my life, this fuckin' guy was behind me, telling me to calm down and just brace myself the best I can.

"I'm gonna die. I'm gonna die. I'm gonna die. I'm gonna die. Oh my fuckin' God! I'm gonna die. Don't tell me to calm down. Don't say shit to me! Don't say a fuckin' thing to me. I'm gonna fuckin' diiiiiiiiiiiiiiiiiie! Pleases God Pleeeeeeease! I don't wanna die. I don't wanna die!"

At this point, even the guy that I was doing my tandem jump with, was screaming his ass off. Now that didn't do me any justice at all. Alls that did was just assure me that we were really gonna hit the fuckin' ground and die. I was so damn scared that I even started to cry. I had no idea what happened after that—I just passed out from fear. Before I knew it, we had landed on the ground. I had no clue about whether I was dead or alive. It was like I was unconscious but I could still hear and see. When I finally came to, alls I heard was everybody laughing hysterically at me. I couldn't believe I was still fuckin' alive. Hell, I was still on the ground, crying like a little panzy ass. Rodger came over and picked me so that I could stand on my feet.

"Holy shit, duude! Did you fuckin' shit your pants? You smell like shit, dude. Turn around." Rodger turned me around and started to smell me. I was still kind of out of it but he started to laugh hysterically. I took a couple steps forward, and yeah, I sure did shit my fuckin' pants. I could feel it in my pants as I kept taking steps forward. They were all laughing at me like it was some big joke. And come to find out, it was a damn joke. They all got together and planned to persuade me into going skydiving. That was the first step—to even get me on that plane up in the air, and to have me jump the fuck out. The second step was to play a joke on me while I was falling from the sky, and say the chute wouldn't open, and that we were gonna die. And let me tell ya, the shit fuckin' worked. I couldn't even get mad because I was just so glad to even be alive. Plus my knees were shaking like crazy. I didn't even know that this dude pulled the parachute. I was so damn terrified that I passed out in the fuckin' sky while gliding down to the ground. Only a person like me could have friends that would do some shit like that to them.

On the brighter side of things, Summer was a fuckin' star. I had turned her into a star, like it was a magic trick. She was on every talk show and magazine that fuckin' existed. Of course, there were people that were calling her a homewrecker and a slut but fuck those people. I mean who were they anyway? A bunch of 9 to 5 slaves, who sat at home and watched TV whenever they weren't being a slave to their jobs. Sitting on the couch with something negative to say about people who refuse to be a 9 to 5 slave.

Hell, Summer was a superstar now. The only thing that was next for her was to come out with a bestseller book, and a movie about her affair with the mayor, and she was set for life. The mayor and Summer were on every fuckin' channel that was important on television. People couldn't even watch their regular everyday shows because it was interrupted with exclusive news about Mayor Luckerman's affair. I was on my way to Summer's house because I wanted to talk to her about another idea that I had that would make us beyond millionaires. I pulled up in the driveway, lifted up the mat where she kept an extra key, just in case I wanted to crash, took it out an opened the door. Summer kept a clean house. I mean it was almost as if you stepped in a magazine whenever u walked into her house—plush furniture, expensive hardwood floors, and paintings that were out of this world. Summer wasn't home, so I had to wait at least an hour for her, she had said. Plus she was always late, so that meant I had time to do my thing.

Now when I say, 'do my thing,' I was referring to a picture that Summer had of her mother that was in the living room. Every time I would go to Summer's house, I would take Summer's picture of her mom off the wall, and I would jerk off to it. Her fuckin' mom was so goddamn hot—hoooooooly shit, her mom was sexy. Every time I looked at that picture, my cock would get hard, and I would take the picture off the wall, jerk off to it, and splash cum all over her face. Then I would clean it off and hang it back on the wall. One time I had just got finished cumming all over her mom's face, and when I cleaned it off, I hung it up crooked. So when she got home, she asked why her mom's picture was crooked. I made up a lie and said, "Oh, I bumped in to it one day." I apologized and she forgave me. Then there was another time that I had done it, and I was so fucked-up from drinking that when I went to hang it up, I just left it on the floor. Luckily, I remembered to clean the cum off of her mom's face because I thought I had forgotten to do so. When she got home, she asked me why her mom's picture was on the floor. So I had made up another quick lie, and told her that Rodger and I were wrestling, and we knocked it over. I got a little nervous that time because she looked at me, and said, "Why is it whenever you come to my house, you always knock into my mom's picture?" But then what made me feel a little better was when she asked me, do I hate her mother. That made me feel 100 percent better because it was better for her to think that I hated her mother than for her to really know how I felt about her mom. If only she knew that I was cumming all over her mom's picture, she would flip the fuck out. But she never thought of it as anything so she just hung the picture back on the wall.

I knew Summer had told me that she was going to be running around, taking care of a bunch of shit. That left me with enough time to at least get it in twice with her mom's picture. So I took the picture off the wall and went straight into the bathroom. I took down my pants and got into the shower with the picture. It was just something about me wanting her mom to suck my cock in the shower that made me go bananas. I put my hands around my dick and I started to get to work. I figured I'd give her mom a nice, slow, hard fuck the first time around, then the second time, I would give her a nice, hard, quick fuck, and then cum all in her face. I mean I had the time to do it. Summer wasn't gonna be back any time soon. I was going in on her mom—I started fantasizing about her mom riding my cock and telling me to bite her tits. Now, of course, you know I had to talk to her. I was really talking to myself, but in my head, I was talking to her mom.

"Yeah, yeah, yeah! You want this black fuckin' cock, don't you? Ride that cock. Ride that cock, you filthy bitch, yeah." Let me tell ya, I was going to town on my cock with my wrist—I had the perfect technique too. My wrist action was genius—pure fuckin' genius—I could write a book on the perfect technique on jerking off.

"Oh my God! Casual, your cock is so big. Shove it in my pussy. Shove it in my fuckin' pussy."

"Yeah, you like that cock, don't you? Open your fuckin' mouth, so I can cum in it."

I was getting ready to explode all over Summer's moms face—I felt it at the tip.

"Oh my God. I'm gonna fuckin' cum in your fuckin' mouth. Oh my God…oh my God…Open ur mouth. Open ur mouth, you fuckin' dirty bitch ahhhhhhhhhhhhhhh."

BOOM! All of a sudden, the door busted open. I jumped back and dropped the picture on the shower floor. And who was standing at the door—it was Summer!

"You fuckin' pervert, Casual, what the fuck are you doin?"

"Damn! Summer, can't you fuckin' knock? What the fuck, yo, that's some rude-ass shit!"

"Rude? Rude? Are you serious, Casual? First of all, this is my fuckin' house, and second of all, I would have knocked if I didn't hear you screaming out, 'oh my God, I'm gonna cum, open your mouth, you dirty bitch.' Here I am thinkin' you're fuckin' some dirty skank in my bathroom."

So here I was, with my cock in my hand, and cum dripping, and where was it landing—right on Summer's mom's face. I was praying that Summer didn't come any closer. But my prayers didn't get answered on that one—she walked right over and looked down at her mom's picture that was covered with cum.

"Casual, you fuckin' pervert! Seriously, Casual, seriously? You have got to be shittin' me right now! I can't believe that you're in here, jerking off to my mom's picture—you sick fuck."

"Shit! Well, if your ass woulda knocked on the damn door, you wouldn't have known. Next time, knock, dumbass!"

"Fuck you, Casual. I can't believe you're jerkin off in my shower to my mom. Who does shit like that?"

# CHAPTER 23

Here I was, sitting in a church with Summer at a wedding that she had begged me to go to. For some reason, Summer loved my company—she said I made her laugh. I was like a fuckin' ping pong ball going back and forth with Rodger and Summer. They both liked having me around. But Rodger was beginning to get on my last nerve with all his depression. He was like a little fuckin' kid—one minute, he was joking and laughing, and the next minute, he was anti-social and wouldn't wanna be around anyone. Summer called me a horrible friend because I wouldn't sit with him when he was going through his bitch phase. I told her it didn't make any sense for me to do that. Why would I sit there and have a conversation with a muthafucka who wouldn't talk?

So now, we were in this church, listening to the pastor say all the shit you have to say to two people before you get married, and the only reason—the only single reason—I was at such an event was because Summer was indeed my friend, and I had told her that I would be her date. Now the reason I say 'such an event' was because here I was again surrounded by a bunch of gay people. Yes, that's what I said, gay people. I could not figure out for the life of me how in the fuck two men could get married in a church. How can that be allowed—this was the sin of all sins. And whoever was in attendance was just as guilty. God was probably in heaven with the most sour face on, just checkin' off the list on who was gonna burn in hell on Judgment Day. I already knew I was on that list any damn way so being in attendance in his house of prayer was the least of my worries. But I just couldn't figure out how a pastor could sit up there knowing damn well that it is dead wrong with that Bible in his hands, and marry two fuckin' men.

"Summer, you do know how wrong this is, don't you?"

"Wrong? How is this wrong? Two people are getting married—what is so wrong about that?"

"Ummm… Summer, you gotta be shittin' me right? You gotta be shittin' me. Marriage is between a man and a woman—not a man and a man."

"Oh, shut the fuck up, Casual. It's love, OK. They love each other, and they wanna spend the rest of their lives together. Who's to say that they can't get married? You're not God."

"Love… Love… That is not love, OK. That is pure… hate. That is just wrong. And you got some fuckin' nerve talkin' about how I'm not God. You don't even know the first thing about God or the Bible. We're both probably gonna get 6 years of bad fuckin' luck for just being here."

"So then why did you come, Casual. I don't wanna hear you sit there and criticize this because you didn't have to come, OK."

"WHAT! Bitch, you fuckin' begged me to come to this devilish event, and I told you that I didn't want no part of this shit. I told you that this was wrong from the jump. But you kept on beggin' me, so finally, I said I would come. Did you fuckin' forget that fast, Summer?"

"Well, you're here, OK. You came. Thank you, Casual. I appreciate it. Now can you shut up and stop complaining and criticizing please?" And that's just what I did. I shut my fuckin' mouth. The worst part about it all was the fact that we were in the third pew back from where they were getting married. So when it was time for the pastor to say, 'kiss the bride'—or well not 'bride' because 'a bride' would signify that there was a woman getting married, it brought me to another question: what was this guy gonna say when it was time for them to kiss and become partners? Was the pastor gonna say, 'I now pronounce you husband and husband' or what?

As disgusting as it sounds, I even wanted to know how he was gonna say, 'You may now kiss the groom'. I mean if you really think about it, this was a really fucked-up event. And the vows, holy shit bro, the vows were the worst part of it all. The one guy was saying his vows to his soon-to-be husband, and he started to fuckin' cry. So now, here you had him crying, and what happened after that—the other husband started to cry! Hoooooly shit! This was a mess, two grown-ass men crying as they said their vows to each other. And let me add, another sick vision to this—one of the husbands had a full-grown beard. And I'm not talking about a shadow or a little shaped-up beard on his face. I'm talking about a fuckin' biker's beard—a long, hairy beard. Oh my God, it was horrible! A big, bearded man crying to another man's vows. I couldn't help it anymore. I reached into my back pocket and pulled out some coke, and just went to town. Here I was, in the 3rd pew of a church, sniffing cocaine because I couldn't stand to continue to watch what I was watching sober.

"Oh my fuckin' God! Casual, are you crazy? Put that away right now! How disrespectful can you be? How dare you pull that shit out and sniff it in a church? We are in a church, Casual—you can't do that in here. Oh my God, you are so fuckin' disrespectful."

"Huh, Huh… Excuse me, you wanna run that by me one more time? Did you just say to me that we are in a church? And did I also hear you say that I'm being disrespectful for sniffing coke in here? Summer, you sound like an oxymoron right now. There are two men getting fuckin' married in the house of God, and you ain't sayin' shit about that. But you have the audacity to tell me I can't sniff in church. Fuck you, bitch! Are we both lookin' at the same shit right now? Look, Summer. Look! There are two men about to tie the knot in a damn church. Hey look, we all gonna burn in hell for attending this shit anyway, so we might as well commit every sin under the sun now."

"Ya know, Casual, I really should have kept your ignorant ass home—you have no class at all. I was thinkin' about maybe givin' you some pussy tonight but you can forget about that shit."

"Class, huh, tell me what is so classy about this? They might as well have gotten married on the damn street corner. I mean, fuckin' really, this is so wrong, I think I might pray before I go to bed tonight." At this point, I wasn't even paying attention to Summer anymore. But what I was paying attention to was this fine-ass woman that kept looking at me in the pew in front of us. I didn't waste any time. I tried to get her attention but I was being too loud. There was no way that I was gonna get her number by whispering loudly in a church. So I grabbed the Bible that was in the pew, and tore out a page. You shoulda seen the look on Summer's face, and the face of the person next to me when I did that. But I didn't give a shit. I tore that page outta that Bible, and wrote a little slick note to this girl. I asked her what her name was, and told her that if she didn't write back, I was gonna keep on tearing out Bible pages to get her attention. I passed it to her, and I saw a smile on her face as soon as she opened it.

It took a minute or two for her to write back but finally she sent me something back: 'Wow, you must have a big set of balls to tear out a page from the Bible, just to get my name—by the way, it's Jasmine.' There was really no more room on the paper to write anything else, so I tore another page out the Bible. I wrote, 'I damn sure do gotta big pair of black balls. But I can show you better than I can tell you.' I folded it up and instead of droppin' it over her shoulder, I tried to be slick and toss it over. But when I did that, it landed on the lap of an old lady. I was fuckin' pissed—this old bitch turned right around and looked at me like I was a fuckin' demon sittin in the pew. Now instead of giving it back to me, what does this old bitch do—she opens the Bible paper and reads the note. She put her hand over her mouth, and turned to look at me with a look of disgust.

"You should be a shamed of yourself, young man, tearing out Bible paper and writing obscene comments on it!"

"Oh shut up, and drop dead, old woman. And gimme my fuckin' paper, please, thank you." I snatched the paper from her and just put it in my pocket. I didn't wanna hand it to the girl because if I did, then she would have looked at the girl like she was some sort of a whore—which she probably was anyway. I finally gave up it wasn't worth it, plus I was just board in the first place. I didn't know what to do with myself but I knew this was the last fuckin time I was going with Summer any where.

# CHAPTER 24

The stadium was packed. Rodger had sold out the American Airlines arena in Miami. I had a hangover from the night before because I had gone to a 'pharm party' with Rodger, just to see what the hell a pharm party was. When he asked me if I wanted to go to this pharm party, I told him, hell no, because I wasn't going to no damn farm to party. I thought it was a party at an actual fuckin' farm. But it wasn't—a pharm party is when people take all the good stuff that comes from the pharmacy, and they pour all the bottles of pills into a big bowl in the middle of the table. Its, sort of like a bring-your-own-pharmacy-pill-bottle party... Depakote, Percaset, Seriquil, Tylenol, Codine, Darvoset—you name it, and they had it. So what you do is you mix all the pills up, and everyone just takes a pill or two. The thing is, you gotta close your eyes and take a pill, so you never know what the fuck you're getting. Therefore, you never know what kind of high you're gonna get.

So here I was, at this sold-out concert on stage with a mean hangover. Rodger was tearing the roof off the stadium. The crowd was loving him. Right in front of my eyes, there were women takin off their shirts, and their bras, and literally throwing them at Rodger, as if he was some sort of fuckin' sex symbol. A whole front row, and then some of women who were absolutely topless—with titties of all sizes from double Ds all the way down to B cups—were just bouncing up and down. And these weren't just your average-looking women. These were fuckin' supermodels and beauty queens, who were willing to do anything just to get to Rodger. Rodger always was a stickler for lighting at his concerts. He wanted strobe lights going off at all times with all color lighting going off at the same time. So it actually looked pretty cool to see hundreds of women in the front row of the concert jumping up and down with a large set of tits with strobe lights going off. You actually got to see all the tits in slow-motion. Loud music and half-naked women would get anybody in the mood to have a good night.

    I was on the side of the stage with Summer, where you could hear the music but it wasn't loud enough to the point where you couldn't hear each other talk. Summer and I had been sipping on some 100 percent agave tequila with no chaser. Now like I said, I was already fucked-up from the night before but like the champion trooper I was, I kept on going.

    "Hey, Casual, let me ask you a question?"

    "Do I have a choice on whether I wanna answer the question or is it mandatory that I give you an answer?" I responded.

    "Yes, you have to give me an answer, and it can't be an 'I don't know' answer. It's either 'yes' or 'no.'"

    I didn't know where the fuck Summer was going with this, nor did I really care. But just to entertain the moment at the time, I drunkenly slurred, and said, go ahead, ask already.

    "OK, listen. If you could feed your newborn baby through your cock, would you do it?"

    Now at first, I really had to think about what the fuck she had just asked me. So I acted as if I didn't hear her the first time, and I said, "What the fuck did you just say?"

"You heard me, Casual. I said, if you could feed your newborn baby through your cock, would you do it? You know, like us women have milk in our breasts, and we are able to feed children through our breast. But what if you guys had milk in your cock, and you were able to feed your child through your cock?"

"Summer, What! What! Who the fuck would come up with some shit like that?"

"You said you would answer the question, Casual—just answer the question."

"I don't even know how to answer that shit. I mean, basically my daughter would be sucking my cock to get milk. Or even worse, my fuckin' son would be suckin' his father's cock to get fed. Hell no, I wouldn't do that shit, Summer."

"OK. OK. Now you say you wouldn't do it but if, since the beginning of time, men were feeding their child through their cock, you wouldn't know the difference, so you wouldn't know any shame."

The crazy thing about this whole crazy conversation was the fact that I actually started to think about it for a minute. I actually pictured my daughter sucking on my cock just to get milk out. Now I knew it was some sick shit, but if since the beginning of time, we had been feeding our children through our cock, we really wouldn't feel any shame. So my answer was still hell no, I would use formula all day everyday.

"Summer! Hell fuckin' no! I wouldn't do that shit. What the fuck is wrong with you?"

"Oh stop, OK, Casual, because you do know that as us women breastfeed, our tits begin to swell up and get bigger. So I say that to say this—what if your cock got bigger from feeding through it. I think that would be so cool."

"I don't think that would be cool at all, Summer. And to be honest with you, I wanna stop talkin' about it because it's fuckin' sick. I mean, are you fuckin' kidding me right now? Picture a wife of mine waking me up at 3 am because the baby is crying at the top of her lungs because she is hungry, and I whip out my cock and put it in her mouth for her to stop crying. And what's worse is, what if it was a boy. So here I am 3 am with my son suckin' on my cock to get milk out. Fuck! That I would never do!"

Summer must have thought what I said was the funniest thing she ever heard in her life because she started to laugh like a muthafucka. Now I woulda expected Rodger to come up with some shit like that, so that's exactly what I said to her.

"Summer, the only person in the world that I could imagine saying some shit like that is fuckin' Rodger."

"Oh my God! It's so funny you said that because you are so right. Rodger and I were hangin' out one night, and he asked me that. I thought it was so funny. I asked him if he had asked you yet, and he said he would never ask you because he said that you would have gotten mad at him."

I knew that something as sick as that question had to come from Rodger's stupid ass. Nobody just thinks of shit like that—not unless they were Rodger or were on some real serious drugs.

The concert was rocking, I mean it was absolutely booming in there. Rodger had already performed his mosh pit songs, so the crowd was basically on calm down mode at this point. This crazy idiot had a sawed-off shotgun in his hands the whole time he was performing, and alls I could do was shake my head. I said to myself, 'I bet this fool lets that shotgun off by the end of this concert'. I knew he would, so I made a bet with Summer that he would do it. She didn't think he had the balls to do it but I knew he had the balls to let that shotgun off in the air. The music had stopped, and here was Rodger, talking to the crowd like he always does during his concerts. I wasn't paying any attention to what he was saying. I was focused on Summer's bright pink lipstick.

I don't know if it was the alcohol I was on mixed with all the drugs in my system or what. But Summer was looking real fuckin' sexy. My eyes zoomed in on her beautiful Barbie doll-shaped lips, and her pearly white teeth. Rodger was still talking to the crowd at this point, and Summer was focused on whatever he was saying to the crowd. I kept staring and staring, and finally, I just seized the moment.

As I went in for the kiss, I was startled by a loud gunshot. I didn't pay no attention to it because I knew what it was anyway. I knew Rodger was gonna let that sawed-off shotgun go. But Summer pushed me away, and ran towards the stage. I turned to see what her stupid ass was running for, and as I looked on the stage, I saw Rodger lying flat on his back. I immediately ran over to him and what I saw froze me right where I stood. There was a hole in Rodger's face. He had put the shotgun in his mouth and blown his brains all over the stage. Security had to keep the fans from running on to the stage to see Rodger's lifeless body sprawled out on the stage. I bent down to pick him up, and I just held what was left of his head against my chest. I just held him. I couldn't let out a tear because of the total shock that had taken over my body. My body turned cold, and pins and needles began to take over my body. I could feel Security trying to pull me off of Rodger but they couldn't free my grip from his body. I held him so tightly to my body that Security was damn near begging me to let him go. I could hear all the fans screaming and crying and shouting, 'Rodger, we love you. We love you, Rodger'. They finally got me to let go of him, and the only reason that happened was because I looked over and saw Summer curled up, letting out cries and screams that would stick in my head for the rest of my life.

The very next day, it was all over the news. Every channel was covering the suicide of one of the biggest rock stars to exist. Rumors were spreading about how Rodger was a stone-cold, depressed, drug addict, and he was a ticking time bomb. Other rumors were spreading about how he worshipped the devil, and this was a satanic ritual to get kids to follow in his footsteps. Magazines, newspapers, radio stations and daytime talk shows were covering Rodger's suicide. I had no idea how much impact Rodger and his band had on kids all around the world—Japan, Germany, Africa, Switzerland, Australia, China, Russia, Brazil, and of course, the United States. There were fans crying all over the place, girls and guys. As I sat in front of the television with a bottle of tequila and a table full of coke, I couldn't fuckin' believe how much love Rodger had all over the world.

Who would have ever thought that Rodger would make history the way he did. But why did everything have to end like this? I felt as if my life was haunted by a dark cloud. I knew now that my life was doomed to hell. I mean, first Lacey jumps 50 stories from a building, Then Patricia cuts her wrists in the bathtub, and now Rodger takes his life. This had to be a fuckin' nightmare. But as I took another gulp of tequila, and snorted another line of coke, I said to myself, Maybe it was time to turn my life around and move out of the country. I mean I had the money to do it but I had to get it in my mind that this was it. I didn't even go to Rodger's funeral because I couldn't get up the strength to attend. My heart and my soul were just to weak to attend my best friend's funeral. Some of the cats in Rodger's band got a little upset that I didn't attend but I didn't give a fuck. Summer and I had actually gotten into a really big argument about it but I didn't give a fuck. I tried to explain to her that this was my best fuckin' friend. I had nothing left in me at this point.

There was nothing left to do but to turn my life around. I had told Summer that I was planning on moving out of the country and if she wanted to come, she was more than welcome to do so. I didn't feel as if I had done too much to change my life around, and I knew that this was the perfect time. Summer had actually thought it was a good idea, so for the next couple of months, alls we did was argue about where we were going to move to. Not to mention all the arguments I had with Rodger's band about what was in the future for the band. It got so heated that one night, I pulled my gun out on all of them, and told them I didn't give a fuck what they did, I didn't want any part of Suicidal. I wanted to erase that part of my life totally out of my mind. I didn't even wanna hear the word 'suicidal' anymore. I was really fucked-up with Rodger's decision to kill himself, and the way I felt, I would have shot every single band member in that room that night.

Summer saw the pain in my eyes as a tear fell down my face and I dropped to my knees, and just put my head between them and began to cry. I was turning into a fuckin' wrecking ball. My temper was getting shorter and shorter. I had road rage beyond all belief—I mean something as simple as just cutting me off on the road could lead to me chasing them down and trying to run them off the road. The only person I could be around without snapping was Summer. She was my medicine. She would always try to get me to go to therapy but that wasn't me. Hell, black people didn't go to fuckin' therapy—that, to me, was a white people thing. Until Summer said one day, "Well, I'm white, and I'm perfectly normal. You're the black guy that's acting like a total maniac."

So I actually took her advice on seeing a shrink, and it turned out the shrink was a beautiful Columbian woman who had been married for 15 years. Instead of me getting my head fixed, I was having a full-blown affair with this woman. She was absolutely amazed by my story and how I was best friends with Rodger. She didn't believe me at first but after I showed her video clips and pictures of me and Rodger, the tables turned immediately. I was her shrink, telling her how to live her life. It was all going quite well until her husband found a text message in her phone about how I love when she chokes on my cock, and how I can't stop thinking about splashing cum all over her glasses. And let me tell ya, I didn't feel bad at all. I was becoming to be a full-blown sociopath. Rodger's death fully transformed me into a madman. And I was spinning out of control.

Summer thought it was funny that I was sleeping with my therapist. I blamed her for even sending me in the direction of a therapist. If you ask me, the bitch made me worse than earlier. I was so fucked-up with what was going on in my life that I forgot the bitch was married. I was sending her text messages while she was out to dinner with her husband. I had been all fucked-up from drinking and snorting coke all day and it totally slipped my mind that she was married. I fucked-up a perfectly happy home, and alls that did was make me drink and get high even more. I didn't know where my life was heading at this point. Months went by, and my mind was still blank. Alls I knew was that I wanted to move out of the country, and start all over.

## CHAPTER 25

As time went on, things were beginning to get a little easier to cope with. I wasn't snorting up as much coke as I use to, and I wasn't drinking as much either. But I still had groupies come and party with me at night—as if I was the fuckin' backup singer for Rodger's band. The only thing I didn't like was when reporters were kicking down my door, willing to suck and fuck me all night, just to get an inside scoop of Rodger's life and why he killed himself in such a manner on stage in front of all his fans. But after a while, it dawned on me that I could actually make an honest living off of telling Rodger's story all over the world. I mean nobody knew Rodger like me—not even his own band members. We drank together, got high together, partied together, burglarized houses together, and even murdered together. There was nobody other than me that could tell Rodger's story better than me. I could write a book, do a documentary, or hell, I could even do a full movie on his life. I had the connects to make it happen, and I knew Summer would help me as much as she could.

Hell, speaking of Summer, I was on my way to meet her at a lounge. She had met a dude that she had actually fallen in love with, and they had set a date to get married, and this guy was dying to meet me. Summer had changed her life around 360 degrees. She didn't even get high anymore—just an occasional glass of wine and that was it. I had made her a promise that I would take to my grave. I promised that I would never mention the blackmail scheme that she and I had. She knew that I was planning on writing a book and producing a movie on Rodger and my life. She actually thought it was a great idea but she made me promise that I would never mention that in my book or the movie. Summer didn't wanna look back on anything. She just wanted to move forward and put all this shit in the past, and I didn't blame her. She wanted to get married, have kids, and just live a normal American life. I knew if I put what we had done in that book, it would incriminate us, so there was no way I was adding that anyway.

I met her and her future husband at the lounge, had dinner and conversation, and I bounced out of dodge right after. I was really happy for Summer, even though this guy that she was about to marry was a total fuckin' geek to me. But for that matter, anybody that didn't come from the life that I lived was a fuckin' geek. The important thing was that this guy was genuinely in love with Summer. All he talked about at the table was how in love with her he was. I actually had to tell him to shut the fuck up. I asked him doesn't he have anything interesting to talk about. Summer kicked me under the table for being an asshole, so I snapped back to reality. But this was what Summer needed though—a guy in her life that was going to treat her the way she always dreamed of being treated. Because the bottomline was that Summer was a good girl—she just met me, and I turned her life upside down. I turned my own life upside down. At times, I would just sit at home and watch Rodger in concert—it was amazing how many people loved this dude. I couldn't believe that Rodger was actually going to go down in history, and I was the one that had the information that the world needed to get his story out there. I was this dude's best friend, which meant I too was going to go down in history.

I had it all planned out. I was even going to write a book about being addicted to drugs and the tools needed to kick the habit. If I could even take a tour across the world, talk to all teens, and tell them how important it is to stay away from drugs and stay in school, it would make a big impact on the young kids in today's society. And I knew they would listen to me instead of their parents, so that would be my payback to society for all the wrong I had done. And I knew for a fact that I would reach all kids across the world because I had actually been attending rehab classes myself. As I sat there and listened to people's drug problems, I said to myself, 'Holy shit! These fuckin' people are fucked'. Some of them were so damn deep in the drug world that, in my opinion, there was no coming back. Now as deep as some of their stories were, I knew that they couldn't reach the kids of today because to kids today, they were considered nobodies, losers, addicts, fuck-ups. But me, I was different—I had a name, and I had something that I represented. I was part of the biggest rock band in history, I was a multi-millionaire, plus I made this fucked-up type of life look good.

When it was time for me to introduce myself, and tell my story about how I got addicted to drugs and what it did to me, everyone's face dropped. Their eyes were wide open—talk about giving me full undivided attention—when they found out that Rodger was my best friend, and I was not only a member of the most inflencial, most famous rock group in history, but I was a huge part of the band's success. I brought in tapes of concerts, footage of us hanging out backstage, even signed autographs and took pictures after class was over. The point I'm trying to make here is that if I was a regular dude with regular drug problems, they would not have tuned in the way they did. I even got some of them to really consider leaving this drug shit alone. And the real fucked-up shit about it all was I was fuckin' high while I was in rehab class. I would take breaks to go to the bathroom, and get sniffed the fuck up while someone was telling their story about how they lost their family, their job, and damn near everything they had.

I remember during this one class, this guy was fuckin' bawling his eyes out because his wife had left him due to the fact that his dick wouldn't get hard. Now that wasn't the funny part. The funny part was this fuckin' asshole melted down some Viagra, mixed it in with his heroin, and stuck the needle in his dick vein. I thought that was the funniest thing. I mean it didn't help that I was high on coke but that shit was fuckin' funny. And to top it all off, his dick still didn't get hard. I said out loud, "Holy shit. You went through all that and you still couldn't get a fuckin' hard on. Either your wife was a disgusting fuckin' pig or your dick needs to get cut off." I mean you really hear some fucked-up stories in this fuckin' class.

The guy next to me told another story—he owed his dealer money, so his dealer wasn't giving him anything until he paid up in full. This guy begged his dealer to loan him a fix but the dealer wasnt hearing it at all. So in the middle of the fuckin' winter, the dealer told this guy to go and get him a slice of pizza, which was at least 10 minutes walking distance away. He told this poor guy that if he could get him that pizza, and bring it back to him without it being cold in the dead winter of Chicago, he would give him a fix. And he had to run—he couldn't take a cab or anything. So can you believe this fuckin' asshole actually ran full-speed to the pizza shop in the dead winter, and actually tried to bring this dealer a hot slice of pizza? So he ran to get the pizza, ran back to the dealer, of course, with a cold slice, only to find that the dealer had left. The poor guy couldn't understand why the dealer wasn't there.

Now across the room, there was another heroin addict, who jumped in and decided he wanted to compare heroin-shame stories. This guy said, "Shit, you think that's bad?" And he started telling the class about how he had no money, so he attempted to sell his daughter to the dealer. The fuckin' dealer told the guy, I don't want that bitch. First of all, I already fucked her, so you better come with something better. Now when he said that, I thought that was the end of the fuckin' shame. Because to me that was some shameful shit—you are so desperate for drugs that you attempt to sell your daughter to get high, only to find out that the dealer had already fucked her. But that wasn't it. The dealer told this fuckin' guy, if you want a fix, bring me a pillow. So the guy says, "A pillow? Why do you want a pillow?" The dealer tells the guy, "Just bring me a fuckin' pillow." So the guy brings him a pillow. Now here's the crazy part—are you ready for this shit? The dealer told the guy to cut open the pillow and release all the feathers. So the guy did as the dealer said—he cut open the pillow and released all the feathers into the wind. After he did this, he looked at the dealer and said, "Is that it?" The dealer said, "Hell, no. That ain't it. Take your raggedy ass, collect all them feathers, and put 'em all back inside that pillow. If you can do that, then I will give you double the fix that you want."

Everyone in the class was looking at this guy, waiting for him to say whether he did it or not. And sure enough, he started to cry and said, " I had to try and do it—I needed to get high." Now I don't know what it was, but I was the only person in the class that thought it was absolutely the funniest thing I had ever heard in my fuckin' life. I mean what in the hell made this dude think that if he released feathers from a pillow into the fuckin' wind, he would be able to retrieve them all? I knew my problems were nowhere near any of these guys' fuckin' problems but I did know where I was taking my career from here on out.

Summer would always tell me that I needed to find a nice girl to settle down with. But I just wasn't ready to be a nobody's husband or long-term boyfriend. Hell, I loved my midnight whores and sluts that would come over and do anything I asked them to do. Who the hell would wanna settle down when you could have that every night? By this time, I was working on my book, and jotting things down that I wanted to put into Rodger's documentary. My goal was to come out with the book, the documentary, then the movie. And believe me, I was going to be in full control of this documentary and the movie. Being in the industry as long as I was in it, I met a lot of people that did a lot of things in terms of movies and shit like that.

Meanwhile, as time went by, I started doing inspiring speeches to motivate people. I would show up to fully-packed auditoriums, gymnasiums and hotel ballrooms, and give motivational speeches on how to tackle success. People actually thought my path to success was pure genius. They loved the fact that I started off burglarizing homes to get money for my drug habit and ended up where I was now. Every now and then, I would show pictures of me and Rodger before he became a rock n' roll icon. I showed them pictures of us down and out when we didn't have a dime, snorting up lines of coke and guzzling bottles of liquor.

People everywhere loved my charisma—they loved my outlook on life. I had professors in prestigious colleges quoting my lines. Doctors, lawyers, and all types of political figures, tuning in to what I had to say about tackling success—taking the initiative to grab life by the fuckin' balls and never to accept no for an answer. Being a star to me was never a dream that was out of my reach, ya see, before I was the shit, I always acted like I was the shit. Way before I became a star, I always acted like a star. Confidence is always key in anything that you want out of life. I never cared about what people thought about me, and why the fuck should I care—those thoughts are your thoughts! If you think that way, then you have to deal with it, not me. My philosophy on life was, 'hey, I'm selling me. If you don't want me, then that's your loss'.

I can't—and will not—sit around, and try to convince any man or woman that I am the shit, and that my presence is an asset, and without it, you by your self are a liability. If I feel like I'm trying to convince you, then I'm stepping off, and its bye, see you, later, and I'm never coming back, if you don't believe that I'm the shit, then you just don't. But there are way too many people out there that believe it, so I gotta get them—I don't have time for you. And people loved to hear me talk this way at conventions and all types of other events, and they paid me good money for it.

By this time, there were rumors being spread around that Rodger and I were responsible for the murder of Fritz and that little girl. All because of the gun that was used to rob that store. I guess the police had tracked the gun back to the murder, and they were just putting the puzzle together so that they could charge me. Neither one of the cops had contacted me but I knew what they were up to. They figured, if they didn't contact me, I would think that everything was OK. At this point, I knew that I had to get out of the country, and that is exactly what I was planning on doing. The bottomline was that it wasn't a fuckin' rumor—we had really murdered Fritz and that little girl that night. And I was going to have to live with that for the rest of my life. So I had to get outta Dodge. I was not going to jail for the rest of my life. Fuck that! They weren't gonna take me alive—that was for sure. Those cops were gonna have to kill my fuckin' ass before I spent the rest of my life in a dirty, rotten cell. I was thinking about maybe South Africa, or some place interesting, like Australia, or maybe China, or Japan. And then, once I was settled, I could send for my kids. I knew Summer would have loved to see how I calmed down somewhere in a foreign country being a father to my kids.

# CHAPTER 26

It was a rainy Friday night, and I had planned a party for Summer because she was getting married in two months. It wasn't anything big because I didn't believe in having a whole bunch of naked men grabbing on the wife-to-be as a celebration for getting married. Her friend was begging me to plan that, and I just flat-out said, "Fuck no". I told her that this party isn't about her ass. It's about Summer having a nice little celebration before she marries this guy. Quite frankly, I didn't like her anyway. I just tolerated her to get the party planned.

One late night, we were finishing up all the plans for Summer's celebration, and I just had the urge to get my cock sucked. She was talking on the phone, and and I was just staring into her mouth. So I just stood up, pulled my dick out, and placed it on her lips as she was talking. And can you believe it—this bitch bit my fuckin' cock! I couldn't believe it—and man, did that fuckin' shit hurt like hell! So to this day, I fuck with her ass—I say, "Well, at least you had it in your mouth. Whether you bit it or not, you still had my cock in your mouth."

Summer was having a great time, and she was drunk as hell, dancing on top of tables and doing all types of stupid shit. She actually had a little mushy moment, and leaned forward to kiss me. "What the fuck are you doin, Summer? I think it's time for your ass to go home," I said to her.

"Ohhh. I know exactly what I'm doing. I'm gonna suck your damn face before I get married because after that, I ain't gonna be able to do it no more."

"Well, damn, Summer, let's at least go to my car, so your friends don't see me and you kissing in this place."

Summer agreed, and we both walked to my car, and as soon as we got in, she grabbed me and kissed me. And it wasn't a passionate kiss—like she was in love with me—it was a dirty, raunchy, hard, tongue-kiss. I guess she had to get it out of her system before she walked down that wedding aisle. For some reason, I turned on the car and just started driving. I asked Summer if she was really ready to get married, and if the guy that she was with was the guy that she could see herself with for the rest of her life. And she was absolutely sure that she wanted to be with this guy for the rest of her life. She said she had never been so happy in her whole life. This guy was exactly what she needed, Summer said, and you know what, I believed her. She had said that nobody had ever showed her so much affection and attention. Now even though this guy hadn't lived half the life that Summer had lived, and wasn't half the party animal that she was, for some reason, they just were fit for each other. She kept going on and on about how she wanted to have a bunch of kids and was going to be the perfect housewife for him, staying home, baking apple pies, and preparing big weekend dinners for her whole family.

As she was talking, her voice was fading out because in my rear view mirror, there was a cop car that had been following me for the whole damn time I had been driving. It didn't really bother me until

I saw another cop car pull up in front of me, and press on his breaks. I said to myself, 'I am going to drive right around him and speed up'. Now once I passed him, and sped up, either of two things were going to happen: he would chase me or he would drive off and go about his business. And if he chased after me, I would know for sure what it was all about—and they weren't going to haul my ass off to jail. So I swerved past the cop car in front of me and sped up. And lo and behold! That muthafucka flipped on his lights and chased after me. I looked in the rearview mirror and saw about 7 cop cars behind me with all their lights on.

    I already knew what it was all about—they had figured out that I was the one that was responsible for the murder of Fritz and that little girl. At least Rodger's ass was dead and gone, so he didn't have to worry about doing time for the rest of his life behind bars. I was not about to spend the rest of my life behind bars willingly. These bastards were going to have to fuckin' catch me. I slammed down on the gas and pushed that Ferrari all the way to the fuckin' max. I had to be doing over 100 mph easily. They even had the helicopter in the sky following my ass. I was swerving and dipping until I got to the back roads. I was finally able to get to the back roads where I just opened up that car and was moving like lighting. This chase had been going on for about 15 minutes at this point. I couldn't believe I had gotten as far as I had but I just couldn't shake these muthafuckas. They were trying to run me off the fuckin' road and everything. I'm thinking to myself, 'Damn! These cops are trying to kill my fuckin' ass'. Alls I could think about was me going to jail for the rest of my damn life.

    This was not in the plans—I was supposed to be on a plane heading to some foreign country before they even confirmed that it was me that had committed that grizzly murder. These cops were not letting up. I mean I had a godamn Ferrari, for Christ's sake, and they were still on my ass. These couldn't have been no damn regular cop cars chasing me. I knew that I was probably on every news channel in the country.

## A SUICIDE STORY

Every single radio station everywhere was probably announcing that I had been leading the biggest police chase ever. I looked up in the sky to see two helicopters with the light shinning down on my bright, yellow Ferrari. I was fucked. I was absolutely fucked. And what made it even worse, there was a dead-end sign that flew past. It looked like there had been some construction or some shit, but I didn't know what was ahead of me. Alls I knew was I was not about to spend the rest of my life in nobody's fuckin' jail. If it meant I had to crash into this dead-end and kill myself, then so be it. That's exactly what I was going to do and that's exactly what I did. I figured, 'Fuck it! I'll just end everything right here. I'd rather kill my fuckin' self than do jail time.' I crashed through the guard rail as I came to the dead-end, and it was a fuckin' cliff. And I as I flew off the high cliff into the air, I said to myself "OHHHHHHHHHH SHIT!"

I had forgotten that I had Summer in the fuckin' car. She had been screaming and hitting me to let her out of the car, but I was way too caught up with trying my best to avoid going to jail that I totally tuned her out to the point where I didn't even hear her screaming at me to let her out of the car. It was like I totally blacked out. I was so concerned about myself that I forgot that I had her next to me. I was commiting suicide with no regards for her at all—that's how selfish I was. Alls I knew was that I was going to end my fuckin' life because I was not about to spend my life in jail. Before I could turn and say that I was sorry, the fuckin' car smashed into the rocky mountain. The last thing that I saw for some reason was Summer and me as little 12-year-old kids sitting on the curb, and we were sharing my jacket, and I was holding an umbrella over our heads because of the heavy rain. We had nowhere to go and she turned to me, and said, "I'm so cold, Damion."

When I finally woke up, I found myself handcuffed to a hospital bed with tubes in me. There were cops all around me, and a really pretty-faced nurse with green eyes told me that I was lucky to be alive. All I could think of was Summer. I jumped up and started yelling out her name. " SUMMER! SUMMER! Where is she? Where is Summer?" The nurse told me to calm down and that I needed to relax. I yelled at her and said, "Bitch, I am calm. Where the fuck is my friend? The doctor that was beside her held me down and told me that she didn't make it. All my air just came out of me, "What the fuck do you mean by she didn't make it—what the fuck did you do to her?" "Sir, we didn't do anything. She died from the impact of the crash, Sir. We are terribly sorry, Sir but she passed."

For the first time in a long time, I actually felt heart-broken. I had fucked up. I had fucked up bad, and there was no way for me to apologize to her at all. I was so selfish and so caught up in my own self that I had killed Summer. I was trying to kill myself, and I ended up killing her.